MW01146196

JAY CROWNOVER

Recovered
(standalone romance coming March 2018)

Getaway Series
Escape
Shelter
Retreat

The Saints of Denver Series
Salvaged
Riveted
Charged
Built
Leveled (novella)

The Breaking Point Series
Dignity
Avenged (crossover novella)
Honor

The Welcome to the Point Series
Better When He's Brave
Better When He's Bold
Better When He's Bad

The Marked Men Series

Asa

Rowdy

Nash

Rome

Jet

Rule

ESCAPE

Cover design by:
Hang Le
www.byhangle.com

Photographed by and Copyright owned by:
Wander Aguiar Photography
www.wanderbookclub.com
Model: Sebi Perner

Editing by:
Elaine York, Allusion Graphics, LLC/ Publishing & Book Formatting
www.allusiongraphics.com

Copyediting by:
Amy Donnelly
www.alchemyandwords.com

Interior Design & Formatting by:
Christine Borgford, Type A Formatting
www.typeAformatting.com

THE
GETAWAY
SERIES

ESCAPE

NEW YORK TIMES BESTSELLING AUTHOR
JAY CROWNOVER

Dedicated to your first and your forever, and to the ones who were lucky enough to find both in the same person.

INTRO

I WANT TO DROP A quick heads-up about the start of *Escape*.
I wrote it in third person, but the rest of the book is in first,
told in alternating POVs, as are most of my books. I know a lot
of readers have strong feelings about third person vs. first person,
I'm asking that you don't let the first few pages throw you off.

The reason I chose to write the beginning the way I did is
because when I was putting the words on the page, I was getting
distinctly uncomfortable watching it all unfold. It felt like I was
a fly on the wall watching this train wreck going down in front
of me and wanting desperately to scream "STOP IT!" I felt like a
spectator to tragedy instead of being lost inside the moment inside
one of the characters, and I guess it made sense to make all of you
reading as uneasy as I was while everything unfolded. I wanted you
stuck, skin crawling, eyes wide, words on the tip of your tongue
wanting to spill forth right along with me.

These two have such a complicated history and so much unrequited love and lust that I seriously doubt the prologue will be
the only parts of this book that were tricky to write and even more
complex to read! Isn't that the best?!

It's going to be a long road home for the final Wild Warner—
buckle up and enjoy the ride.

Additional side note: When I initially wrote Brynn, and made
her part Native American, I didn't think that all the way through.
Specifically, with regard to having to write about her experiences

growing up on a reservation and needing to make that as authentic as possible. Remember this series was inspired a lot by old westerns and the TV show *Longmire,* which uses a reservation as one of the main settings. It is shockingly difficult to find someone to talk to about growing up on a reservation, even harder to find a woman who happens to be within my limited reach to pick their brain. So, there are parts of Brynn's backstory where I admittedly took creative license. Fact and fiction often go to war when you are trying to tell the best story possible. I based those parts of her story on the documentary *Hidden America: Children of the Plains,* and various YouTube videos where Native Americans speak at length about their experiences both on and off the reservation. Again, there is a shocking under-representation of women in this situation that one can use as reference tools. So, while I tried my best to give a true-to-life experience for Brynn's story, I'm sure I got some things wrong. Don't hold it against me . . . or do, but know I did my best.

Love & Ink
xoxo
Jay

PROLOGUE

Yes or No

"WILL YOU MARRY ME?"

A hush swept through the engagement party that now had an ill-fated proposal smack-dab in the center of it. The silence wasn't one of breathless anticipation and silent delight. No, the silence that seemed to echo and bounce off the walls of the rustically decorated home was one that was laced liberally with something closer to horror and noiseless despair.

The words should've had the women bright-eyed and giddy and the men shifting with anxious expectation. Instead, they fell like a lead weight, and instead of every eye in the place landing on the woman who was staring at the handsome cowboy who was on bent knee before her, they drifted helplessly to another man in the room. The one who was leaning against the farthest wall away from the couple. The one who was watching the romantic scene in front of him with narrowed blue eyes and a jaw so tight it was a miracle his teeth didn't shatter from the pressure of them grinding together. He was still, so still. It was as if the question hung in the air waiting for the dark-haired man to react—as if the question didn't exist until he acknowledged the words were there in the room, hovering between him and the woman staring in horror at the ring offered to her by a man that wasn't him.

All eyes were on Lane Warner, not the proposal.

"I know we haven't been together for very long, and this might seem sudden, but I know you're the one, Brynn. I love you, and I want to build a life with you. So, what do you say, will you marry me?" The blond cowboy named Jack asked the question with hope and love shining out of his bright eyes.

Jack was ernest and clearly nervous. He clearly loved the woman who was standing in front of him, her hands shaking as she covered her mouth and blinked back the tears in her dark eyes. Jack was a good man, and he was right, this was sudden and unexpected—but not really. He had been around that he wanted to move toward something more serious, something more permanent over the last few weeks. Danger and mayhem tended to make people react without thinking. All the other people standing in that room could have told the handsome cowboy that she wasn't ready for that kind of commitment, that there was a good chance she might not ever be ready, but he didn't ask. Jack went out and bought a ring, sure the beautiful woman who had effortlessly stolen his heart was as in love with him as he was with her.

He hadn't been paying attention. If he had, he would have noticed the dark-haired man who seemed to be sucking all the air out of the room well before now. He would have been aware of the way the woman he loved let her gaze drift to wherever the blue-eyed cowboy was in the room and how it lingered. If he looked closely, he would have seen the way her eyes followed that dark-haired cowboy with undisguised longing and soul-deep regret. The hopeful cowboy would have spotted the way that she quieted and stilled when they were alone, leaving only part of herself in his hands. But they say love is blind for a reason, and the man holding the ring and pleading to the woman with his eyes didn't see any of that until the room vibrated with tension so thick it was hard to breathe through. Only then did he see what was right in front of him all along. He loved her, but she loved someone else.

"Umm . . . Jack—" Her hands shook even harder, and her typically sweet and melodic voice sounded rough and husky, laced with tears, and something that he would soon learn was remorse.

Before she could finish the sentence and before she could drop the single word that would change the life of the blond cowboy who worked on the ranch next door irrevocably, the dark-haired man pushed off the back wall, straightened and left the room. It was like every bit of confidence, and wishful thinking had vanished with him. It was almost as if he took every ounce of love and hope with him when he left. All that remained was a shaking woman, a desperate man on his knees, and a gathering of friends and family who didn't know if they should look away or rush to prevent the inevitable train wreck that was taking place right before their eyes.

"I'll go after him." The deep rumble of Cyrus Warner's voice finally broke through the stranglehold on everyone caused by the lack of an answer from Brynn. The thud of boots on hardwood sounded in time to rushing heartbeats as the oldest Warner brother went after the youngest. It was his job to protect, and that's what he was going to do.

Lane Warner had been present for every proposal that took place on this ranch, and it seemed his reaction to every one of them was getting worse.

When Lane was eighteen, he tried to be Brynn Fox's hero. He was the first cowboy who got on his knee and asked the beautiful girl to marry him even though they hadn't so much as shared a single kiss. They were best friends, close in a way his brothers and several of their classmates would never understand. Brynn needed someone safe, a protector and a confidant. Lane needed someone who saw him. Someone who thought of him as more than the youngest Warner. Someone who knew he was as far as could be from the easy-going jokester that he presented to the world.

They were honest with one another; they were each other's truth. Brynn owed him too much to let him sacrifice his entire life and his youth for her, so that first proposal had ended much the way this one was going to.

The trembling hand that covered Brynn's mouth dropped, and her spine stiffened. The tears that were threatening escaped the lush cage of her lashes and started to fall freely. She took a step back, and a collective exhale seemed to be breathed out by the rest of the people in the room. Her answer didn't just change Jack's life forever; it changed everyone who had watched Brynn and Lane torture each other with unrequited and unspoken love for years.

"Jack, you're great, really. I . . . I had no idea you were so serious about us . . . about me. I . . . well . . . I'm not ready for something as big as marriage. I'm so sorry. I wish I could give you the answer you want to hear." It was evident in her voice that there was a part of her that honestly wanted to be able to tell him yes. If anyone asked about her relationship she told them that Jack was easy. Jack was kind. Jack was a fresh start. What she never could say out loud was, Jack didn't own the other half of her heart. Lane Warner did, and he had since she was twelve years old.

Jack seemed to wilt. He dropped the hand holding the ring and ran his fingers through his shaggy blond hair. "Brynn?" Her name was part question and part plea.

Brynn took another step back and shook her head, sending her fiery hair swinging. She ran her hands down the front of her jeans, palms obviously sweaty. "I'm so sorry, Jack. But I can't." Everyone in that room aside from Jack knew that she really couldn't. It wouldn't be fair, and it wouldn't be the first time she told a good man "no".

Slowly, the blond cowboy climbed to his feet. Belatedly his gaze swept around the room. Brynn's family was there minus the Warners. Lane and Cy had disappeared to God knew where. Sutton, the middle brother, had left for California a couple of months ago. Jack's boss, a woman named Ten, who just happened to be a longtime friend of the Warner's was there.

Tennyson McKenna was watching them with guarded eyes and a fierce frown. She'd warned Jack to be careful. She'd told him in no uncertain terms that anyone with the last name Warner had a complicated relationship with love. Jack had laughed it off and reminded Ten that Brynn was technically a Fox, in more ways than one. She was only a Warner out of necessity, not because she wanted to be. Ten asked him how sure he was about that. Right now, Jack was wishing he had been able to read between the lines sooner. Because the audience witnesses him going down in flames at the boots of the woman he wanted to marry were people Jack couldn't easily avoid when this was all over. There would be no place to hide his broken heart and disappointment in this small town and within this tightly knit group of people.

Brynn's younger sister, Opal, was there. She watched everything with wide eyes and a pale face. Her hand was wrapped around an older woman's, whose face was pinched and twisted in the same kind of pain that seemed to be ripping Jack apart at the moment. Brynn's mother was visibly horrified by her daughter's reaction to the proposal, even though she had never met the man asking for her eldest daughter's hand in marriage.

Brynn didn't mind that her sister was present for one of the most vulnerable and tragic moments of her life. Opal had been invited to the festivities that had nothing to do with the messy display today, but Brynn would have rather walked through lava barefoot than deal with her mother's response to this nightmare. The older woman had latched onto her youngest's invite like a leech, refusing to let her come to the party unless she got to tag along. The only reason Brynn's mother had made an appearance was because there was free food and she couldn't pass up the opportunity to see who was gathered at the Warner's ranch. Brynn's mom was always looking for her next meal ticket, and the Warners knew all the influential people within several hundred miles. Brynn should have let Cy throw the older woman out when he offered, but she hadn't wanted the scene to distract from the celebration. Her mother knew how to make the happiest of moments awful and unforgettable in all the worst ways.

All Harmony Fox wanted in life was to be taken care of and treated like a queen. Brynn's mother spent her life endlessly searching for someone to take care of her and provide for her. It was obvious Harmony couldn't believe her oldest daughter was walking away from that, that Brynn was willfully turning down the security and safety she'd always been willing to kill for. Her expression quickly switched to anger as she pushed her youngest child's hand off her arm and started for her oldest, a determined slant to her mouth.

Jack's best friend and his cousin were also in attendance, as well as a few faces who were new to Sheridan, Wyoming. A man whom Cyrus had hired to help run the luxury vacation portion of the business when the middle Warner left, and another man who was a few years older than him. The latter looked so much like the hired hand there was no mistaking the fact that they were brothers.

They had all been lured to the ranch by the promise of free booze and prime steaks as they celebrated another engagement, one that had gone off without a hitch. When Cyrus Warner got on his knee and asked Leora Conner to be his wife and to spend the rest of her life with him, she couldn't say yes fast enough. The petite redhead had thrown herself at the oldest Warner with enough force that they both ended up on the floor. The joy and rightness of the two of them being together forever had seeped into everyone who was lucky enough to witness *that* engagement. This party was supposed to end the same way. Jack thought it was perfect timing, he felt it at his very core. He couldn't have been more wrong.

Everything with the Warners was changing, which meant everything in Brynn's world was changing. For a long time, the Warners and their ranch had been her entire world. The boys' dad, Boyd Warner, had stepped in when Brynn turned Lane down back when they were teenagers. Brynn was a few weeks away from being legally able to walk away from her circumstances, but she was stuck in a no-win situation. No one questioned the possibility that the next time she was sent home to the reservation where she lived—trapped, with her mother and sister—might very well end up being her last. Things had taken a turn for the worse recently, but there were few legal means for anyone outside of the reservation to do anything to help. Boyd hadn't wanted his youngest son to offer up the rest of his life to save his best friend either. Nor had he wanted Brynn to continue returning to a home where she wasn't safe.

The patriarch of the Warner clan knew his days were numbered. He'd been sick for a while, fighting and pushing back against a disease that was slowly stealing minutes of his life away. His boys didn't know, he kept it from them on purpose, but he'd told Brynn. Confided in the girl that his youngest couldn't live without, and promised her that if she took his last name, no one would be able to hurt her again. At least not physically, because words could sting and rumors would wound.

They'd called Brynn a gold digger. They'd blamed Brynn for his death. To this day they talked about the fact that not one, but two Warners had offered to change poor, pitiful Brynn Fox's last name, and only the older, wealthy, established one had managed that feat. It took forever for Brynn's skin to thicken to the point it was almost bulletproof. She was safe. She was home, and she was loved no matter what the small-town gossips had to say. What Brynn never got over was the way Lane had looked at her after she agreed to his father's outrageous plan. As soon as that ring hit her finger, their friendship had ended, and every second Brynn spent loving Lane seemed irrelevant and wasted. Those closest to the two of them watched as Lane went from the most important person in Brynn's entire life to a virtual stranger overnight. The fact that the rest of the family had immediately taken Brynn in and welcomed her regardless of the circumstances hadn't helped things. The other brothers had no problem joking about their hot-as-hell stepmother, but Lane never found the situation funny.

Eventually, Boyd Warner came clean about his disintegrating health and why he brought Brynn into the fold the only way he knew how. When he passed, they all grieved the man who gave them a home and taught them how to be a family, and none of the brothers were surprised when their old man left a portion of the ranch to Brynn in his will ensuring she would always have a safe place to call home.

As time went on, Lane and Brynn fell into an always awkward but easy pattern. She pretended not to notice he turned into the town Lothario, sleeping his way through every available woman—and even some who weren't—he came across. He ignored the fact that Brynn was living the life he tried to give to her without him. Reasonably happy and content in the only place she ever felt wanted and safe.

They were both miserable, but neither one knew how to break down the walls they constructed to keep the hurt that the other inflicted at bay. Now, with Cyrus getting married and settling down and Leo stepping up to be his partner in every single way, the role Brynn had played for so long was less defined and less necessary. She had been the one who took care of the Warners, but now they were all moving on and finding the women made for them. They found the other half of their hearts, and it was no longer up to Brynn to make sure they ate right, remembered to rest and didn't work too hard. She was no longer in charge of holidays and making sure the strong-willed brothers didn't bash each other to death with their stubbornness and egos. Brynn was sure they didn't need her anymore, and that was scary, but nowhere near as terrifying as giving it all up and marrying Jack would be.

"Brynn, honey, take a breath for me." Leo's voice was calm and soothing. Everyone in the room focused on the man whose heart she had just stepped on and abandoned, but Leo didn't work that way. She always had an eye on the big picture, and there was no way she missed how hard it was for Brynn to hurt a man who didn't deserve it. She took careful steps toward the woman who had become one of her closest friends, hands out like she was approaching a wild animal.

Brynn merely shook her head again and bolted from the room, bouncing off Cy as she went. The big man caught her as he was coming back into the room, giving the top of her head a gentle kiss before letting her retreat. His looming presence and unspoken command had everyone in the room turning to look at him questioningly, except for Jack. Jack couldn't tear his gaze away from the spot where the woman of his dreams had just disappeared. The man looked like a stiff breeze would blow him over, and no one dared to touch him because it was evident he was ready to break apart.

"Lane left." Cy's raspy voice filled the room as he pulled his fiancée toward him.

Leo barely reached the big man's chin when she stood directly in front of him, lifting her hands to rest on his cheeks. Her fingers were pale against the salt and pepper scruff that covered the lower half of the man's face making him look both distinguished and rugged.

"What do you mean he's gone? He probably just needed some air. I think we could all use some space to breathe." Normally that would be when Brynn swooped in to offer everyone a drink or something sweet to eat, but considering the pretty redhead was the whipping winds of this particular storm it was up to the future lady of the house to smooth all the rough edges that were still very much working to slice everyone open. She motioned lightly to Brynn's still-stunned little sister and told her, "Why don't you go check on our girl. Tell her I'll be up in a minute." Her sharp gaze lit on Jack's people and she inclined her head sharply in the direction of the dejected man telling the people who loved him, "I'm sure this is the last place he wants to be right now. Take him somewhere that has good whiskey and a dark corner. Don't leave him alone."

The cousin and best friend jumped to do her bidding like she was a tiny, bossy general giving them orders for war.

"I think it's pretty clear the party is over, at least for today. We want to thank everyone for coming, but right now our family needs some time to figure some things out." She plastered a pleasant smile on her face and congenially ushered everyone who wasn't a Warner or soon-to-be Warner out the door. If anyone bothered to look closely, they would have noticed that Leo's smile was more a baring of teeth because she was every bit the fierce predator that would do anything to protect her pride. She lived up to her namesake fully.

Cy's voice wavered, and his hands weren't steady when he pulled his woman into his arms. "He's gone, Leo. He got in his truck and told me he didn't know when he was coming back. Said he didn't know if he could ever come back."

The ranch was in their blood. Cy had never wanted it, Sutton had resented the hell out of it, but Lane . . . Lane loved it. He was his father's son. When Sutton decided his happiness was somewhere other than the sprawling property in Wyoming, no one had been surprised. To hear Lane say he might never be back was unfathomable. He was the heart and soul of the Warner Ranch. If he abandoned ship—the place he'd always called home, his legacy, and a dream—it would be nothing more than soil and responsibility. There would be no love without Lane. There would be no light, no songs, and laughter. There would be no music. Everything would be quiet and dull.

Leo rested her head on Cy's heart. She ran her hands down the taut muscles of his arms and locked their fingers together. "He'll be back." There was no doubt in her tone.

Cy heaved a sigh and leaned forward so he could rest his chin on the top of her head. Her curly strawberry blond hair tickled his face the way it always did when they were this close. "How do you know, Sunshine? How do you know he'll be back?"

Leo kissed the hollow of his throat and whispered with certainty, "Because he belongs here, and he would never let you down. Besides, Brynn is here, and we both know that no matter how far he runs he won't ever be able to get away from the way he feels about her. It's followed him around for over ten years. It's time he turns around and faces it."

Cy heaved another sigh and wrapped his arms around the woman who brought the light back into his life. Everyone knew that if Cy had his way, he would never let her go. He knew better than anyone there were a lot of emotions you could ignore and overlook, but love wasn't one of them. No, there was no escape from love once it got its claws into you. Sometimes the more you struggle, the more you hurt yourself when those talons dug into all your tender, soft places. All Cyrus Warner could hope for was that his youngest brother didn't bleed out by the time he was done fighting the fate that he'd been running from for far too long.

CHAPTER 1

Want or Need

LANE

WHEN I CLIMBED INTO MY truck with nothing more than my wallet, my boots and my car keys it didn't occur to me that I was going to need much more than that to get to wherever it was I was going.

I had to stop somewhere in Idaho to buy clean socks and underwear, and I needed to make a pit stop in Washington somewhere to pick up a couple of clean shirts and another pair of jeans. I hated shopping for that shit. I was the type who was still wearing crap that was lying around from my high school days. My ass hadn't changed much over the years even if my thighs and entire upper body had bulked up and broadened. I was good with denim and cotton, with some flannel thrown in to keep things interesting. Everything I owned was variations of the same thing, so I hated having to work in new shit I didn't know what to do with. I was very much an if it ain't broke, don't fix it kind of guy, but that scene back at the ranch had been beyond broken, and there was no way in hell that I was going to be the guy who stepped in to try and fix it. I'd done that once before when Brynn Fox was in trouble, and it didn't end well for me.

When I tore out of the ranch like my ass was on fire and the devil was chasing me I had no real destination in mind. All I knew for certain was that I needed to put as much distance between me and Brynn—and her new fiancé—as I could. I felt like I was suffocating in that room. I was watching another man, who wasn't me, jump in to save the day, and it killed me. Brynn was supposed to be mine to protect, mine to guard and shelter from all the terrible shit her mom landed her in. She was meant to be mine to cherish and defend, but I never got the chance because someone else was always there waiting to rescue the damsel in distress. Last time it had been my dad. Brynn was in big trouble; the kind silly kids couldn't get her out of, and my old man stepped in with a solution that changed the one constant in my life that I'd come to rely on. She didn't need me, and she didn't want me. I wasn't sure which of those daggers did the best job slicing my heart open repeatedly.

Before she could say yes, promising herself to the hired hand, I bolted like the coward I was. I couldn't hear it. Not again. I couldn't stand to see the happiness on her face that was put there by a man who wasn't me. She had always been unattainable and just out of my reach, but if Brynn married Jack, she would no longer be a Warner. She wouldn't be my family, and I would go back to being the odd brother out. The one who wasn't as ambitious or as focused as Cyrus. The one who never had any drive or ambition. I would go back to being the brother who followed Sutton around to keep him out of trouble when he got into one of his moods, the one who was always there for comic relief and to keep the other two from killing each other. Without Brynn in the family, there would be no one there who recognized I was a man who worked his ass off to make his family proud.

Sure, I loved the ranch and everything dad left us—buckets more than either of my brothers—but that didn't mean making a go of the business wasn't backbreaking labor. Both the ranching side and the luxury retreat side were grueling. I wanted to do my dad proud and be the kind of man he was. One who gave everything to his family and put his neck and reputation on the line to help out a young girl just because his son cared about her. Nobody saw that I worked day and night to make the ranch a place my mother would regret walking away from. No one noticed that every move I made was to ensure that the Warner Ranch was going to live and thrive long after the original Warner blood no longer called it home.

Nobody noticed how much of myself I gave to my family and our home except for Brynn.

I was going to fade into the shadows, disappear in the small print on the bottom of the brochure, and become nothing more than a caricature of the perfect cowboy when she was gone. I was going to be a hollow shell filled with nothing more than the dust of my failures and disappointments when she left.

Mindlessly, I headed west once I got out of Wyoming. At the time, I didn't realize I was going to California. It didn't hit me until after I spent a couple of days in Seattle and a couple more in Portland that I was making my way down the coast toward Sutton. Both of my brothers always had my back and would be there to offer me a stiff drink and some no-bullshit advice. Cy was too close in proximity to the newly engaged couple, so Sutton it was. I needed him, even if he was halfway across the country.

My middle brother had managed to knock-up his new girl-friend within the first few months of claiming her as his own. It was hands down his best mistake to date. The woman was stunning, forgiving, and had a backbone forged of solid steel. My tempera-mental and destructive brother tended to create chaos with very lit-tle effort. Emrys Santos was the eye of his storm. When everything else around him was flailing in the chaotic winds of the maelstrom, she was the calm center and his safe place. With Em in Sutton and his young daughter Daye's lives, it became clear that one could indeed dance inside of a hurricane if Emrys was around to offer a few moments of peace and tranquility. She was also pretty damn good at keeping other people from getting caught up in the storm that always seemed to sweep through when Sutton was around. They had pulled through some serious hardships together and at the end of the day decided some new scenery might be nice as they started their own little family. Em was originally from Northern California and during an extended visit with her folks after learning she was carrying her and Sutton's baby, the first Warner in over a hundred years who had been born and bred on the ranch decided to make his home somewhere other than the sprawling property in Wyoming. Forging his own path with his newfound family, putting his hopes and dreams on a goal that didn't involve Warner obligations . . . and I was damn proud of him.

There was no question of my welcome when I showed up out of the blue with barely anything more than the shirt on my back and a face full of scraggly whiskers from over a week spent on the road. I made sure to stop and get Daye a present because she wouldn't let me in the house without a treat, but other than that I was a man without a plan and with no sense of direction for the first time in his life.

After a few days with my family, Em tried to bring up the proposal and mentioned she wanted to talk to me about how it all went down. I appreciated her concern and the fact she was worried about me, but I refused to engage in the topic. I had no desire to know what happened after I walked out of that room. I told myself it was finally time to let whatever this thing I had with Brynn go. It had been strangling me for more than a decade, and I needed to breathe. Em accepted my avoidance and let the topic drop. She skirted around the issue the rest of the time I was there and made sure all impending nuptial talk remained firmly on Cy and Leo's wedding. Daye already claimed the illustrious role of flower girl, so there was no containing her youthful enthusiasm for flouncy dresses and the new wedding shoes that were going to sparkle.

It was nice spending time with my brother, and I adored both his girls, but it was weird and hard to get my head around the fact he had a whole new life that I wasn't around for. I'd been in both Sutton and Cyrus's back pockets since I could toddle after them. They were my whole world, and everything I did was in search of them noticing me and approving of my efforts. I wanted to be just like them, but now one was having a baby, his second kid, and one was getting married for the second time. It took both my brothers a couple of tries to get things right.

I was admittedly jealous that I'd never had the chance to screw shit up for the first time. Everyone who mattered the most to me was moving on and away from where we had always been, and it left me feeling hollow and aching all the way down to the center of my bones. For a man who thought he would live and die spending every minute caught between the shadows his brothers' cast, I found myself thrust into the light of day and boy did that sun scorch when you weren't ready for it.

Sutton and Emrys didn't mind letting me couch surf as long as I needed, with the understanding that I would check in with Cy every few days and assure him I was doing all right. I lied through my teeth and told my older brother that everything was fine; I just needed some space. What I needed was a whole new history and to have never stepped in and stopped Danny Turner from pulling on Brynn's fiery pigtails when we were both in grade school. Even back then I knew she was a game changer. One look into those mysterious, secretive dark eyes and suddenly there was someone I cared about just as much as my brothers. I wanted her to stop crying and being scared. I tried to destroy everything and anything that dared to hurt her. She was my wounded bird with more than a fractured wing, and I knew it was going to be my job to teach her how to fly.

Fuck . . . I missed her.

The trip to the coast and the subsequent visit with my brother and his family was the longest we'd ever been apart. She was always there. One of the threads of my family that made the fabric tough and resilient. I couldn't fathom what I was going to do when that material started to fray and unravel as her thread got yanked out of the weave.

To distract myself from the constant worry and fear of how everything in my life was changing, I offered to take Daye to the beach one afternoon so Sutton and Emrys could have a couple of hours alone. They weren't shy about showing affection or touching one another, but I could see the gleam in my older brother's eye as he watched his woman when she wasn't looking. He wanted to pounce, which he couldn't do with his baby brother and his daughter hovering. I earned myself a steak dinner and a bottle of my favorite tequila for my troubles. Plus, I liked spending time with my niece. She was mouthy and bossy but sweet as could be. I missed having her underfoot and asking me questions about everything under the sun.

The weather cooperated by being temperate and slightly breezy the day of our outing. We didn't boil and bake as Daye dragged me to the water's edge and splashed around gleefully. She demanded that we make sandcastles and then chased the remnants out to sea as the tide crashed into them and washed them away. We played a short-lived game of catch that ended when Daye dropped the ball and wasn't fast enough to catch it before the waves claimed it. After that, we both plopped down on the huge beach towel Em had shoved into my hands on my way out the door, falling together into a fit of laughter.

Daye's blond ringlets were kinky and wilder than usual, but her dark green eyes that looked so much like her father's eyes were steady and serious. She'd lost her mom recently and watched her father struggle with addiction and recovery. She also witnessed him fall in love and now had to share him with not only Em but also the new baby. She'd always seemed older than her years, but now, looking into those solemn eyes, I wondered if she knew more than the rest of us ever had. Knew that life wasn't as complicated as it appeared to always be, but was as simple and as uncomplicated as loving hard and laughing often. As if she almost knew that adults muddied up the waters with pride and emotions and other things that didn't matter.

"Why are you so sad Uncle Lane?" She twirled a curl around her finger and kicked her sandy feet in the air. "You're never the sad one. That's always Daddy."

Perceptive little shit. God, I loved her something fierce. I gave her a grin and dragged my finger down her nose. "What's Uncle Cy?"

She giggled and stuck her tongue out at me. "He's the mean one, and you're the nice one. You're the funny one who makes everybody laugh, but not right now. You haven't laughed once since you got here. I don't like it." Her mouth contorted to a very practiced pout. Very rarely did she not get her way when she pulled that expression.

I sighed and threw myself onto my back, blinking up at the sky through my sunglasses. "Hasn't been much to laugh about lately, Goldilocks. Your Uncle Lane wants something he can't have, and that's no fun."

The little girl crawled on top of me dragging sand and sea with her. She ended up sitting in the center of my chest, her hands clasping my cheeks as she stared intently down at me. "Did you ask for it again?" I tried not to wince as her knees dug into the still healing bullet wound on my side. It hurt almost as much as my broken heart.

I pushed my sunglasses up to the top of my head and tickled her sides making her squeal and roll off of me. "What are you talking about, little bit?"

She held her sides as she laughed and shook her mop of crazy hair out. "When Daddy tells me I can't have something, I hate it. Especially if it's something I really, really want." She lifted her tiny blonde eyebrows up and batted her long, golden lashes at me with exaggerated sweetness. "But sometimes if I wait long enough and plan for just the right time, if I ask him again he says yes, and I get it anyway. And sometimes if I ask Em instead of Daddy, she says yes even though he already said no. So, if you really, really want something you shouldn't stop asking for it."

I sighed and climbed to my feet so we could start to shake the sand off everything and get cleaned up. It would have been smart to bring a pair of trunks to change into, but the only shoes I had were my boots, and that wasn't a look I was brave enough to sport, even a million miles away from home. I was going to take Daye out to dinner and then for ice cream to ensure we didn't interrupt whatever Sutton and Em were up to in that big empty house. "I don't think that works when what you want belongs to someone else. I think you just have to let them have it and realize it was never meant to be yours. We can't always get what we want, little bit, even when you flash those big puppy dog eyes and flutter your pretty lashes."

She huffed a little sound of aggravation and let me rub her down and put her dry shoes back on. She held my hand tightly in hers as we made our way back to the truck. She chattered on about a girl in her class who wanted a new horse and how she had gotten Sutton to offer to teach her new friend how to ride in case her dream came true. She told me that I was the best and that I should always get whatever it was that I wanted because she loved me and wanted me to be happy. It was so sweet and innocent, the way she loved. It made my chest tighten. I refused to tell her that when your happiness was irrevocably tied to another person, you weren't always in the driver's seat on the road to your happy ever after. She had a lifetime to learn about all the ways love could hurt, and many years before she had to find that out the hard way.

I was invested in her bubbly chatter, so relieved that everything that had happened back at the ranch wasn't playing over and over like a horror movie I couldn't turn off, that I didn't notice the woman leaning against the front of my truck watching us. I didn't see the way her dark eyes tracked us or the single tear that slid down her cheek.

Daye had no such problem recognizing we were being watched and were under intense scrutiny. She halted mid-sentence, pulled to a stop, and then let out a scream of delight so loud it sent a flock of gulls angrily into flight. She tugged at the hand I was holding too tightly, keeping her from pulling free and running.

"Daye, what in the heck? What are you doing?" My brother would skin me alive if I let her loose. She'd been through enough; there was no way she was getting hurt or worse on my watch. It burned deep in my chest, the ache where the bullet had shattered my ribs. My ribs throbbed as memories of what happened to her the last time I took care of her darkened our peaceful afternoon. I wouldn't let my mind wander back there and I sure as hell wasn't going to let her get hurt as she tried to bolt from my grip.

She pulled frantically on my hand, her pink, glittery canvas shoes digging into the sand deep enough to gouge out holes. "It's Brynn! Let go! I want to say hi and hug her. Brynn! Did you bring me a present? I missed you!" Every single word was shouted across the sand louder than the one that came before it.

I let her little hand drop from mine only because my body went numb. I couldn't believe what I was seeing, so I pressed my fingers to my eyes and blinked rapidly against the sting.

Sure enough, there was a familiar figure bending down to meet Daye's unchecked and enthusiastic greeting. I knew that hair colored with fire and flames anywhere. I dreamed about those midnight eyes and jerked off to the thought of those endless legs wrapped around me when I was alone in the dark. I would know her anywhere, even here, where she shouldn't be.

Her long hair was caught up in a messy bun on the top of her head, but the light breeze was doing a good job picking it apart. Her hair looked like a halo of fire flickering around her head, and she had a determined slant to her lush mouth as I approached much slower than Daye had.

I shoved my hands into the pockets of the wet and sandy jeans I was wearing, wishing I had my Stetson on so I could hide under the brim. It had been weeks since I last saw her and somehow, she looked completely different. One thing hadn't changed though; her all-important ring finger was still naked and unadorned. I couldn't stop my heart from jumping in excitement at the sight, relief and something so much bigger than that filled my throat and made breathing difficult.

"Brynn. What are you doing here?" The question came out sounding far harsher than I had meant. I wanted to ask her about the proposal, about Jack, but I didn't think I could stand to hear her answers. I was regretting not letting Emrys break the news to me when she'd tried. I had nowhere left to run.

The stunning woman squeezed the little girl who was trapped in her arms and looked at me unwaveringly over the top of her head. The corner of her mouth kicked up into a familiar grin, but I could see the way her fingers shook, and how her lower lip trembled as she answered, "I came to bring you home, Lane. The ranch needs you. Your brother needs you. Webb needs someone to keep him in line and show him what he needs to know. Leo misses you. Things aren't the same with you gone. Nothing has felt right since the moment you left."

That was all nice to hear. It assuaged some of the fears I'd had when there had been nothing but endless road and doubt while I was driving, but none of it was enough to have me packing a bag and hightailing back to Wyoming.

"What about you, Brynn? Why are you the one who came to get me? Why not Cy if he needs me so badly?" I was a dick, pushing for something when I didn't even know if she still belonged to someone else. I was putting my return entirely on her slender shoulders when I was intimately acquainted with the heavy load that slim frame already carried. Getting me home was the rock, and I was the hard place, so fucking hard, and she was stuck directly between the two of us.

"Oh, Lane," her voiced dipped, and I heard her suck in a shaky breath. "I don't need you to come home."

I fell back a step like her words were a bullet that pierced through all my toughest armor. I was getting ready to grab my niece and toss her in the truck so I could get as far away from this woman as I could, when one of her hands reached out and touched the side of my face. I felt the tremor in her fingers and the truth in her pulse as it raced in the wrist lying against my jaw.

"But I *want* you to come back with me more than I've ever wanted anything ever. I want to see you at the breakfast table and hear your stories about the tourists that can't ride. I want to pass you in the hall and share that same smile we've shared since we were kids. I want to bitch at you to separate your damn laundry, so I don't have to, and I want to yell at you to put the toilet seat down. I want to patch you up when you get thrown from a horse and agree with you that Cy is an overbearing ass most of the time. I want you in my life, Lane. I don't know how to live without you there." She looked down at the tips of her boots which were as worn as the ones I had dangling loosely in my hand, and just as out of place on this beach. "I feel like I'm missing half of myself when you aren't around. It hurts."

I pulled my eyes away from the hope in hers and looked to where Daye was examining the shells she'd collected on the beach earlier. She seemed oblivious to the heaviness of the conversation going on around her, but I knew better. The little sprite was sharp as a tack. If I didn't answer the right way she was going to have something to say about it and no doubt she would give Em and her father an earful when we got back to their house.

I let Brynn's words sink in.

We'd always been friends until I couldn't handle it because I was so confused about the way she made me feel and terrified if I admitted to wanting more, then everything would fall apart. Maybe she was right and having part of her was better than having nothing. I'd cut her out of my day to day to save myself the heartache of seeing her knowing I couldn't ever let myself have her, but I missed the little stuff she was talking about. The familiar camaraderie that I'd shut down because it made sharing the same life but moving in opposite directions so hard.

I tunneled my fingers through my damp, dark hair and looked down at my feet. They looked naked without my cowboy, and I suddenly realized everything about me was exposed and vulnerable out here in the world so far away from the one that was meant for me. A sigh so heavy, so thick, that the waves wouldn't be able to carry it out to sea, escaped. I had no idea what the right thing to do was anymore, but constantly running away from her hadn't gotten me anywhere. I couldn't deny that her finally chasing after me was doing something to my insides. I was so confused, but one thing was clear. If she cared enough to come after me, I could show her that I cared just as much by going back with her.

"I want you in my life too, Brynn. Even if that means that you come with someone else. I've been stubborn and selfish. I've been acting like my mother, wanting things to be different than they are but not doing anything to make the situation better. When things got hard she left, I did the same damn thing—not once, but twice." And wasn't that enough to make me feel lower than low? The one person I never wanted anyone to compare me to was the woman who ruined what love meant for all the Warners. I wanted to be the man my father raised me to be, but I'd been acting like the son my mother left behind instead. It was shameful, and for a second I wallowed in that until I remembered the woman in front of me saw someone worth fighting for.

A heartbreaking smile split her beautiful face and her entire body sagged with relief. "Does that mean you'll come home with me?"

I hesitated because I still wasn't sure it was the right call. After a few moments, I nodded and moved forward to wrap both Brynn and my niece up in a rib-crushing hug which made them both squeal. That embrace felt so much like home it made my knees weak.

There was no escaping the way Brynn made me feel. Those feelings didn't stay in Wyoming, they followed me to California. There was no screwing it out of my system or shoving it down into the pit of my soul. All I could do was face those emotions head on and hope I didn't get crushed under the enormity of how vast and heavy they were.

CHAPTER 2

In or Out

BRYNN

FOR THE FIRST TIME IN days, it felt like my world was set back to rights.

Everything was crooked and off center the minute Lane walked out of the house in Wyoming and disappeared. I couldn't think straight. Every step I took was wobbly and unsteady. From the moment I opened my eyes, to the second I fell into a fitful sleep at night, it was like I saw things through a grainy black and white filter. There was no color in any of my days when Lane was gone. There was no joy or light. There was only a massive void where I knew I should be able to feel my heart hurting and my soul suffering, the way they always did when it came to the youngest Warner, but when he left there was nothing.

I thought I knew what it felt like to have everything inside of me freeze and shatter. When word came that Lane had been shot while trying to protect his niece from a madman hell-bent on destroying everything that was important to Sutton, I was sure I would never be able to breathe or feel again. That icy pain, that frigid fear had nothing on the numbness that followed when Lane walked out the door seconds after Jack dropped to his knee. At that moment, I knew I was supposed to focus on the man asking me to share his life with him, the one who wanted me for me, and not because he was driven by some chivalrous need to save me from my messed up family and tumultuous home life.

But I hadn't been focused on Jack. All I could see was the resignation and regret flashing through Lane's pale blue eyes. We were both reliving the moment another man had asked me to marry him. Only that time, Lane hadn't been able to escape the outcome. He'd been reminded of it for years, every waking moment when I'd technically held the title of his stepmom. I was something neither one of us could get away from no matter how hard we tried. It was amazing how much one little yes could change everything.

Now that he was standing in front of me, looking much thinner and more haggard than he had even when he came home from the hospital, I finally felt like I could inhale again. Everything that was fuzzy and blurred around the edges pulled back into sharp focus. I could look at the sky behind his tousled head and see that it was the same stormy blue as his eyes. I could also focus on the lines of tension and stress radiating out of the corners of those eyes and the bruised, dark hollows underneath them. Without him, nothing felt like it mattered. There was no home. There was no peace of mind. There was no safety and security.

When he was close, the littlest things felt hugely important and essential. The twitch of his lips into a wry grin spread warmth that chased away the emptiness for the first time in what felt like forever. The heat radiating off of his long, lean body made my heart kick back to life. When his arms wrapped around me for a seriously overdue hug, I finally felt alive. Finally felt something other than the echoing loneliness and hollowness that consumed me the minute he turned his back on me. Even with Daye trapped between us, I still felt a tingle at every single spot where his body touched mine.

"It's so good to see you." I meant it with every fiber of my being. Looking at him, even as worn and as drawn as he appeared, settled something deep inside of me.

Lane gave me another hard squeeze that made Daye squeal from where she was caught between us. She wrapped her thin arms tightly around my waist. The little girl looked like she had grown a couple of inches in the months that had passed since I last laid eyes on her, but I was happy to see that her green eyes were clear and bright. Missing was the cloudy fear and anxiety that had engulfed her after the ordeal with her father's tormentor and the death of her mother.

"It's good to see you too, Brynn." He stepped back, and I could feel the reluctance in his touch when he dropped his arms. He put a hand on Daye's head and gave her curls a little pat. "Why don't you let Brynn go, and we'll find something to eat. I'm sure your dad and Emrys have worked up an appetite while we were gone." Lane gave me a conspiratorial wink and smiled at me. "Did they tell you where to find us?"

I took a step back so I could lean against my rental car and pushed my hands through my hair. It was a tangled mess from the flight and endless tossing and turning as I tried to sleep the night before. I'd never been more than a few hundred miles outside of the Wyoming border. I didn't hesitate one second when I made the decision to jump on a plane to chase down Lane and bring him home, just like he never hesitated to stand between me and whoever was trying to hurt me.

His protectiveness may have started when he pushed Danny Turner down for pulling on my pigtails, but it never seemed to end after that. If anyone dared to tease me about my torn, ugly hand-me-downs, Lane was there to set them straight. He was quick with his fists and faster with his sharp tongue. No one wanted to be on the other side of his wrath. If anyone dared to touch me, they ended up with matching bruises. When the girls picked on me for not being pretty enough, popular enough, nice enough to fit in with them, Lane was the one who made them regret it. He was all the things I wasn't so when he decided that someone hadn't treated me right he wasted no time using his good looks and legion of admirers to show them what being on the outside looking in really felt like. I existed in a protected bubble at school because he couldn't protect me at home. He was the cushion between me and the harsh reality of most teenage experiences, at least he was until that bubble popped.

Going after Lane meant my first time flying, my first time seeing the ocean. It was also the first time I'd seen Sutton and Emrys since they announced they were expecting a baby. When Em answered the door to their cute little house on the coast, her rumpled appearance, inside out shirt, and bright red flush didn't register because I couldn't tear my eyes away from the softly round-ed curve of her belly. Honestly, I was a tad bit jealous of that baby bump. She was beautiful, and the way she had healed Sutton and pulled him back into the fold of his family was nothing short of a miracle. All I wanted was to do the same thing for the youngest Warner brother. I wanted to bring him home and make him see that no matter what happened between us or to us, we would always be family. He would always be the most important person in my world. He was the person at the center of it, even when I didn't want him to be.

"Em told me where you were. I didn't get a chance to see Sutton. I . . . uh . . . think I interrupted them. I was anxious to see you, so I didn't hang around for too long." It was easy to feel the sexual tension and heat circling Emrys as she hastily gave me directions to the beach. I smiled down at Daye who was still watching me with wide, expectant eyes. "I did have time to grab you something at the airport before I flew out. I would never forget about my girl." I dropped into a crouch and took the little girl into my arms. It felt so good to hold her close while knowing she was happy and healthy. She was practically vibrating with energy and excitement, so much like the Daye that existed before the events in her parents' lives had twisted her day to day into tight, painful knots. This little girl found her safe place and settled into her new home. It hurt that it was so very far away from where those places were from me, but anything that made her look young and innocent again was a good thing.

Evergreen-colored eyes glinted mischievously at me as she practically strangled my neck in a return hug. "I missed you, Brynn, and so did Uncle Lane. He hasn't smiled the whole time he's been here, not even when I took him to see the horses at Daddy's new job." She pulled back and put her small hands on my cheeks. Her tiny face screwed up in a severe and intent expression. She always seemed to know more and see more than normal girls her age. I thought I was immune to being examined by an inquisitive seven-year-old, but the way she saw through me was still unnerving and unsettling. She shouldn't have that much knowledge of how screwed up, and flawed people could be at such a young age. "I'm glad you brought his smile with you, and I'm happy you brought me a gift. Can I have it now?"

Lane broke into our quiet conversation that wasn't quite as quiet as I'd hoped. "Later, Daye. Let's grab some food and give Brynn a few moments to relax after traveling all day. I'm sure your dad and Em are excited to spend some time with her too. What do you feel like eating, little bit?"

Daye turned around in a flurry of blonde curls and excited sounds. She clapped her hands together and smiled up at her uncle, showing every one of her missing teeth. "Sushi!" She said it with such glee that Lane had to struggle to hide his horrified expression. I swallowed down a laugh after catching the look on his face. There wasn't anything close to traditional sushi in Sheridan, Wyoming.

Lane ran a hand through his nearly black hair, messing up the dark strands even more than they already were. "You like sushi? Since when?"

My guess would be the little girl's tastes were widening and expanding in any multitude of ways now that Emrys and her father had shown her just how big and exciting the world could be. I'd never wanted anything more than to find my place and make my home in the familiar comfort of the Wyoming wilderness, but Daye, she was too smart and had already lived too much life to accept *what was* as *what will always be*. She was embracing change with vigor and excitement only found in youth.

"She's a California girl now. Of course, she likes sushi." I let the laugh out as Lane scowled at me, still barely containing his disgust at the idea of eating raw fish. "Don't worry. I'm sure they have something on the menu that you can eat." I inclined my head toward the rental car. "Want me to follow you or meet you at the house?" I was going to have to GPS my way back. There were a lot more roads in northern California than there were in Sheridan and a lot more traffic. Everything was busy and moved so fast, driving felt like a full-contact sport on these roads. Getting back to Sutton's place was going to take nerves of steel and white knuckles on the steering wheel now that I didn't have a missing cowboy to distract me and occupy my mind.

Lane gave the sensible rental a once over, and then shifted his gaze to where his lifted, beast of a truck was parked. I'd seen the mud-splattered, red four-by-four from a mile away, and the familiar sight made my heart thump so loudly I couldn't hear the blaring horns honking at me as I dared to drive the speed limit. That truck meant Lane was close by and everything would be okay once I could touch him, and talk to him. Everything would go back to normal and the home I had sacrificed for would once again be a place where I felt like nothing bad could ever touch me again.

"Follow me. We'll eat there and grab something to take back to the house. That gives Sutton another hour to do whatever it is he's doing with Em." The knowing gleam in his gaze said he knew exactly what it was that his older brother was doing with Emrys. "We can drop Daye and the food off and then head back to the airport so you can ditch the rental."

I blinked at him in surprise as I tried to follow his train of thought. "I was just going to drop it off when I flew home." I didn't see any reason to make an unnecessary trip to the airport. All the people coming and going was overwhelming. It was like I'd stepped off the plane into a whole new world, one that was waiting to swallow me whole and run me over.

"When were you planning on flying home?" Gentle curiosity colored his tone as he watched me carefully.

I shifted anxiously on the heels of my boots and nervously tugged on the ends of my long hair. "I don't know. I bought a one-way ticket since I didn't know how long I was going to have to beg and plead with you to come back to the ranch. I figured I would leave my options open in case you sent me on my way without hearing me out." Dread that he wouldn't even see me when I came all this way ate at my insides from the moment I stepped on the plane until his arms had wrapped securely around me in a hug that I would never forget. Being in his arms felt more like coming home than any time I'd walked through the door of the ramshackle home my mother kept on the reservation, or anytime I'd managed to hide away at the Warner ranch.

He cocked his head to the side and narrowed his eyes at me. "I've always listened to what you had to say, Brynn. Even when the words hurt."

The "yes" that ended everything we may have been to one another. I could still feel the way that word ripped my heart to shreds and turned my future upside down.

I sighed. "Things are different now, Lane. You left." I couldn't keep the hint of betrayal and hurt that colored my tone hidden.

A frown pulled at the corners of his mouth as he moved away to put his boots on. He was looking at the ground, tension tight along the line of his broad shoulders when he muttered, "I know I did. I took the easy way out. I thought things would be even harder than they already were if I stayed."

I scoffed and gave my head a shake. "Things were worse with you gone." At least I was far worse without him there.

I broke Jack's heart, and that made me feel terrible. He didn't deserve to come in second to a man who couldn't or wouldn't love me the way I'd always wanted. But as bad as hurting Jack made me feel, the guilt of those emotions couldn't touch the gnawing ache that consumed my insides at not being able to talk to Lane about how wrong everything had gone. He was my constant. He was my equilibrium.

When he left, he took years of reassurance and comfort with him. I didn't belong on the ranch when Lane wasn't there. The place I tried so hard to make mine felt like it was too wide and open when the youngest Warner wasn't there to take up the extra space with his effortless wit and charm. I didn't fit without him there to fill in the gaps. He represented my reason for being there. With Cy doing his thing with Leo, and many roads and state lines separating Sutton from Sheridan, Lane was the last stronghold for my place on the ranch. Without him there, I had no purpose and was left floating adrift and not tethered to anything.

He arched a dark eyebrow. "I'm in no rush to get back to the mess I'm sure we both left behind. I was planning on hanging out with Sutton for a few more days then making my way back home. There's no reason we can't make the drive together . . . unless you would rather fly?"

I stared at him in silence for a long moment, weighing his words carefully. It had to be more than a thousand miles between Sacramento and Sheridan. That was hours and hours of him and me alone in his truck. We purposely avoided being alone when we were at the ranch. There were many awkward moments of silence and words we wanted to say but couldn't. On the one hand, it was all I ever wanted. Lane Warner, with no place to escape me and our tangled, tormented history. We would finally be forced to put the past to rest, whatever that meant for us moving forward. On the other hand, the idea of being alone with him, trapped in that horrible, uneasy silence that plagued us since the second I said "yes" all those years ago made my skin crawl. There was no guarantee that Lane was ready to lance the wounds we'd both caused that had long been infected and festering. He seemed content to pretend things were fine when they were anything but.

He rubbed his thumb along the corner of his mouth and gave me that grin of his that ensured he got whatever it was he wanted. "We can even take a few days and go to the Grand Canyon and Vegas if you don't mind adding a few stops and several hundred miles onto the trip. I've never really been anywhere outside of home and who knows when we'll get the chance to see it all again."

He was so persuasive with that charismatic smile and the soft look in his eyes.

Daye caught my attention as she reached for my hand. She was bouncing on her toes, eyes as excited as her uncle's. "You have to say yes. It sounds like so much fun. I want to go to the Grand Canyon one day. Did you know that you can ride horses down to the bottom?" She had the Warner charm already and did she ever know how to use it.

"That does sound like fun, but are you sure I wouldn't cramp your style? Especially in a place like Vegas." I couldn't disguise the hesitation in my tone.

Lane never made it a secret that he liked the ladies, the flashier and easier the better. Vegas was built for a guy looking for a good time, and Lane was always up for some fun. There was no way I was hitching a ride with him if it meant that I was going to have front row seats for all of his bedroom antics. I was willing to suffer through a lot to get him back where he belonged, but my battered heart couldn't take watching him with other women anymore. That was one thing about our tenuous relationship that had to change.

He chuckled softly and hooked his thumbs into the front pockets of his jeans. The action pulled the denim down low on his hips flashing a strip of hard, tanned skin. I knew that under his t-shirt he was rocking more than a six pack and had a body littered with carved muscles and sharp lines. Ranch life had blessed all the Warner boys with bodies to die for, but somehow Lane ended up looking the best of all of them. He was the quintessential cowboy, rugged and rough in all the best ways. Too bad he knew it and used every inch of that delectable body to his advantage. I couldn't remember the last time he spent the night alone. All his conquests had to creep past my bedroom door to make their early morning getaway, and there was always a steady stream of them.

"No, Brynn. You absolutely won't cramp my style. In fact, I can't imagine anyone else I would want to drive around the country with. I think we could both use the break from our reality and time away from it all. I promise to behave. So," he lifted his eyebrows and gave me that panty-melting grin. "Are you in or out?"

We watched each other, neither of us giving anything away. I wanted to go with Lane more than I wanted my next breath but I couldn't tell if he wanted me to tag along with the same ferocity. It was the story of my life, a vicious cycle of wanting Lane Warner. Me wanting him and him not deciding what he wanted.

Was I in or out?

Of course, I was in . . . I was all in. I was in so deep with him there was no hope of me ever finding my way out. There was only one response to his question that I could give, my brain and my heart wouldn't allow any other one.

"I'm in."

CHAPTER 3

Close or Far

LANE

MY OLDER BROTHER WATCHED ME out of the corner of his eye as we sat on the back deck of his house. Sutton had moved his family close enough to the ocean that I could hear the rhythmic sounds of the water lapping against the shore. Every breath I inhaled held the flavor of the sun, salt, and sand. It was calming in an entirely different way than the vast quietness and stillness of Wyoming.

I could see why Sutton loved it here. He'd found his place and his peace. He even looked like he fit in with the laid-back California vibe that seemed to be everywhere. His sandy hair had lightened a couple of shades, making it gold where it hung long and shaggy around his face. He'd traded his boots for a canvas pair of Vans, and his too-tight Wranglers were nowhere to be seen. Instead, he was wearing loose board shorts that he'd paired with a plain white wife beater. He looked like he was ready to catch some waves and nothing like the guy who taught me everything I knew about roping and riding. But it was more than just the clothes he wore that had changed; there was something different about him . . . something more settled and less chaotic than he'd always been.

He also looked happy.

But at this moment, there was deep concern shining out of his dark green eyes as he continued to watch me sip the beer Emrys brought out to me a couple of minutes ago. She also brought Sutton a can of soda and a kiss. The brush of her lips was partly because they couldn't keep their hands off one another, but I could sense the apology in it as well. Sutton wasn't drinking, not now, and not for the foreseeable future. It was a new development, one that was necessary and drastic, but we'd almost lost him to the bottom of the bottle and demons that didn't want to be exorcised. I couldn't hide how thrilled I was that he didn't so much as glance at my beer longingly.

His attention was focused solely on me and my reaction as he asked pointedly, "You sure you're up for this, kiddo? That's a long ass drive with just the two of you, and you've barely been able to be in the same room together for the last decade." That was more on me than on her. I didn't know what to do with the Brynn who turned me down when I asked her to marry me. I had no idea how to navigate her being my stepmother, even if it was just a technicality. So, I dodged and deflected to avoid dealing with the inescapable truth of our circumstances.

The truck was packed, and we were ready to go after a long weekend of rest and relaxation. Brynn spent most of her days helping Emrys get ready for the baby. They shopped more than I knew was possible. She spoiled Daye rotten and did a good job pretending she hadn't just walked away from a man who would have given her everything. At night she would disappear, and no one commented when she came back to the house with her face tearstained and her feet covered in sand. A midnight stroll along the beach was as good as anything else when it came to helping deal with the onslaught of emotions she must be feeling.

But, Sutton was right. Not once when she slipped out the

door did I get up and follow her. I didn't ask her if she was okay or what I could do to help because I knew I was part of the problem. I figured she didn't need the guy who ruined everything good in her life trying to make amends. She had enough on her plate, and I hoped with this spontaneous road trip back home, we could finally get back to the place where she shared every morsel from that plate with me without stopping to think. When we were younger, what was mine was hers without question, and vice versa. It hadn't been until we got older and our friendship changed that we started picking and choosing which parts of ourselves we were going to share with one another. I missed having all of her, and I was sick and tired of hiding all the parts of me that were hurting and damaged from our history from everyone, including her.

I used my thumbnail to pick at the peeling edge of the label on the bottle in my hands. "Brynn's always been my best friend, Sutton. She gets me in a way no else ever has. I miss being able to talk to her about anything. I miss knowing I have someone at my back and on my side no matter what." I blew out a heavy sigh. "She's always been the most important person in my life, even if I didn't treat her that way. I'd like to fix our friendship if nothing else, and I think this trip can do that. We're not going to have anyone else to talk to but each other." And I had a lot to say. An entire lifetime's worth of apologizing to do. I needed the time with her to figure out if I could risk losing her by asking her for more than I'd ever asked from her before.

Sutton used one sneakered foot to push off the deck and rocked his chair up onto two legs. He pulled his gaze away from mine with a scowl. "You know Cyrus and I have your back no matter what, and we're both going to be on your side forever. You're never alone when you're a Warner. You don't need to drag Brynn halfway across the country to know that."

I cringed not thinking that his older brother instincts would hone in on that. "I know you do, Sutton. Both of you have been there for me whenever I needed anything, but it was different with Brynn. Whatever I did, whatever mistakes I made, she never made me feel like I was letting anyone down but myself. She let me be me, not the impulsive little brother, or Boyd Warner's youngest son. She stood by me because she wanted to, because she believed in me. Not because of familial obligation. She forced me to see that Mom leaving and continually finding fault with everything I did was about her, not about me."

Knowing I had someone to lean on like that had gotten me through my oldest brother leaving for college, my mom appearing and disappearing for the entirety of my childhood, and finally my dad's illness. When Boyd Warner told his boys he had stage four prostate cancer, and the prognosis wasn't good, his oldest had immediately shifted gears to get his ass home. His middle boy had shut down emotionally but effortlessly stepped into the role of ranch foreman with no question. And me as the youngest, the one who was his happy, jokester son had pulled on a brave mask and taken on the part of family cheerleader. No one was allowed to wallow and be fatalistic and grim. I took it upon himself to make sure his father's last days held nothing but good memories, laughter, and cheer. But underneath that mask, I was a wreck. I was shattered. I cried every night alone in my room and wondered what I was going to do when my dad was gone. He was my hero. My mentor. I was lost and so alone, not wanting either of my stoic brothers to see the way I was breaking inside. I tried to hold my family together, but Brynn, she was the only thing keeping me from falling apart.

She let me cry on her shoulder when no one else was around and didn't make me feel weak for breaking down. She made sure we all stayed fed and that Boyd never once missed a doctor's appointment. She was the one who tried to make me laugh when I was exhausted beyond measure trying to do the same thing for everyone else. She was the person who stayed hopeful and optimistic, even as it became apparent the end was getting nearer. And possibly the most important thing she did was remind all of us every single day that our dad loved us and that even when he was gone that love would remain forever.

Brynn knew. She never let me wear the mask around her. She held all the ugly jagged pieces of my broken heart in her hands, holding onto them for me until I was strong enough to put them back together. There was no artifice with Brynn, and I missed that. I couldn't hide behind my smile and charm with her. She saw how angry at my mother I was and how devastated I was by the inevitable loss of my father. She knew how desperately I wanted to live up to the expectations set by my brothers before me, and how I struggled to find my own identity coming up in life behind the both of them. She never underestimated me or discounted that I could be as ruthless and merciless as my older siblings when it came to protecting mine and those I was loyal to. She was there right alongside me as Boyd raised me to be a man who knew what was important and how to fight for the things that mattered. Defeat wasn't in the Warner vocabulary, which is why I was determined to use this trip home to repair all the damage that we did to our relationship over the years. I couldn't take the divide anymore.

Sutton's chair rocked back even farther. "Brynn is family."

I knew that.

Brynn being family is what ruined us in the first place. "I know that. She went from being mine to protect and care for, to all of ours." Maybe I wasn't good at sharing, after all, I was the youngest. I grinned at the thought and turned to look at him. "I want to fix things between us. I don't want to go back to the ranch and have it feel like we are opponents facing off in the ring anymore. Neither one of us is going to win that fight. We both belong on the ranch." We were so close day in and day out, but so, so far away from each other in all the ways that mattered. We lived lives that ran parallel to one another, never crossing and never connecting, but somehow always intertwined. That gap was steadily widening, and soon there would be no way for either of us to reach across to touch the other.

Sutton grunted in agreement and pointed his colorful can in my direction while keeping his gaze trained out on the horizon. "You gotta know that if it isn't Jack or the next cowboy who comes calling, that eventually there will be someone who comes along and gets her to look at them the way she's only ever looked at you. They're going to see those legs and that hair and refuse to take 'no' for an answer. They're going to find out how sweet and caring she is, and they're going to hear about her nightmare of a childhood and move mountains to give her the kind of life she deserved from the start. Brynn might belong on our ranch, but she deserves the kind of love and the type of life that she might not be able to find if that's the only place she ever is." He tilted his head to look at me, his expression stern and thoughtful at the same time. "She doesn't think she'll fit in anywhere you aren't, Lane. You're her anchor, and it's up to you to keep her steady and safe in the waves, but you have to realize you can also sink her so fucking deep she'll never sail anywhere. I'm all for you making an effort to fix your friendship with her, that's been a long time coming, but do not use the ties that have bound you together for so long to trap her when there is so much more out there for her. You'll hate yourself if you take those opportunities away from her, and eventually, she'll hate you too."

I wanted to tell him he had no idea what he was talking about, but the truth was he knew better than anyone else what it felt like to be trapped in obligation and responsibility. Neither Cy nor I had noticed what our father's legacy was doing to Sutton until it was too late. He had drowned right in front of me, pulled under by the weight of expectation and the fear of the unknown.

My hands curled around the bottle, and I lowered my head to look at the deck between the scuffed toes of my boots. "I don't want to hold her back." But I couldn't say I didn't want to hold her down because I did, preferably while she was naked and I was pounding my cock as deep inside her as I could get.

Sutton sat forward, the front legs of the chair thumping loudly on the deck. He reached out a hand, and the familiar feel of the work hardened palm on the back of my neck and calloused fingers squeezing me there pulled a relieved sound out of me. He might look like a new and improved version of Sutton, but at his core, he was still the older brother who let me follow him around and showed me everything I would need to know to be the best rancher I could be. The parts of him that I loved the most were still there under the new packaging. "I'm not saying you're holding her back. I'm telling you that you might not be the one who can give her what she wants and if you recognize that, then you need to do the right thing and let her go once and for all." He gave me a little shake like I was a misbehaving dog that made me scowl at him. "Cy called and told me what happened at the engagement party. You hightailing out of there when you saw that ring tells me you were scared shitless she was going to say yes. That tells me you *want* to be the guy who gives her what she wants, but you don't know how."

I was scared, terrified that everything I knew about her and me was going to change. "I tried to give her what I thought she wanted when I asked her to marry me a hundred years ago. I got it wrong then, how am I supposed to know I'm getting it right now?"

I still felt her rejection deep down inside of me. It used to throb and ache incessantly. Over the years the pain had dulled to a low hum until someone randomly bumped into a memory that triggered it. If she belonged to someone else, for real, not just in name, maybe I could finally let the simmering attraction and prickly want that crawled under my skin go. If she were no longer a Warner, I wouldn't be torn between the way I felt for her before and the way I felt about her after she let my dad sacrifice everything for her.

He made a noise low in his throat. "Brynn's not going to say yes to anyone who isn't the right person. Not after what happened the last time she said it. She may have gained a family and a safe place to call home, but she lost her best friend and her dream of a happy ever after. You have to know as scared as you were when Jack whipped out that ring, she was just as scared when she heard you took a bullet to the chest. No one is that scared for another person without a little bit of love being involved. You're the most important person in her life too, Lane. Don't take that lightly."

I watched as Sutton absently rubbed the spot in the center of his chest where the bullet he took while trying to save Emrys from being raped and tortured had ripped through him. That was another thing about Sutton that hadn't changed. He had a hard time letting go of every mistake and misstep he made along the way, with his family and the woman he loved.

I lifted my hand and pressed on the spot on my side where my bullet wound was still healing and tender to the touch. "Does it ever stop hurting?" I wasn't talking about the injury so much as the memories of how we each ended up with the marks in the first place. I could still see Daye screaming and struggling in the arms of the man who shot me. She was crying, screaming her head off for her dad and me. All I could do was keep my head above water as the bastard who took her dragged my bleeding, barely conscious body into the river. I was supposed to protect her, and I failed. The knowledge of that burned worse than any of the surgeries I'd needed to fix my punctured lung and shattered ribs.

He pushed even harder on the mark that was peeking over the

collar of his wife-beater. It was still red and raised even though it was long healed. It was a constant reminder that he risked his life for the woman he was going to love.

"Eventually I started to remember that every single day I get to wrap my arms around her and hold her close instead of seeing the look of terror on her face when it all went wrong. It takes time, but sooner or later you focus on the fact the person you tried to save is still here and not on the fact you almost lost them. The pain of watching someone you love suffer never goes away, but ultimately it's a good reminder to stay vigilant and to make sure you cherish the people who matter most because you can lose them in the blink of an eye." Like Daye lost her mom. Like we lost our dad.

I shook my head and bent to put the empty bottle down on the deck by my feet. "I would never be able to look you in the eye again if anything had happened to Daye. I can't imagine forgiving myself for letting that psychopath get the drop on us. I should have done more, been more vigilant." It was a sore spot that I hadn't stopped picking at since the day I woke up in the hospital and Cyrus gave me a rundown of what happened at the river that day.

A smile pulled at my brother's mouth, and the curled hand around the back of my neck gave the tense muscles there a squeeze. "We all could have done things differently, Lane. You don't get to take all that guilt on yourself. That is too heavy a burden for one person to carry alone. My little brother and my daughter got to go home, and the man who hurt them will never see the light of day again. It was a hard-won victory, but it's a victory nonetheless."

He cleared his throat and dropped his hand. Emotion made his voice thick and deeper than it usually was as he told me, "I'm proud of you, Lane. You are an amazing brother, a fantastic uncle, and you are a good man. You have the best parts of all of us in you, which is why I know you will do right by Brynn, even if it means staying to face all your fears."

Any time one of my brothers told me that they were proud of me and appreciated the man I had become, warmth spread throughout my chest, and my heart swelled double in size. All I wanted was to be like them and to be the kind of man they were honored to have stand with them. Their praise made me feel like I had taken everything my father taught me and put it to good use. I wasn't letting my dad down if I had Cyrus and Sutton's approval.

It was my turn to clear my throat and battle back the clog of emotion that was threatening to choke me. "I'm proud of you too. I'm so glad you finally found what you needed to be happy. That's all I ever wanted for you."

His answering smile lit up his entire face, and for a second all I could see was the carefree teenager I used to play football with in the pasture behind our home, and the guy who taught me how to chase girls and what to do with them when I caught them. "Got a lot of reasons to be happy now, and one on the way. It's hard having all of that here while you and Cy are back home, though."

His grin dimmed just a fraction so it was my turn to reach out and clasp the back of his neck so I could give him a reassuring squeeze. "Your happiness is so big, so immense, we can feel it all the way in Wyoming, Sutton. The distance doesn't matter, what we fill it up with does, and our distance is full of good shit. We don't have to be in the same state to share all the great things happening in your life. Though, we both know there isn't a chance in hell Leo is going to let Emrys bring that new baby into the big, bad world alone."

That got me a snort and a nod. "Trust me, I know. Em already told me if only one of us is allowed in the birthing room, it's gonna be Leo." He didn't sound upset at that, but then again, he probably knew his pregnant woman was kidding. Sutton was a wonderful dad and a committed partner. He wasn't letting any baby of his come into the world without being the first person there to whisper soft words to them and comfort them, all the while ensuring that Emrys was well and healthy and that Daye welcomed her sibling into the world right along with them.

Leo Connor was Emrys's best friend, a former California girl as well. She was a fiery redhead with a savvy business mind and my oldest brother's fiancée. She was the glue that had filled in all the cracks where we Warners had fractured.

I hadn't realized how much I missed her smart mouth and meddling ways until I brought her up. I didn't recognize how much the world around me was changing until I called Leo Cy's fiancée in my head and teased Sutton about the upcoming birth. One brother was getting married, another one was having a baby, and here I was stuck in the same old rut. Caught between what I wanted most and what I told myself I could never have. Could I really risk loving someone the way I wanted to love Brynn from the start, knowing there was no guarantee she wouldn't eventually walk away? That old fear was thick and hard to cut through, but I was starting to see all the good things on the other side of it.

It was time for something to change.

It was time for me to change . . . and not just because I was trying to keep up with, or trying to prove something to my big brothers. No, I needed change so I could have what they had . . . happiness.

CHAPTER 4

Help or Hinder

BRYNN

I T WAS A TWELVE-HOUR DRIVE from Sacramento to the Grand Canyon. I figured Lane would pull the typical 'I-can-make-the-whole-drive-in-a-day,' thing most men were known for. He surprised me by offering to stop in Joshua Tree National Park for the night so we could camp and see the desert. It was out of the way but since we were playing it by ear and sort of going where the wind took us it made sense to divert our route. When he said he wanted to take his time and see as much of the West Coast as he could, he meant it. He even offered to spend the day at Disneyland with me, but I wasn't close to being ready to spend any time at the happiest place on Earth when my insides felt like they were at war with each other. I passed on getting to meet Mickey but readily agreed to a trip through the Mojave Desert on the way to Vegas, which was closer than the Grand Canyon, making it our next stop on this possibly ill-conceived adventure. The barren sprawl of the desert and the clear night skies were more my speed than a crowded theme park anyway. I was hoping the quiet and emptiness would calm the riot of feelings fighting for control inside of me.

The first couple of hours flew by in a mostly companionable

silence that only broke when his phone's GPS told him to turn or warned that we were about to get stuck in California traffic. When he swore at the other drivers on the road it made me smile and laugh but didn't exactly open the door for conversation. He didn't like the traffic any more than I did and his massive truck had a much harder time navigating the packed freeways than my little rental. He sang along to the radio, often sounding better than Blake, Luke, Keith, Garth, and Sam.

I recalled that it was when we started middle school that Lane became determined to find something that pulled him out of the shadow of his older brothers. Cy was the town golden boy, the prodigy. Sutton was the Big Man on Campus, the most popular guy in school, and Lane was simply Cy and Sutton's little brother. Nothing more. It drove him crazy that everything he did or didn't do ended up being compared to one or both of his brothers. His accomplishments were never celebrated for what they were worth because his brothers had already been there and done that. In seventh grade, a classmate brought in his dad's guitar for some project and Lane watched, enthralled as the other kid pitifully strummed a terrible version of "Brown Eyed Girl" by Van Morrison. After class Lane rushed home to beg his old man for a guitar of his own. Unfortunately, Lydia Warner surfaced at the same time and proceeded to break her son's heart, like she always did when she was around. She told Lane there was no point in getting a guitar unless his father ever agreed to leave the ranch. She told her disheartened son that as long as the Warners were stuck in Wyoming and tied to the ranch, that all they would ever be good for was shoveling horse shit and playing babysitter to a bunch of worthless cattle. According to her, musicians belonged in the city and had no place in a depressing, desolate place like the home Lane and his brothers loved.

Lane knew he was never going to leave his father or the ranch, so he forgot about the guitar and refused to tell his dad all the awful things his mom had to say about their home. Not that her words or actions would have surprised Boyd. The man loved Lydia to distraction, but he was beyond familiar with her disdain for everything he had worked so hard for. He would never tolerate the vile woman poisoning her youngest child's dreams, though. His boys were the only thing in the world Boyd wouldn't let Lydia tear apart and disparage. So, when I told Lane's dad how desperately Lane wanted a guitar, and how excited he was before Lydia got ahold of him, Boyd Warner wasted no time in getting his boy an acoustic Martin that would've made Johnny Cash proud.

Lydia took the gift as an opportunity to pick one of her final fights with Boyd. She accused him of giving the boys false hope and dangling the prospect of having more than they were destined for in front of them like a carrot. She took off, again, and missed Lane being a natural when it came to making music. He learned by ear, not needing lessons at all, his voice, when he sang, was raspy and rich. Unique to Lane and guaranteed to make women sigh in appreciation and men stomp their feet and want to two-step. The boy was already irresistible with that killer smile and inherent cowboy swagger. When he had a guitar in his hands, and a love song slipped from his lips, he was more potent than the oldest whiskey and the strongest drug. Cy couldn't carry a tune to save his life, and Sutton was all thumbs, so making music effortlessly was the one thing Lane had that was all his own. Lane found the thing that set him apart from the rest, proving his horrible mother was wrong. He used his guitar to make the overnight trips from the ranch which people paid the Warners a lot of money to go on, more enjoyable and lively. The tourists loved to hear him play, and Lane loved that he brought something no one else in the family did to the business.

That was Lane to a T. He was the guy who wanted to be useful, invaluable, needed by everyone who mattered to him. That was ultimately why we fell apart. I didn't *need* Lane Warner to save me, but I *wanted* him to love me. I wanted him, period.

"You doing all right over there? You're pretty quiet." His gruff question broke into my meandering thoughts and pulled me back to the present.

I gave myself a mental shake and played with the end of my long braid to avoid looking at those questioning blue eyes. "I was just thinking about the first time you ever sang to me. It's been a long time since I got a private Lane Warner concert. I haven't heard you sing in years. I think you sound better now than you did back then."

I watched his eyebrow quirk from the corner of my eye. He had a ball cap on with the ranch's logo, and that, coupled with the quizzical expression on his face, made him the poster boy for what a rugged yet adorable, Country Western sex-god should and could look like.

"I play all the time. I guess I don't play much at the house anymore. I save it for the paying customers." His full lips twitched up into a familiar grin, making heat coil low in my belly. All this time and his littlest expression lit me up from the inside out. He was more than potent with age; now he was straight up lethal. "I remember learning how to play Taylor Swift when you were deep in your Swifty phase. Man," he shook his head ruefully. "I did everything I could think of to make you smile back in those days." He lifted an eyebrow. "Now all the teenage girls I take out for rides fall in love with me because I can play their favorite songs."

That wasn't why they fell in love with him, and he damn well knew it.

I chewed relentlessly on my lower lip to keep from blurting out that he hadn't done any of the things that would guarantee I never stopped smiling. He never kissed me. He never wrapped his arms around me in a hug that wasn't full of friendship. He never looked at me longingly the way I looked at him. He never let himself love me.

I returned a strained smile that never quite formed fully and turned my head to look out the window. "It didn't take much for you to get a smile out of me back then. Anytime I saw you it made me happy. You were the one good thing in my life for a long time. When I saw you, I could leave all the garbage that was going on at home behind and pretend to be a normal kid. I knew you weren't going to let anything inside the walls of that school hurt me." I suffocated on the reality of my day to day, trapped in the same house as my mother, and all her desperate choices. But when I was with Lane, I could breathe.

He made a sound low in his throat and tapped his fingers on the steering wheel to a beat only he could hear. "When did that change, Brynn? When did looking at me start to make you cry instead of smile? And don't tell me it was when I proposed, and you decided to tell me 'no'. Things were off with us long before you let my dad step in to save you instead of letting me slay your dragons. I'm still not sure how we went from friends to strangers overnight."

Clueless. He was clueless. He always had been. I'd gone out of my way to keep my feelings for him to myself because I didn't want to scare him off. I couldn't fathom a life without Lane in it, so I played the part of his best friend without complaint, until being around him while he ignored me and chased other girls made it just as hard to catch a breath at school as it was at home.

"Do you recall asking me to go to homecoming with you junior year?" There was so much in that simple question, and I knew he couldn't miss the weight of it in my voice.

I could see his reflection in the glass of the window I was looking out. His handsome face screwed up in confusion as he tried to pull up a long-forgotten memory that was insignificant to him. It was a memory that meant everything to me. I could clearly remember the excitement and thrill when he asked me to go. I couldn't care less about getting dressed up and going to the dance, but I was elated at the idea that Lane might finally be looking at me as something more than his buddy, his pal, his bestie. I said yes so fast it was embarrassing, but not nearly as embarrassing as the crushing disappointment that followed when Lane explained that he wanted to take Shelby Donner to the dance, but her parents wouldn't let her go with him. By that time Lane had earned a bit of a reputation as a man-whore, one that was well deserved and sadly accurate. I figured that he only wanted to take me to the dance because he knew I didn't have a date and then ditch me once we got there so he could hook up with Shelby. If her parents thought he had another date to keep his wandering hands busy they were more than likely going to let her go. He wanted to use me as a smokescreen so he could get laid, and he had no clue that his asking me to cover for him crushed me.

I went, but I didn't bother dressing up. I didn't pretend to have a good time. I walked into the gaudy, tackily decorated gymnasium, accepted Lane's one-armed hug of gratitude, then turned and walked right back out. I surprised my mom and her most recent boyfriend when I got home early and ended up with a black eye and broken wrist for the perceived violation. They were pissed I showed up early. Mom's latest mistake thought it would be fun to shave my little sister's long, beautiful, raven black hair off while I was supposed to be gone. Because if I had been home, there was no way I would have let him get as far as he did. He claimed her beautiful, long, black hair was too much work and made her look too ethnic. He was pissed because he swore that whenever he took Opal off the reservation that people in town looked at him like he had kidnapped her. He didn't like the whispers and stares, or the fact that she was so obviously not his kid.

My mom wasn't doing anything to stop him. She never intervened when she had a man who was willing to pay the bills and warm her bed. My sister was screaming, fighting with everything her tiny body had in it, and when she caught sight of me, she looked at me like I was her very own hero whose sole purpose was to save the day. I was sixteen years old. Way too young, and vulnerable, to be anyone's hero, but I took on my mom's brutish boyfriend and managed to save my sister's hair.

Sadly, that particular boyfriend caught Opal on a sick day when she was home alone and buzzed her head anyway. I wanted to kill him, would have tried, but I was still healing from the previous beating. Instead, I sheared my locks down to the scalp, so my sister didn't feel alone and embarrassed by her unwanted haircut. Lane freaked out when he saw me the day after, but by then I could hardly speak to him without wanting to burst into tears, so I didn't try and explain. He always asked about the bruises and marks I couldn't hide, but the story was always the same, and I was tired of the ending not changing, so I was done telling it.

I got a little choked up when I remembered that a few days after that he'd popped up at school wearing the same Mr. Clean look as me and my sister. Of course, when he did it, it started a trend, and soon everyone was walking around with shaved heads . . . well, the boys were. The girls looked at me like I was a freak, but even though I wasn't talking to him and had started to put distance between us, Lane still refused to let anyone make me feel like I was less than something utterly special.

"Of course, I remember. You told me you would go, but then as soon as we got there, you ditched me. I spent an hour looking for you until Sutton told me he saw you slip out the side door as soon as we walked in." His blurry reflection frowned, and I could feel tension fill the space that separated us in the cab of the truck.

"When I saw you at school on Monday, you wouldn't look at me when I tracked you down and asked you what was up. Not that you could look me in the eye because your eyes were swollen nearly shut. I remember your wrist was all fucked up and you wouldn't let me take you to the emergency room to get it looked at. That was the first time you told me to leave you alone." He sighed, his tapping fingers picking up tempo as their movements became agitated. "It felt like you slapped me across the face when you said that to me. You were the only person who always seemed to want me around, and suddenly you didn't want me to be anywhere near you. So yeah, I remember all of that, why?"

I exhaled long and slow. I leaned forward so I could rest my forehead on the cool glass of the window I was looking out of and tried to force my thundering heart into a regular rhythm. "That's when things changed, Lane. That night was when we went from friends to something else." We would never be complete strangers, but I did realize then that maybe I didn't know everything about him after all.

I heard him shift in his seat and all the history and hurt between us swelled to nearly bursting. I could practically taste the bitter tang of those memories on my tongue.

"Why? What was it about that night that changed everything, Brynn?" He sounded genuinely perplexed and old pain laced through every word.

I lifted my head and let it drop back against the window with a small thud. "The only reason you asked me to go with you was so that you could screw Shelby Donner in the cab of your truck." How could he be so oblivious to how awful that was for me at the time?

A sharp laugh huffed out of him which pulled my head around. Our eyes locked and I couldn't look away from the tick in his cheek where a muscle was twitching. "Everyone wanted to screw Shelby Donner back then. I still don't understand why you walked away from me."

I let out a low groan and plowed shaking fingers through my long hair. I refused to cut it beyond a hefty trim when it started to grow back. It took forever to get past my shoulders, and every time I caught sight of the shiny, flame-colored length, it reminded me of everything I'd had and lost in my life. It made me appreciate the little victories when I spent so much time losing.

"I wanted to be the girl you were trying to get naked in your truck. I wanted you to ask me to the dance because you wanted to be close to me. I wanted you to ask me so that you could slow dance with me and cop a feel. You were everything to me. Everything. And all I was to you was some girl you had to take care of when you weren't too busy fucking your next conquest. I loved you, Lane, and for a while, I could take all those other girls, but then one night I couldn't." There it was, the unvarnished truth. My jealousy was bigger than my fear of being without him. My need to protect myself outweighed my wanting him to want me back.

His handsome face twisted into a furious scowl. His dark brows lowered over his pale eyes, and that lush mouth that was so quick to smile, instead turned down into a frown so fierce it sent a chill dancing up and down my spine. Lane didn't get angry often, but when he did it was like a storm rolling in over the summer sky. Angry clouds gathered in his sky-colored eyes, and his emotions rumbled with the force of booming thunder through the small space we were enclosed within.

His head cocked to the side, and his voice was barely more than a rough growl when he bit out, "If you loved me, then why did you tell me no when I asked you to marry me, Brynn? If you wanted me, why did you reject me?"

It was the one thing he admitted to being terrified of. Loving someone and having them leave the way his mother had left them over and over again. He was scared to death of the fact that sometimes love wasn't enough. I'd loved him, but that didn't seem to be enough, and that was the impenetrable wall we could never seem to climb. It was there, made of bricks of regret and mortared with remorse.

It was more than wounded pride and hurt feelings that kept him from trusting me and caring about me the way he had before. I always accepted him and recognized what it was that made Lane so special, but when I told him 'no' when he asked me to marry him, all he heard was his mother telling him he wasn't good enough. I wasn't his former best friend; I was exactly the same as the one person who was supposed to love him always but only ever found him lacking.

"I told you 'no' because you never kissed me." One kiss. That was all I needed from him. It would have changed everything. I needed a sign that he could feel for me what I always felt for him. "All you ever saw were the bruises and the black eyes. You had no problem kissing my boo-boos and patching me up, but you never kissed me for real. You saw me as a victim, not as a potential girl-friend or lover. I was a charity case that you could fix. If you had shown one iota of interest and passion toward me—the real me, not the beaten and broken version—I would have said yes even though we were both too young and it would have been a terrible idea." He'd asked me to marry him while I was in a hospital bed, groggy and terrified that as soon as the doctors released me, they would send me back to my mother and the man who had put me there in the first place. It was the least romantic proposal ever. It was something that was necessary in Lane's eyes . . . yet it was tragic in mine.

My mother's worst mistake was a man who was worse than the bully who beat me up and shaved my sister's head. He was dangerous and was tangled up with some really bad people. A month before my eighteenth birthday he'd tried to drug me and sell me to one of his business associates as payment on a loan he was behind on. Lucky for me, one of Opal's teachers noticed that she had been sneaking leftover food from a trash can in the cafeteria and questioned her about what was going on at home. My little sister broke down and told her that there was no money because it was all going to my mom's new boyfriend, so she was only eating one peanut butter sandwich a day. The teacher called child protective services who showed up along with the reservation police just as my mother's garbage boyfriend was trying to hand my unconscious body off to his cohorts.

The boyfriend and the creepy sex trafficker got arrested, and my mom lost custody of both me and Opal for a short period of time. But native laws tended to be strict and antiquated. It wasn't long before Opal went home to my mother. I refused to go back. I poured my heart out to Lane when he came to check on me at the hospital even though our friendship was fractured. I told him I was running away and that I was taking Opal with me. There was no way I was ever going to be in the position of being used as human currency again, and I wouldn't risk my sister.

Lane immediately dropped to his knee and asked me to marry him. If I was his wife, my mother's rule and tribal law no longer had any say in my life and in my sister's future. I wouldn't have to risk my life by waiting until I was eighteen to get out if I was married.

I told him 'no.' I had to, but three days later Boyd Warner approached me with a serious expression on his ruggedly handsome face and a ring in his hand. He explained that Lane told him what was going on under my mother's roof and he explained that he wanted to help. With tears in his eyes, he laid out that he only had a year or two left to live, the cancer was progressing fast. All Boyd wanted before he passed was to make sure his family was okay, and Lane was not okay with me being in danger every time I walked in my mother's door. He asked me to marry him in name only and told me if I agreed he would talk to my mother and make sure that she had no reason to risk Opal's safety anymore. If we were married, he could take an active role in protecting Opal, and the tribal police couldn't fight him on it because he would be family.

I said yes. I had to. I did it through tears knowing everything I wanted was going to burn with that single word. I knew deep down if Lane had ever bothered to kiss me, if he had ever given me any indication that he could care about me the way a man was supposed to care about the woman who touched his soul and stole his heart, I would have had a different answer for him from the start.

"It all comes down to a kiss?" He sounded stunned and slightly taken aback.

I sighed and closed my eyes so I could steal myself against the kaleidoscope of emotions that were flashing across his expressive face. "Like I said, you kissed all my scrapes and scratches, but you ignored my biggest injury, the one that hurt the most."

"Your broken wrist?" Some of the grit in his voice had lightened.

"No, my broken heart."

We made the rest of the drive in silence, and I was grateful because anything he had to say, any assurances that what we had was better than what we could have had, would have been too little too late.

CHAPTER 5

Past or Present

LANE

JOSHUA TREE WAS IMPRESSIVE AT sunset. The retreating sun painted the rocks with fiery light and turned the barren ground a thousand different shades of red and gold. The campsite we picked wasn't overly busy, but several families were wandering around snapping pictures and posing next to the famous bushy limbed trees that littered the area. It was quiet, aside from the excited chatter of the other campers, but the silence that stretched long and seemingly infinite between Brynn and me felt heavier and far bigger than the national park we were calling home for the night.

I liked to believe that I wasn't a completely oblivious male. Even as a teenager I paid attention to the people around me. I was good at reading a situation and responding accordingly. I had to be to survive my parents' prickly, unpredictable relationship. I learned to play whatever part was needed to keep the peace, and I learned to be whatever kind of son my father needed me to be when my mom bailed time and time again.

But looking back it suddenly hit me that it was Sutton who pointed out that Brynn was growing into her coltish legs and filling out in ways that had the rest of the guys at school taking notice. She was almost as tall as I was back then, luckily, I'd had a late growth spurt and now stood eye to eye with my oldest brother who was well over six feet. Her long, red hair was always eye-catching, but at some point, her dark, exotically shaped eyes became her best feature. It took me longer than I wanted to admit that I suddenly noticed that I wasn't the only boy in school keeping track of Brynn Fox's comings and goings. Of course, I knew she was more than beautiful, and my teenage libido recognized how hot she was, but my heart, that sad, confused, mistreated thing could only focus on the fact that Brynn needed a friend just as badly as I did. There was no stopping the refrain that sometimes love wasn't enough to keep the people you needed the most with you.

She was correct when she said that I only ever saw her as a victim. I called her my wounded bird for a reason.

I watched as the bruises got worse the older she got. I seethed with silent rage every time she winced in pain or cowered in fear when someone bigger and stronger than her invaded her space, which was why I started standing between her and anyone I con- sidered a threat. I begged her to talk to someone, to ask for help. I wanted her out of that house of horrors, and I longed for Harmony Fox to get a taste of what she was putting her daughters through.

Brynn told me over and over again that no matter who she talked to or what they did to intervene, the tribal authorities would always return her and more importantly, her sister, back to their mother. Brynn's mother was half Crow, and her grandfather was deeply involved in the politics and struggles of the reservation where she grew up. She told me over and over again that she wouldn't leave her sister since she was the only one standing be- tween Opal and all their mother's twisted machinations. She felt like it was a no-win situation and I felt useless every time I tried to help her.

Back then I thought the way she looked at me might have

changed as we got older. I felt her pull away when I started dating and sleeping with pretty much every single girl in our class who wasn't my stunning best friend. Our hugs no longer felt innocent and harmless. There was something else trapped between us, and I couldn't figure out a way to get around it or get over it. There was no way in hell that I was ever going to treat Brynn like I treated other girls. I needed her too much to risk our relationship. For me sex was fleeting, a way to pass the time and feel good while my home life remained shaky and unsteady underneath me. My dad tried to give us a little bit of everything, but he could never make up for the fact that our mother never missed an opportunity to let us know how each and every Warner ruined her life. The ranch was failing, as many were when the economy crashed, and my older brother was getting ready to leave for college. Brynn was my constant when things were at their worst, so even though I wanted to kiss her and to touch her like I did all the other girls that passed through my adolescence, I refrained. I didn't want to break her heart and give her a reason to leave me; now I knew I'd driven her away instead. I'd forced her to go.

Swearing under my breath, I pounded the final stake into the ground to hold the tent I'd just pitched in place with more force than was necessary. Sutton had hooked me up with all his extra gear, so I'd managed to avoid another loathsome shopping trip on our way to the desert. I grunted as the action pulled at my still healing wound and lifted a hand to touch the tender spot under my shirt. I had another scar that sliced across my abs from where I'd needed emergency surgery on my intestines. The bullet I'd taken protecting my niece shattered a rib, and somehow a tiny, sharp piece of that broken bone managed to nick part of my intestines. The infection and repeated surgeries that followed did more to put my life on the line than the bullet did. I was lucky to be here, regardless of the tension between us that felt like it was going to crush us both. And it was fortunate that Brynn was here as well, instead of enjoying her engagement to a cowboy who wasn't me.

I stood up with a groan while twisting and turning to try and work out some of the twinges that pulsed underneath my skin.

"Are you all right?" Brynn's quiet question pulled me from my bumpy trek down memory lane.

She was standing by the lowered tailgate of the truck fishing around in the coolers for provisions for dinner. Camping was second nature to both of us. Brynn was also no stranger to roughing it, so we divided up tasks without speaking because each knew the other's strengths. She could make a gourmet meal with nothing more than a propane camp stove and a few scraps, and I was as comfortable under the stars as I was in a five-star hotel. I didn't want to think about the fact that we only had one tent and it would be the first time we'd spent the night together since we were teenagers. A familiar current buzzed and popped between us but now it seemed charged with something new and undefined . . . and that made it feel dangerous and a bit overwhelming.

"Just moved wrong. It's nothing." I pressed on the sore spot and flinched involuntarily as a stinging, sharp pain stabbed all the way down my side.

She made a sound that indicated that she clearly didn't believe me. I heard her approach, but it still made me jump when I felt her hand land on my back between my shoulder blades. It'd been a long, long time since Brynn put her hands on me voluntarily. I felt the impression of her slender fingers like a brand through the cotton of my shirt.

"You look pale, and you have those white lines around your mouth that you only get when you're in a lot of pain. Remember when Gentry first bucked you off and you dislocated your elbow?" I could hear the soft censure in her tone that reminded me she knew I far too often pushed myself so hard that I broke.

Of course, I remembered that. Gentry was the first horse that my old man bought just for me. He was mine to break in and to train. I wanted to make my dad proud; I wanted to show him that I was as good as my brothers, that I belonged on the ranch with him no matter what my mother said. I was overzealous in my desire to prove myself and didn't take the time and care that was needed to get Gentry used to me. I didn't give myself enough time to earn his trust. I rushed it, and the horse had let me know in no uncertain terms he was having none of it. When I got tossed, I landed wrong and not only dislocated my elbow but also tore a bunch of tendons in my knee. It took both me and the horse months and months to have any confidence in one another again. The worst part was I felt like I let Boyd Warner down. He believed in me, gave me a huge responsibility, and I let my ego and need to prove myself get in the way of being the son he believed me to be, the son I so desperately tried to be.

"It's my ribs. They take forever to heal. Sometimes I move wrong, and it hurts like a bitch. I should wrap them up for the next few days since we're sleeping on the ground tonight and logging some major hours in the cab of the truck." I'd learned that trick when I left the ranch and headed to Sacramento. Stabilizing the spot seemed to help with the shooting pain that randomly caught me off guard.

Brynn shifted behind me, and her hand fell away. I felt the loss of her touch all over my body. It was like someone had dumped a cold bucket of water over my head. A shiver worked down my spine, and I ordered my wayward emotions to behave. I was getting ready to ask her what she was making for dinner when she waved her hand toward the back of the truck. "There's a First-Aid kit in there somewhere. Come sit on the tailgate, and I'll wrap your ribs up for you."

I was no stranger to this woman patching me up and putting

me back together. We both did our fair share of playing nursemaid, but something about letting her tend to my aches and pains now seemed significant and more important than her slapping a Band-Aid on my scraped knee.

Blowing out a breath, I snatched my hat off my head and raked my hands through my hair. I was annoyed to see that there was a slight quiver in my fingers as I started to work on the buttons of my faded plaid shirt. I'd tossed on one of the new ones I picked up on the road over my plain, black t-shirt when the sun went down. And maybe subconsciously I was looking to put as many layers of clothing between me and Brynn's pretty, golden skin as possible. I burned where her fingers had touched. I was going to go up in flames if I ever got her naked body next to mine. I was supposed to be on my best behavior, I promised her. So, I was going to behave, even if it killed me.

Thinking too slowly to come up with an excuse for not needing her help with the problematic injury, I tucked my shirt into my back pocket and worked the cotton of my t-shirt over my head. I propped a hip on the edge of the tailgate and watched as Brynn rooted around in the chrome toolbox that was attached to the bed of the pickup. She held up a small white box with a red cross on the front victoriously, but the smile on her flawless face faltered when she turned and noticed that I was half naked.

Her midnight-colored eyes raked over me. They were soft and so dark it felt like velvet dragging across my skin as she checked me out from head to toe. A gasp whispered out between her parted lips when she caught sight of the jagged and still-raised scars that adorned my skin.

She moved across the bed of the truck and lowered herself so that she was sitting on the tailgate next to me with her long legs dangling. Her face was tight with an expression I didn't recognize, and her mouth flattened into a tight line. She put the medical kit on her lap and dug around until she found an Ace Bandage.

"Come closer to me and let me wrap you up." She crooked a finger at me and spread her legs, making room for me between her slender thighs.

It was a place I dreamed of being when I let myself wonder what *could* be before I remembered how awful it *would* be if she left me.

Our eyes met briefly before hers shifted and landed on the scar that started below my shoulder blade and circled to my front, ending right near my nipple. I stepped into the space she created for me and heard Brynn suck in a breath. The proximity had my blood heating and things behind the zipper of my jeans twitching and throbbing in a way that wasn't very comfortable. I was the one fighting back a strangled moan when her fingertips landed on the lifted ridge of the scar on my stomach. It was a four-inch line that darted from the base of my belly button and disappeared into the top of my jeans. Her gentle caress left a trail of fire across my skin as she examined all the things about me that had changed from the last time she saw me without my shirt on. The tightly packed muscle and corrugated abs were the same, as was the light dusting of dark hair that spanned my chest and faded to the thin line where it turned into a happy trail. It was the marks of violence and the visual reminder that even a Warner couldn't win every fight that changed how we all looked on the outside just a little.

"You almost died, Lane. I don't think anything has ever hurt as much as knowing you were barely clinging to life and there was nothing I could do about it." When she looked up at me, I could see every second of pain and every ounce of agony she'd been through when I was too out of it to assure her I would pull through. "All I ever wanted was to be able to take care of you the way you always took care of me."

I lifted a hand and pushed at a strand of her hair that stuck to her cheek. The red looked even more like fire and flames in the setting desert sun than it normally did. I wound the silky strand around my finger, forcing her to lean closer to me the tighter the loops got.

"I didn't die though. I'm right here." I lifted my eyebrows up as her hands landed on my shoulders. She was so close I could see the lighter brown in the center of her pitch-black irises, and I could count each of her rapid breaths. When her tongue darted out to slick across her bottom lip, I could practically taste her. I knew she would be just as sweet as all the things she spent hours baking in the kitchen back home. I brought my free hand up and rubbed the pad of my thumb across the lush curve of her lower lip, catching the moisture left behind. I licked her flavor off my finger and watched as her dark eyes blew out with awareness and something deeper. "I'm here. I'm standing right in front of you, not walking backward through the past. I can't change the things we did back then or the way we hurt each other. All I can do is tell you that I never want to be where we have been for the last decade again."

She tried to lean back but I had her head trapped between my hands, and there was nowhere for her to go unless she shoved me away. I dropped my forehead so that it was touching hers and told her with every ounce of sincerity I had in my body, "What I can do, what we can do, is start over. When we were kids, we were caught up in choices that everyone around us was making for us and reacting. We can make our own choices now, Brynn. What do you choose?"

Her gaze dropped and her hands ghosted over my skin until they stopped to rest at my waist. My very interested dick twitched, and heat swirled low in my gut.

"I always chose you, Lane. Always." Her nails dug into my sides, and her eyes were glittering like the night sky when she lifted her head to glare at me. "You were the one who wanted anyone and everyone else but me."

I let her hair unwind from my finger and brushed my knuckle along the narrow blade of her cheek. My voice was raspy and uneven when I told her, "I wanted them for a couple of minutes or a few hours, so I wasn't lonely. You, I wanted to keep. From the very beginning, since before I was old enough to know what it meant, I wanted it to be you and me, Brynn." I huffed out a frustrated breath and rubbed the tips of our noses together. "We fell apart without a kiss. Maybe we can put ourselves back together with one."

She opened her mouth to argue or maybe to tell me to go to hell, but I didn't give her the chance to say anything. I swooped in and closed my mouth over hers, stealing away any protest she might have had. I moved in close, pressing my bare chest against the softness of hers. I held her head in an unbreakable hold, tilting her face up for my voracious assault on her pliant mouth. Her thighs tensed and shook where they rested on the outside of my legs and her spine arched as our hips aligned and every hard, aching part of my body, hit the welcoming heat of hers.

There was no way it could feel like a first kiss. Not with our history and all the things we'd been through together. It was impossible for it to be a kiss that was teasing and exploratory. We knew each other too well for that. I wasn't tender. I wasn't considerate. I wasn't gentlemanly or polite. I didn't kiss her the way that the younger me assumed she wanted. No, I devoured her the way the adult me had been dreaming of doing since he realized he was never going to care about anyone the way he cared about this woman.

My lips slid across hers, wet and slippery. My tongue flicked against hers, eliciting a startled gasp that let me go deeper and taste even more of her unique flavor. She was as sweet as I imagined, but to my surprise, there was a bit of spice mixed in there as well. She tasted as complex and as alluring as she looked. She was a combination of so many things, and I couldn't get enough of all of them.

Her teeth dragged along my lower lip, and I swallowed a whimper as her legs tightened against the outside of mine. My hips kicked forward involuntarily, and I bit down on the tip of her tongue and sucked hard when my cock pressed against the notch at the top of her spread legs. I'd been looking for a place where I seamlessly fit for what felt like forever. Of course, that place would end up being locked between Brynn's legs. We slid against one another, bodies writhing and unconsciously arching into one another. Every sweaty, sensitive place slotted together almost as if we were made to be joined together from the moist heat at her center to the scalding press of her lips against mine. I dropped a hand to the delectable curve of her ass and tugged her closer to the rigid length of my straining cock. When she responded by wrapping a leg around my hip and pulling me deeper into the bend of her body, it was my turn to gasp.

She took advantage of my sudden surprise and twisted her tongue around mine. She wasn't shy when it came to kissing me back since I wasn't giving her a choice in the matter. She kissed me like this was her only chance, and she had to make it count. She kissed me like she was making up for lost time. She kissed me like she wanted me to regret all the years we'd missed having this between us, and I did regret it, every last moment of what we could have been.

It was such a waste.

Neither one of us had much good to fall back on when we were growing up. This was better than good, it was beautiful and bright, and all ours.

I squeezed the rounded swell of her ass and grunted as her nails dragged up my sides. She wasn't handling me as if I would break and I continued to kiss her like I had something to prove. We couldn't get enough of one another, and for that brilliant, blazing moment neither one of us remembered where we were. It was only her and me and this thing that had been between us from the start. Finally letting it loose, and setting it free consumed both of us. I felt like there was no way to get close enough to her, it was impossible to touch all of her at once and to find all the secret places where her different flavors lived. But I was doing everything possible to try.

My palm was sliding across the smooth skin of her stomach, and her fingers were dragging into the short hair at the back of my head when reality rudely interrupted us in the form of a disembodied voice shouting for help and demanding to be released.

I pulled back with a start and blinked at Brynn. I was foggy like I'd been woken up from a dream and wasn't ready to get out of bed just yet. Her face was bright pink, flushed prettily along her cheeks and neck. She wore the same bewildered expression that I was sure I had. I knew without a doubt that I would have had her jeans open and my hands all over her most private of places if we hadn't been interrupted.

That shrill voice reached out through the desert again and caused Brynn to stiffen against me. She cleared her throat and lifted her eyes to mine. "Let me wrap your side up and then we should go see if whoever is screaming is injured or needs help."

I nodded out of reflex and stepped back so I could lift my arms up as high as they would go. When her hands touched me this time, they were efficient and moved quickly as if she didn't want any more contact with my bare skin than was necessary.

That kiss had been a long time coming. There was no way to know if it had been enough to reset our hearts back to the beginning, back before all the damage we had inflicted all that damage on each other's most defenseless parts.

CHAPTER 6

Bold or Timid

BRYNN

IT WAS AN HONEST TO God struggle to stop myself from bolting into the darkening desert around me.

My fight or flight response was going crazy. Half of me wanted to get as far away from Lane and the lingering heat of that kiss as I could. It was everything I'd ever imagined kissing him would be like, and it was nothing like I dreamed about in those moments when loneliness and grief got the better of me. All of the intensity he kept tamped down and glossed over dripped from his lips and pulsed from his fingertips when he touched me. There was nothing easy or relaxed about him when our bodies pressed together. I got pure, unfiltered, and unchecked Lane when he kissed me and that had my fight response fired up and ready to throw down. We burned together. There was a spark as soon as our lips touched and our breath mingled. As soon as he was close enough for his heart to beat against mine, there was no past, no uncertain future. There was no yes or no, and there was no right or wrong. All that existed was the heat that poured across every inch of my skin and fire that licked along my nerve endings. He obliterated the memory and significance of every other first kiss I'd ever had. He forced this to be the only first kiss that could—and would—ever matter . . . and it kind of pissed me off.

When Boyd took me in and promised to keep my sister and me safe, I resigned myself to a solitary life spent as his caregiver while pining away uselessly for his youngest son. To my surprise, it was Boyd who encouraged me to get out and meet new people. He told me over and over again that no one deserved to have their childhood stolen away from them the way I had. He desperately wanted to see me happy, and I think fall in love with someone who could allow themselves to return my feelings.

So, I dated, quietly and infrequently, but only after he passed away. There was already so much talk and so much gossip surrounding our unorthodox relationship that I refused to add more fuel to the fire when he was alive. I didn't want him to be haunted by the rumors that I was a gold-digger just like my mother, that he'd replaced one ungrateful, awful wife with another. I didn't want him to have to defend me when it took all of his waning energy to get out of bed each morning. But after he was gone, I did what he told me to and looked for men who were available and ready for something serious. I didn't bother with anyone who looked at me sideways or who approached me with questions lingering in their eyes. I had no time for a man who thought I was a sure thing simply because of what they heard in town. Boyd forced me to come to terms with my value and worth, and I refused to squander that gift.

I was lucky that there had been good men in my life, great men, and my first kisses with some of them were not moments I took lightly or wanted to forget. But all I could feel was the slightly frantic slide of Lane's mouth across mine and the sense of rightness that settled in my soul when I finally got a taste of him. All this time I'd been trying to find someone to replace him, and with one kiss he destroyed everyone who came before him. I was never going to forget that kiss, and I knew all the way down to the marrow in my bones that I was never, ever going to be able to replace Lane Warner in my heart.

"There are rattlers and sidewinders out here so watch where you step." His voice was smooth and smoky from somewhere behind me.

I gritted my teeth together and cast a look down at the ground, making sure to watch where I stepped after the warning. We had all kinds of wildlife in Wyoming that could kill you in an instant, so I was typically more aware of my surroundings. That kiss was still swirling around my senses, making me careless and rushed.

"I'm not sure where we should be heading. I don't really know which direction the yelling was coming from." When I heard somebody in distress, it sent all my inner alarms trilling. So many nights I called for help whenever one of my mother's mistakes got out of hand, and every time my cries went unanswered. It was only the next day when Lane caught sight of new bruises or took note of the fact I was limping that someone offered a helping hand. I don't know what I would have done without him, and now that I was an adult, not scared to stand my ground, I could never look the other way when someone might need me the way I needed Lane back then.

"Take a left up here. I don't think it was coming from the area where the tents are set up. It didn't sound that close. The RV section is over there a little way, maybe it came from there." I could feel the whisper of his words against the back of my neck.

I looked over my shoulder and realized he was very close to me, blue eyes scanning the darkness, jaw locked in a hard line of tension. I didn't say anything when he retrieved a wicked looking, black handgun from the glovebox of the truck before we set off. The Warner boys were practically born with a firearm in their hands, and after Lane's ordeal down by the river with Sutton's stalker, it was no surprise he was going to be prepared for anything waiting out there in the dark. He might have lost Round One, but there'd be no Round Two if he had anything to say about it.

"We can't be the only ones who heard that scream. It sounded like someone was struggling. Why isn't anyone else making sure everything is okay? This campground is more than half full." My frustration was evident and ingrained deep within me from a lifetime of being let down by others.

Lane grumbled something I couldn't make out under his breath. His warm palm landed on the back of my neck, his fingers biting into the tightness that made my whole-body stiff. The rough caress sent a shiver shooting down my spine and forced my hands to curl into fists so tight that my nails dug painfully into my skin. He was always physically pulling me closer while inexplicably pushing me away.

"People tend to turn a blind eye to problems that aren't their own. They like to think their inaction doesn't matter, but it does. They tell themselves that it's someone else's responsibility to do something about it, but we both know the only way to make sure everyone is safe is for all of us to account. All humans need to take some ownership of what happens to other humans, especially those who aren't in a position to defend and speak for themselves." His voice dropped off, and his hand constricted to the point where it was almost painful.

I wasn't sure if he was thinking about the way I'd been left behind and forgotten about over and over again when I was younger, or if he remembered the way everyone in our hometown let Sutton's ex slip through the cracks. Our entire town knew the woman had a drinking problem and that she was a danger to herself and her child. Instead of helping her and protecting Daye, they ostracized the woman and let her drown in her misery and despair. No one tried to throw her a life preserver, and no one who wasn't family offered Sutton a hand out of the water when he started to sink right along with her.

I gave a nod of agreement. That sense of responsibility, that deep-seated need to protect and defend, was something all the Warner men shared. It was only a small part of what made them all so very special.

The first RV was a tricked-out rental occupied by a young couple who were so stoned I doubted they would remember us stopping by to ask them if they heard anything concerning. They offered to give us a baggie full of brownies that Lane turned down with an amused snicker. The next RV belonged to a family that was visiting from Canada, I could tell by their accents on certain words and their unfailing politeness even though our questions made them obviously uneasy. The dad was outside with a couple of teenagers, and they all looked at us with thinly veiled suspicion when we stopped to inquire about the screaming. Admittedly Lane was a big guy, and his current scowl wasn't very friendly, but he kept his posture relaxed and let me handle asking the questions. They all muttered that they hadn't heard anything, but none of them would meet my gaze when I pressed and insisted that I'd heard someone screaming not that long ago. The next few spaces were empty, and the next three had RVs parked in them that were dark, indicating the owners were either asleep or out and about elsewhere.

My frustration mounted with each step and unease slithered under my skin as I recalled the panic echoing through the air in that scream. Lane looped a heavy arm around my shoulders and pulled me into the curve at the side of his body. His lips ghosted over my temple in a barely there kiss. I could feel how tense he was; his disappointment as palpable as I'm sure mine was.

We were retracing our steps back to the entrance of the RV park when one of the teenagers from the Canadian campsite suddenly called out for us to wait up a minute. I shared a wide-eyed look with Lane, and he pulled to a stop and subtly shifted so that I was stationed somewhat behind him. The teen couldn't be any older than sixteen or seventeen. However, he was taller than I was and had quite a bit of muscle on him. I would bet good money on him being an athlete of some kind. I noticed that his father was no longer hanging out with the kids outside of the camper and that his brother and sister were watching the exchange with obvious concern. The kid wasn't even slightly out of breath as he jogged his way over to where we were standing.

He pushed a nervous hand through his hair, his eyes skimming over Lane. "Sorry about my dad. He has a very firm 'don't talk to strangers, no matter what' policy." An anxious giggle burst out of his mouth, and he shifted uneasily in his sneakers. "He also thinks every single American is carrying around a machine gun, so he's been very cautious this entire trip. This is only our second stop. We're all hoping he loosens up after the first week. My brother and sister and I were kind of hoping we could talk to some kids our age in the places we're visiting, but so far he hasn't even let us do that." He laughed again, but I could see his apprehension plain as day.

I put a hand on Lane's lower back, right next to the spot where he had his handgun tucked away and tried to give the kid an encouraging smile. "Your dad is just trying to keep you safe. Can't blame him for that. It's always a good idea to be cautious and aware of your surroundings. Are you sure you should be talking to us? I don't want you to get in trouble." I kept my voice even and steady. The kid was like a wary animal. I was afraid he was going to bolt any second, and I didn't want him to get in trouble for doing the right thing, not at the start of his family vacation.

He looked Lane up and down again and swallowed audibly. "It's fine, but I don't have long. He had to make a work call, but he wasn't getting good service, so he walked out toward the entrance of the park. He's only going to be gone for a couple of minutes, and he left me in charge." He looked down at the ground and then back up at us, his eyes locking on mine. "The reason he was so weird when you stopped by and asked about the screaming is that we heard it too. My little brother and sister were outside playing tag when they heard someone calling for help. Dad freaked out and ran outside to check on the kids, and while he was out there, he said he saw a guy around my age being dragged by the arm to an old RV that used to be parked a space down from ours. Dad said the kid was struggling, telling the guy to let him go, but the guy doing the pulling laughed it off and mumbled something about brats acting out. My dad was worried about getting my brother and sister inside and out of harm's way. He said he got a bad feeling from the guy who was manhandling the kid. He didn't like the way the older guy looked at my brother. As soon as Dad had the kids inside, he went out to write the license plate of the RV down, but it was already gone." The teenager looked down at the ground and shifted his feet. "He was trying to do the right thing. He feels bad they disappeared before he could alert the authorities." He cleared his throat. "He was just trying to take care of us like you said."

Lane's chin dipped in an understanding gesture. "I get it. And from the sounds of things, it's good your old man is keeping such a close eye on all of you. You said it was an old RV? Anything else about it stand out?"

The teenager rubbed a hand over his face and turned his head to look at his siblings who were still watching us closely. They were a tight unit, watching out for one another. It reminded me of Lane and his brothers who also wanted to do the right thing and refused to let anyone take advantage of their valiant streaks that ran a mile wide.

"It was practically rusted out, man. Like I have no idea how he drove it away without leaving the muffler behind. The windows were covered too, which I remember thinking was really weird.

Why come camping somewhere as cool as this if you aren't going to look at the trees and if you can't watch the sunset?" His head snapped up, and his eyes popped wide as his hands fluttered excitedly in front of him. "There were stickers on the back. They were faded and looked like they'd been there for a long time." He went on to describe the stickers, and I could see his eyes light up when he remembered, "I'm pretty sure the license plate said Texas. It wasn't from California, I'm sure of that. We were playing spot all the different license plates on the way down from Vancouver."

"That's good information. You have been very helpful even though you don't know us. I'm sure your dad will be proud of you for doing the right thing especially when it's kind of scary." I gave him a reassuring smile as his brother called his name.

"That kid, ummm, you think he's in trouble? Do you think that guy was hurting him?" The obvious distress coming off the kid pulled at every heartstring I had.

I plastered a hopeful smile on my face and leaned into Lane's solid form. "I hope not. There's a good chance it was nothing more than a family squabble that got out of hand." My mother had used that very excuse more times than I could count. I could feel the weight of those empty words settle like lead in my gut. "I have a very good friend who works for the National Parks service back home. I'm going to give her a call when we get to our campsite and see if she can call in a favor or two. We'll try and get the right people to check on the kid and the guy in the RV. Your description of the RV should help the right people be able to locate them."

The teen's chest puffed up, and a wobbly smile pulled across his achingly innocent face. "I hope I helped."

Lane clapped a hand on the kid's shoulder and gave him a tiny shake. "You did good, kid. Now, go back to your brother and sister. Be sure to tell to your old man and let him know you talked to us. He might be mad at first, but it would make him even angrier if you tried to hide it. He needs to know he can trust you, and I bet he'll be proud that you're a young man who understands what it means to take a stand in a difficult situation."

Lane and I both exhaled noisy breaths as the kid turned on his heel and darted back to his family.

Lane's arm landed back on my shoulders, and I hooked mine around his narrow hips as we headed back to our camp. I was ice cold everywhere that wasn't pressed against him.

"You think he was kidnapped?" The quiet question felt like it was shouted in the stillness of the night around us. My voice cracked and shivered like I was naked in the middle of a snowstorm instead of fully dressed in the desert.

Lane swore and rubbed his calloused fingers up and down my arm. "I dunno. Could be that, could be sex trafficking. This place is pretty remote, all things considered, and it is on the way to Vegas where a lot of sex trafficking rings are known to be based out of. Though, could be nothing more than a pissed-off teenager fighting with his dad."

I huffed out a sound and burrowed deeper into his side. "You don't believe it's nothing." I knew him better than that. Every bruise I showed him, every black eye I couldn't hide was another reason for him to go to war for me. Going up against someone who was abusing the weak and defenseless was a battle he was willing to fight with very few questions asked.

"The covered windows are concerning. The kid was right about that. Who goes camping with blacked-out windows? Doesn't make sense." He gave me a squeeze that was more reassurance than a hug. "Let's call Ten and see if she can do anything with the rundown of the RV like you suggested. Not much else we can do."

Tennyson McKenna was a long-time friend of the Warner family. She had a history with Cy that went back almost as far as my history with Lane, and aside from being a badass rancher, she was also a full-time forest ranger in Wyoming. The woman was better with a gun than any of the Warners were, and she was fearless. She was sharp as a tack and would know what to do in this situation. I hated feeling hopeless and useless. If there was anything I could do to make sure nothing bad was happening to that kid, then I had to do it . . . there was no other choice.

CHAPTER 7

Bitter or Sweet

LANE

NEITHER ONE OF US GOT much sleep that night.

I could tell Brynn was worried about all the things she couldn't do to help the kid. Unfortunately, Ten hadn't offered any reassurance or platitudes. Without a license plate number, there wasn't much anyone could do to track down the mysterious RV, and without a formal complaint filed, or a verified missing persons report she could link back to the kid there was no legal leg for anyone to stand on when it came to hunting the missing travelers down. As of now, it was nothing more than an uncomfortable confrontation witnessed by a couple of strangers even if something deep within my gut told me there was something much more to it. Ten promised to put some pressure on the park rangers that patrolled the area where we were camping and assured us that if anyone came across the RV, she would have them do a welfare check on the young man. It was something, but it didn't feel like nearly enough. And I knew Brynn felt the same way.

How many times had the authorities stopped by her mother's trailer to check on her and her sister, only to walk away and leave them in the care of a woman who couldn't see past her vices?

Harmony Fox was a master manipulator and a skilled liar. When she needed to play the role of caring and concerned mother, she did, and Brynn was left in that house fighting to survive whatever trials and tribulations her mom's newest conquest put her through. Back then all I wanted to do was drag her out of that ratty, rusted trailer and take her home with me. I wanted to hide her away somewhere she would never be found by the people who left bruises all over her and that taught her to flinch whenever somebody reached out to touch her. Now, all I wanted to do was protect her from the pain that being unable to help someone she so clearly sympathized with was causing her. She didn't want anyone else to suffer the way she had, and that made the feelings I had for her swell even bigger inside of me. Her compassion and kindness were endless, and I couldn't help but be affected by it.

The close quarters didn't help matters either. Every time I closed my eyes, I was enveloped in her sweet and spicy scent. Every way I moved I felt the whisper of her soft skin or the slide of her long, silken hair. My heart beat in time to her choppy, aggravated breaths and when she twisted and turned in her sleeping bag I could feel the air churning between us with sexual tension and a lifetime of dismissed desire. Now that the passion and hunger were allowed out of the cage I'd kept them trapped in, those feelings were starving, ravenous, and barely controlled. I could feel them clawing at my insides, twining up my spine and tangling around my throat. I was close to being a savage, controlled by nothing more than the primal instinct to take, to claim, to devour what my inner animal always considered MINE. There wasn't a single part of me that didn't want every single part of her, but for the first time ever, Brynn was the one who wasn't ready.

She was still skittish from that soul-scrambling kiss, and I could see the way her heart was hurting from having to hurt Jack. It was clear she didn't trust the sudden shift in my willingness to see what she'd put in front of me from the very start. I'd spent so long ignoring all we could be to one another, that it was hard to blame her for being wary of my intentions. All she knew was how I treated her when she was my best friend, and how I treated her when she broke my heroic heart. She had no idea how I would treat her as a woman I wanted to make my own, and frankly, neither did I considering there hadn't ever been anyone besides her that I wanted to tie myself to for the long haul.

Since neither one of us slept more than an hour at most, we were up in time to watch the sunrise over the desert, and if the circumstances were different I would admit to the sight being as beautiful and as breath-stealing as the woman standing next to me. A landscape that was so stark and hostile shouldn't feel warm and dynamic, but each color that shot across the sky, and each grain of sand that sparkled a different shade in the awakening sunshine painted a picture full of life and experiences. It reminded me of home.

Brynn and I worked quickly and efficiently together to break the tent down and paused only long enough to eat a quick breakfast. We spent the morning in contemplative silence, but it wasn't uncomfortable. Vegas was still on the agenda, but some of the excitement about visiting Sin City had waned. Suddenly a city where anything was allowed with very few consequences wasn't as appealing as it was before that panicked scream in the night had ripped Brynn and me apart. We were both intimately acquainted with the results of what happened when someone wasn't afraid of consequences. I'd taken a bullet, and she'd lived a life ducking thrown fists and wandering hands.

The drive was only supposed to take a little over three hours which I was grateful for. While I was too keyed up the night before to sleep, staring at the road and the flat desert landscape that was stretched out in endless, rolling miles ahead of us, was enough to lull my eyes into a series of heavy blinks and to have me fighting back yawn after yawn. Brynn used her phone to book a couple of rooms at one of the flashy, glittery casinos on the Strip and I couldn't wait to face-plant in the center of the king-sized bed. I didn't question her when she said she got two rooms. It was clear she needed some space to work through the way things were changing between us, and I assured her that I was going to be in the suite next to hers all alone unless she decided she wanted to keep me company.

Since I left the ranch, I was running on nothing but nostalgia, remorse, and adrenaline, not to mention I was still healing from major surgery. I was drained, both physically and emotionally. Having my hands tied when it came to helping out that kid who may or may not be in trouble was the last straw. My well was dry, and I needed a good night's sleep, a steak, and a shot—or six—of good whiskey to recharge. I also wouldn't turn down another taste of the woman sitting silently beside me, but I didn't want to be greedy.

"Do you mind stopping at the next rest stop or gas station?" Brynn's question pulled me out of my sleepy musings. She held up an empty bottle of water and gave it a little shake. "I drank one too many of these this morning, I think."

We left the campsite so early that we would hit Vegas before most things besides the casinos were even open. We weren't in a rush, so I didn't feel like I was racing a clock. I told her I would be happy to stop as many times as she needed me to.

She gave me a little grin of appreciation, and I felt the way my blood heated in reaction swirling in my veins. I forgot how great it felt to be the reason she smiled. Even now she didn't do it enough.

"I forget that it's okay to ask for what I want and that I'm allowed to say what I need. Your dad was the one who drilled that into me. He was the first adult I ever met who didn't make me feel bad for asking for more." She fiddled with the ends of her hair. "He was also the one who taught me that just because you asked, didn't mean you were going to get it. He told Lydia over and over again what he could do to make her happy, and when he told her what she could do for him and you kids, in turn, she practically laughed in his face. Boyd was such a good man. I will never understand how he loved someone as selfish as your mom for as long as he did."

I grunted and felt the way my face twisted into a dark scowl. My dad had done everything he could to make sure my brothers and I had a great childhood, except protect us from our mother's frigid indifference and heartbreaking disappointment. He let her ruin our family time and time again because he couldn't stay away from her or tell her no. Not until he got sick and she finally committed the ultimate sin. Dad wanted her to come home and help out with the ranch and to keep an eye on Sutton and me since we were still in high school. He told her that he was dying and that he wanted to spend his last few years as a family, together. He'd been sick for a little over a year at that point without any of us knowing about it. My mom practically laughed in his face. She told him that as soon as he was gone, she was selling the ranch and taking the money to buy a house in Dallas. It was the coldest and harshest she'd ever been, and it was finally Dad's breaking point. He could deal with Lydia not loving him, and not loving his kids, but there was no way he was going to tolerate her not loving and caring for his ranch after he was gone.

Discarding his family's home like it was as disposable as their love had been, taking the only thing left of his legacy away from his sons, he wouldn't stand for it. So, he filed for divorce the next day and put the wheels in motion, cutting Lydia out of everything in case he died before the divorce was final and leaving everything to my brothers and me equally. When Brynn became family, he also left a portion of the property to her, a portion my mom had tried to wrest away from her after my dad passed. She was convinced she could contest the will and prove that she was the rightful recipient of the inheritance due to the length of her marriage to my old man, and because of all the questions surrounding his union with Brynn. Brynn had only been a Warner for a little under a year at that point, but she was so much more a member of our family than Lydia had ever been.

Mom lost, and nothing made me and my brothers happier than to see her go down in flames. The rage she had at no longer being able to dangle my dad at the end of her rope was immensely satisfying, but none of it made up for her years of jerking all of us around.

"He always said there was something special about her. There was something about her he couldn't let go of. Maybe because she was the first person he'd ever loved? Maybe because she gave him three boys to carry on his birthright? Who knows? He never looked at anyone the way he looked at her, even when she broke his heart every time she left." I cut a look in Brynn's direction and let out a sigh. "I used to pray she wouldn't come back. Every time she left I wished it was finally the time she'd had enough of us, enough of the ranch, and she would stay away. She never did." My hands curled around the steering wheel so tight that my knuckles turned white. "She always ran out of money or got bored with whomever it was she was sleeping with. Whenever real life got too hard, she came back to us with her tail between her legs. She was only conciliatory for as long as it took her to drop her bags at the front door."

I spotted a sign for a gas station at the next exit and shifted lanes so we could get off the highway.

"The Warners also have a really hard time admitting they're wrong. Dad held onto Mom for as long as he could, Cy would have never walked away from his first wife even though they were never a good fit, and Sutton put up with Alexa and her madness far longer than he should have. We never seem to get it right the first go around." Which was why I hadn't bothered to try up until now. She made me look at taking that risk in a whole new light. Maybe we were the very definition of it being better to love and lose, than never having allowed ourselves to love at all.

Brynn let her head drop back against the headrest and worried her lower lip with her teeth. "Do you think you're ever really able to let go of the person you love first? Is that love the biggest, brightest love that will eclipse any other love that tries to take its place? Is there no seeing around the love that ultimately teaches us how badly loving someone can hurt? Does first love taint all the other love that follows after it?"

I hit the brakes too hard when I pulled off on the exit. We both jolted forward getting caught in the seatbelts. I hated that I was her first love and that she called all the different ways she felt about me back then tainted. I never wanted her to think of the way she felt about me as dirty or ugly. Even when I didn't know what to do with it or how to return it, I thought the way she loved was the most beautiful thing in the whole world. I'd never seen anything like it until my older brother met Leo, and then again when Sutton allowed himself to fall for Em.

I rubbed a hand roughly over my exhausted face and pulled the truck to a stop at the pumps. "I think first love is important because it shows you how strongly you can feel about another person, both good and bad. Then I believe there is a forever kind of love which is the love that simply feels right. It's the kind that you know was meant to be yours all along. Everyone in my life has been burned badly by first love, but my brothers held out and fought for the forever kind, and they sure seem happy. They didn't have a problem finding their way around whom they loved first, or second, for that matter. They all made their way to the person who could love them the right way, except for my old man. He ran out of time before he had the chance to find the kind of love that wouldn't hurt him every single day."

Brynn reached for the door, cocking her head to the side as she climbed out of the cab. "So, you think it's all a matter of patience? That forever love will find whomever it's meant for?"

I followed her out of the truck, boots landing with a thump on the cracked asphalt. The gas station was quiet, we were the only people at the pumps, and aside from a lone semi parked off to the side, there didn't seem to be any other customers. I watched Brynn through the space between the open doors, and she watched me back just as intently.

"I think that both your first and your forever are important. I don't think you can have one without the other, and I don't see any reason why your first can't also be your forever as long as it's the right person. Someone special."

Her rust-colored eyebrows lifted and another one of those grins that shook me to my very foundation crossed her face. I was starting to think of them as my smiles, ones she only gifted to me. I was going to covet them and collect as many of them as possible before we got back to the ranch.

"I'll keep that in mind. I'm going to run in and do my thing. You want me to grab you anything while I'm in there?"

I tipped my hat back with a finger and smiled at her. "Funyuns."

She wrinkled her nose and made a face of utter disgust. "You still eat those gross things?"

"Yep." I made sure to pop the 'P' on the end and added a wink for good measure. She handled all the cooking and most of the grocery shopping, not only for the family but the guests at the ranch as well. If I wanted a Funyun fix, I had to go into town, and I typically only ate them when I was out on a trail ride. They were my survival rations when I did the tours like the one Emrys and

Leo had initially gone on, the ones where guests paid to live off the land and really, truly rough it for a week. The Funyuns were a lifesaver after five days of fish and whatever else they foraged from the forest.

She rolled her eyes at me and muttered, "gross," just loud enough that I could hear her.

I propped my boot up on the back wheel of the truck and watched as the gas gauge ticked up and up. Fuel out in the middle of nowhere was damn expensive. I was wondering if it would have been smarter to fill up when we got to Vegas when I was jolted from my thoughts at the sound of a vehicle pulling up along the opposite side of the tanks. The RV rattled and shook like it was about to die when it rolled to a stop. I frowned when I realized the ugly machine was more rust than metal and the hair on my arms lifted when I realized all the windows in the ancient vehicle were covered up with wilted and sun-faded cardboard. I couldn't see the plates, but I had a feeling if I walked around to the front of the RV they would be the familiar white and blue ones from the Lone Star state. There couldn't be that many RVs in the desert with blacked out windows.

I pulled my hat down low on my forehead and watched as a burly man hefted himself out of the driver's seat. I watched as he lumbered around the front of the RV, head down while he muttered to himself. The guy was several inches shorter than I was but about twice as wide and it wasn't from middle-aged spread. He was built like a damn bull, and there was no way that a scrawny kid would be getting away from him no matter how hard they fought.

The guy ran his card through the machine and finally noticed me leaning against the side of the truck. We considered each other silently for a long, tense moment until he tilted his chin up in a brisk greeting.

"Afternoon." The voice was bland and disinterested, but I got the feeling his narrow-eyed gaze was cataloging every move I made.

I lifted my chin in return. "Afternoon. It sounds like that beast could use a tune-up."

The other man looked at the RV and then back me with a scowl. "It gets me where I'm going."

I rubbed my thumb along the edge of my chin and lifted an eyebrow. "And where would that be?"

The guy frowned in confusion and started to tap his foot impatiently, the big tank on the RV taking forever to top off. "Where would what be?"

I pushed off the side of the truck and shot a look over my shoulder to make sure Brynn was still inside the gas station. I had no idea if this was the same guy dragging that kid across the campsite, but I had a bad feeling about him, and those covered windows were making my skin crawl.

"Where are you going? Pretty sure we were at the same campsite in Joshua Tree, but you lit out of there like you just remembered you left the stove on at home. Just wondering where you're off to in such a hurry." I dropped my arms, so they were hanging loosely at my sides. I wasn't going to let anyone get the drop on me ever again.

The guy took a step back, and his eyes widened in obvious surprise. He shook his head and moved to quickly pull the nozzle out of his tank. "Don't know what you're talking about. I wasn't anywhere near Joshua Tree."

I moved a step closer to him so that I was standing between the gas tanks. "Are you sure? This old hunk of junk is pretty memorable. So was the scene you caused when you pulled that kid through the campsite." I was taking a guess he was the same guy. I was a great poker player and knew when a bluff would pay off. This was one of those times. A mixture of fear and anger moved in a flash across the stranger's wide face. He jammed the gas pump back into the holster and shifted to move around the front of the RV, keeping his angry gaze on mine. I wasn't letting him get back behind the wheel without knowing for sure the kid was okay.

He shook his head at me and took another step toward the open driver's side door. "You're mistaken, man. I'm traveling alone. I bought this beater years ago so I could hit up Burning Man, now I'm just a desert rat, a nomad. I never stick to any one campsite for too long. I need to get back on the road."

I stepped off the concrete divider and with one long stride was in front of the other man. I pointed the finger at the covered windows and practically growled, "Why do you have the windows blocked? What are you trying to hide in there? If you're traveling alone why don't you let me check inside the back of your camper?"

I was pushing it, but I didn't care. If he had a kid in there who didn't belong to him or who was in danger, I was putting a stop to it. I couldn't save Brynn. I couldn't save Daye. But I could do something to help the mysterious kid who should be anywhere else besides inside of this blacked out RV.

'Man, you're crazy. I'm not letting you inside my camper. Get the fuck away from me." The guy reached up and pushed me directly in the center of my chest. My still healing ribs screamed in protest, but I easily knocked his hands away.

"I'm calling the cops." I pointed at the RV again and gritted clenched teeth. "I don't know what's going on, but everything is telling me it's not anything good. You aren't going anywhere until I know you're alone and that you don't have a kid in there." I smirked at him. "I bet they'll impound that rolling garbage can based on your outdated emissions alone."

The guy swore at me, and I anticipated his move long before he lunged at me. I braced for the impact, so he wasn't able to take me to the ground, but his bulk slamming into my body was like taking a hammer to all my still injured places. My back connected with the gas pump and my breath escaped in a whoosh as a meaty fist landed heavily on my side. I managed to get my hands on the stranger's chest and shoved him off of me with all my strength. I tossed an uppercut before I could think about what I was doing and watched with primal satisfaction as the guy's head whipped back so fast I knew it had to hurt. I heard his teeth click together and rolled my eyes when he called me a 'mother fucker.'

"Mind your own fucking business." The guy wiped a hand across his mouth and spat a mouthful of blood in the direction of my boots. I smirked again. I lived on a ranch; he had no idea the crap . . . literally . . . these boots waded through every single day.

"If you're hurting a kid, making him scream and dragging him around, that is my business. If you're lying about being alone so you can hurt that kid, that's also my business. Just tell me what's going on and why you have the windows all covered up, and I'll be on my way. Call me nosey." I shouldn't taunt him, but his evasiveness was wearing on my last nerve, and the longer I kept him engaged, the longer I had to figure out a way inside the camper.

"The only thing anyone is calling you is an ambulance, asshole." The man bent and pulled a wicked looking knife out of his boot. It was the kind that had a thick, rubber handle and a serrated edge. The kind of knife my brothers and I used when we went hunting and had to clean game in the wild. That blade was made to separate skin and muscle from bone. The afternoon sun glinted off the blade and highlighted the deadly intent in the stranger's unwavering gaze. "You ain't getting in my RV and you ain't calling the cops. You're going to walk away and forget you ever saw me. Are we clear?"

The only thing that was clear was that he had something in the back of that RV that he was willing to kill for. I tilted my head to the side and lifted my hands up in front of me in a harmless gesture. "Easy, buddy. No need for the knife."

"Fuck you. Fucking good samaritan. Who gets involved in other people's shit? What kind of moron are you?" The guy sneered at me, taking in my camo hat with the ranch's logo, my tooled leather belt with its belt buckle with the longhorn on it, and my boots. "You're a real cowboy, huh?"

I shrugged. "Just a concerned citizen who worries about those who don't always have someone to fight for them."

The guy tossed back his head and laughed, but it was a harsh, twisted sound. "Your hero complex is gonna get you dead, cowboy."

I shrugged. "Maybe, but that's a risk I'm willing to take."

We were so focused on one another, neither one of us noticed the tall, red-headed woman that slipped into the truck behind me. We didn't see her rummaging around in the glovebox where I stashed my handgun, and we didn't hear her creeping around the gas pump at my back until she called out, voice clear and calm, "Drop the knife and give him the keys to the camper."

I always thought Brynn looked good. She was a beautiful woman, built along the lines of a living fantasy. There was something equally wholesome and mysterious about her, but the sight of her with a weapon, looking strong and steady, ready to defend both of us, kicked my heart in the ass. She didn't need a hero anymore. Maybe she never did. She was her own savior.

The startled stranger faltered for a second before scoffing, "Do you even know how to use that thing?"

Brynn's brows arched and in a flat tone she told him, "I was born and raised in Wyoming." Like that was enough of an answer. She inclined her head to the camper once again. "Let him in."

The guy switched his gaze between Brynn and me, taking stock of how serious she was with that gun. She cocked her head to the side and told him, "I already had the attendant call the police. They should be here any minute. You might as well let us in."

The man let the arm holding the knife fall, and the metal

clicked against the asphalt when he let it drop. He dragged his hands over his face before digging into his pocket for a set of keys. He tossed them to me, but his gaze was on Brynn. "You don't understand. You have no idea what you're getting in the middle of. It's best for all of us if we just go our separate ways. The people I work for . . ." he trailed off and let his head fall forward on his neck like it weighed a million pounds. "You just don't understand. There's no way you could."

Sadly, she understood, and that's why she was willing to pull a gun on him. She wouldn't stop because she knew exactly what she was getting in the middle of.

It took me a minute to figure out which key worked on the padlock that was hanging off a tough looking bracket. That extra level of protection indicated RV guy was trying hard to keep something or someone inside of the camper. I put all my weight behind pulling the rickety door open and when it gave I let out an 'oomph.' Immediately I was engulfed in the stench of unwashed bodies and stale food. The RV was filthy, and there was a graveyard of empty beer bottles, drug paraphernalia, and empty fast food wrappers. It was disgusting, dark, and dank. I suppressed a shiver of revulsion and called out a gruff hello as my eyes adjusted to the dim light filtering in through the spots on the body of the RV that rusted away to nothing.

The space was small, a tiny kitchen with a fold out table and a bunk that folded out. There was no one visible in the main area of the camper, but the bathroom at the back of the RV had a padlock similar to the one on the outside door. Something disturbing and alarming slithered down my spine as I searched for a key that would open the lock. It took me two tries with every key on the ring to get it unlocked, and once I had, it popped, and I tried to shove the accordion-style door out of my way only to meet with resistance that wouldn't give. I put a little more weight into it but stopped immediately when a low groan rose up from somewhere near the floor. I crouched down, sucking in a breath when the form of a very naked body came into view. Even in the dark, I could see bruises and lacerations decorating every spot of visible skin.

"Hang on there, kid. I'll get you out of here." There was another groan and the sound of shifting. The kid moved like a wounded animal, and I knew I was going to put my hands around the neck of that asshole outside and not let up until the cops dragged me off of him.

I rose up and looked in the mess for something I could use to pry the hinges off the door so I could get to the captive teenager when Brynn suddenly screamed my name.

I was out the door between one heartbeat and the next. As soon as I cleared the last step out of the RV, I saw she was no longer holding the stranger at gunpoint. The man was now brandishing his knife at a young woman in a hybrid. He pulled her out of her car while she was shaking and screaming for her life. He unceremoniously tossed the newcomer on the ground and peeled off with a screech of tires and a cloud of dust. Brynn dropped the arm holding the gun and gaped at me. "He moved so fast. There was no way I was going to take a shot with her between us. I'm good, but not that good."

I gazed at the spot where the car had been. "Go see if she's all right. I'm going to get the kid out of the RV. He looks like he needs medical attention. The cops should have shown up by now."

Brynn flinched and moved to tuck my gun away. "I didn't actually have him call. I saw the knife and panicked. The clerk is so stoned I doubt he noticed anything other than the YouTube video he was watching on his phone. I'll call them now and tell them we need an ambulance."

I was about to tell her that sounded like a plan when a voice that was scratchy, and hardly above a whisper begged, "No cops."

Brynn and I both gasped as the naked teenager suddenly appeared at the door of the RV. He looked even worse in the light of day.

His eyes were black and blue, both of them nearly swollen shut. I swore my heart cracked in half when he pleaded brokenly, "I just want to go home."

CHAPTER 8

Straight or Bent

BRYNN

"YOU SHOULD LET US TAKE you to the emergency room at the very least." I tried again to reason with the battered teenager, but just like all the times previously, my concern was met with silence and an unflinching stare.

The kid's face was a patchwork of old and new bruises, mottled blues and yellows that forced me to fight a cringe every time I looked at him. His dark eyes were sunken into his too skinny face, and his long, narrow nose had an obvious bump in it from a break. His hair was stringy and greasy, and so thin in some spots I could see his scalp. His arms and legs were covered in scratches and bite marks, and he was still gangly and knobby, at the stage where he hadn't yet grown into his body.

When Lane asked him how old he was, he muttered that he was eighteen without an ounce of conviction. If I had to guess I would bet he was closer to fourteen or fifteen, even though his eyes looked ancient. When I asked him what his name was, he told me I could call him, Bauer, but didn't mention if that was his first or last name. The kid reminded me so much of myself when I was his age that I felt the ache of those painful memories throb right in the center of my chest.

The woman whose car got stolen wasted no time calling the police, even though the battered, naked teenager was adamant not to involve the police in the situation. When he pulled himself up and grabbed onto Lane's shirt with both hands, the dark-haired cowboy was clearly at a loss. The teen alternated between crying and yelling, frantically telling Lane that all he wanted was to get to Denver where his older brother was. He swore that he was going to take off if the cops showed up. He was in near hysterics when he exclaimed that he wasn't going back to foster care. Somewhere in all the frenzy, he mentioned that he would have never been in the RV with that man, to begin with, if the authorities had just let him stay with his brother in the first place. His desperation poured off of him in waves, and it broke my heart that someone so young knew what that felt like. It also hurt deep down in a place I didn't like to revisit inside of myself that I sympathized with him so strongly. He honestly believed no one in law enforcement was going to be on his side, which led me to believe they hadn't been in the past. Since I'd walked that road myself every time the police in Sheridan passed me and Opal off to the tribal law enforcement, who, in turn, handed us right back to our mother, I knew how lonely and terrifying it was, I couldn't stop myself from blurting out, "We'll take you to your brother."

As soon as the words were out of my mouth, the kid had collapsed back on the ground, drained and drunk with relief. Lane looked at me like I'd lost my mind, but all I could do was shrug. I was going with my gut, and my gut was telling me this kid was going to be a ghost by the time the authorities showed up. If I wanted to help him, I had to get him to trust me. I had to prove that I was on his side.

I managed to get him into a pair of Lane's sweatpants and one of my extra flannel shirts, both of which hung off of his emaciated frame, just as the sound of sirens wailed in the distance. I urged Lane to put the pedal to the metal, so we weren't around when the authorities arrived. He hesitated for a second, but eventually, we were cruising down the highway at a steady clip, putting distance between us and the crime scene.

I looked back and saw the woman with the stolen car waving her arms and speaking loudly into her phone. When we were hustling the teenager into the back of the truck, she had pointed in our direction and yelled that we couldn't leave the scene of a crime. Since we *had* witnessed the assault and theft, she was technically right. That had Lane's jaw tightening even more and a muscle in his cheek fluttering as he ground his teeth together with audible force.

Trying to appease him the best I could and still maintain the gossamer thread of trust I'd built with the kid, I called 911 and reported what we had seen. I gave the dispatcher a detailed description of the man who drove the RV and mentioned they might want to have the police check out the abandoned vehicle once they got to the gas station. I gave my account of what happened when RV guy dragged the woman out of her car and left my number in case the California Highway Patrol had any questions. I wanted to protect the kid, but I had too wide of a moral streak to flout the law completely.

When I hung up, Lane cut me a sharp look out of the corner of his eye. "What's going to stop that guy from grabbing another kid? I don't feel right about not talking to the cops about this."

I was opening my mouth to argue that even if we stayed to talk to the police, there was no guarantee they would be able to catch the man who pulled the knife on him, but they for sure would take Bauer in for questioning. And they would undoubtedly dump him back in the system, when a quiet, shaky voice from the back muttered, "He didn't grab me."

Lane shifted his gaze to the rearview mirror, a frown pulling at his dark brows. "What do you mean? You were locked up in that bathroom. That's no way to treat someone."

The kid looked down at his hands. His fingernails were torn, and there was blood on each fingertip. His knuckles were scabbed over and on the back of one hand was a healing wound that was perfectly round. It didn't take a genius to figure out someone put out a cigarette on the back of the kid's hand. It was on the tip of my tongue to tell him we were taking him to the hospital, no arguments, but I had the feeling if I did that as soon as he was out of my sight he was going to run.

"He didn't take me. I answered an ad I found online. He told me he was taking me to meet my new employers. I went with him willingly." Every inch of the kid's body bled shame and repulsion. I could tell he believed he was supposed to be smarter than that. He'd lived enough in his young life that he was supposed to know if it seemed too good to be true, then it probably was.

"What kind of ad was it?" Lane's initial suspicion that Bauer's abduction was tied to a sex trafficking ring echoed in the question.

The teenager shrunk in on himself and refused to meet Lane's gaze in the mirror. Absently, he traced the wound on the back of his hand, and I watched as he blinked back tears. I needed to get some food into him, and he needed a bath. I was hoping once we stopped to fuel up again I could convince him to let me patch him up, and I wasn't giving up on getting him to a doctor either.

"It's okay. You don't have to tell us anything you don't want to. I know it can be hard to let someone else inside that kind of experience." That kind of pain was personal; it wasn't something you wanted to share with others.

I heard him exhale a wobbly sounding breath as he lifted his head. Underneath the damage, it was easy to see he was going to grow into a rather good-looking young man. There was something almost pretty about his high cheekbones and wide, chocolate-colored eyes. The off-center nose and sharp jawline kept him from being delicate, but just barely. It was all too easy to imagine what interest the creep in the RV had in him, and what he had in store for him when he got delivered to his new employer.

Bauer's fathomless gaze landed on mine, and I could feel him searching for the secrets I had that were so similar to his. He must have seen something that let him know there was truth behind my words because, slowly and methodically, he started talking.

"I'm gay." He whispered the words like he was confessing to a horrible crime. He shook his head when I started to respond that his sexuality didn't matter in the slightest. He held up a hand and whispered, "Let me get it all out, and when I'm done if you want to drop me at the closest truck stop, I'll understand." He shrugged dejectedly. "You oughta know the kind of person you're helping."

Lane stiffened next to me, and he cocked his head so that he could glance at the kid without taking his eyes off the road. "That's not going to happen, kid. No matter what, we're not leaving you until you're somewhere you feel safe. No matter what you have to say, I'm not leaving you until you're with someone who can take care of you. You look like you're in desperate need of it."

The teen made a choking sound and lifted his injured hand to wipe his wet cheeks. He took a fortifying breath and let the rest of the story out in a rush. "My parents are very religious. They didn't take it well when I told them that I liked boys instead of girls." He rubbed both his hands over his face, and I could see that they were trembling. "My dad is real old fashioned. He honestly believed he could beat the gay out of me."

I sucked in a breath through my teeth and put a hand over my pounding heart. "How old were you when you told your parents?" I was barely old enough to tie my own shoes the first time one of my mom's boyfriends hit me. Every memory I had of my childhood ended up filtered through a haze of pain and bitter anger.

"I was"—he paused and looked lost as he sifted through his response—"Uh . . . eleven." His reluctance to give us a hint to his true age drew the word out and caused his gaze to shift nervously around the interior of the truck. "My dad is a big guy. It was never a fair fight. For a while, I thought someone would step in and make it stop. My mom. One of my teachers. The police. It never happened, everyone believed my dad and whatever excuse he had for the marks he left that were visible. I tried to tell him that it didn't matter how many times he hit me, I was never going to like girls, but that only made him angrier. The only person who ever got between me and Dad's fists was my big brother. He always tried to protect me, but like I said, my dad is a big guy, and Mikey was no match for him. I was thirteen when Dad put Mikey in the hospital for daring to stick up for me." The kid's head dropped like it weighed a million pounds and his shoulders slumped with the weight of his story. "I knew that if I stayed under the same roof as my dad, he was going to kill one of us. He told me enough times that he wanted me dead, that I had no choice but to believe him, but I didn't want Mikey to keep getting hurt. The only reason Dad ever hit him was because of me."

Lane made a pained noise low in his throat, and I could feel moisture pushing at the back of my eyes. I was having a hard time keeping my expression even, and it was a struggle to stay in my seat and not launch myself into the back of the cab and wrap the kid up in an unbreakable hug.

"I left before he came home from the hospital. It didn't take me long to figure out truck stops, and lonely truckers were an easy way to make it from one place to another and about the only way an underage kid could make a quick buck." I couldn't hold back the gasp that ripped out of me. He was so young. I knew his story wasn't wholly unheard of or unique, but it still stung all my soft places to hear him tell it so matter-of-factly. "I turned tricks for a long time. Sometimes I made enough to get off the streets and keep myself fed. Sometimes I got the shit kicked out of me and ended up dumped back on the street like trash."

He blew out a sigh and pulled his knees up to his chest. He rested his swollen, abused cheek on the points of his bent knees and closed his eyes. "I was so tired of not knowing what was going to happen to me each time I got into a car with whoever was paying. At least at home, I knew I was going to get knocked around, but on the streets, the nicest guy would turn on me, and for some reason, those hits hurt even worse. One night a guy who was around my age rolled up on me in a brand-new BMW. He wasn't anything like my other tricks, he was cute, the kind of guy I used to daydream about. He picked me up, and we spent the night together. He was the first client who ever treated me like I was a human being. He asked me where I was from and when I told him about my shitty home life he told me he understood and that his parents had kicked him out around the same age. He told me that he used to hustle but found a better way to make money at it. No more shady tricks. No more standing on street corners fighting off junkies for territory. No more shakedowns from other hustlers and pimps. He gave me this website to check out. He told me I could make triple what I was making doing the same thing for a higher class of clientele. He mentioned the BMW and told me it only took him a week to earn enough to pay for it."

Listening to that modicum of hope in his voice, I couldn't resist reaching out to touch him. I was pulled to him because his trauma and lack of options were like a magnet. I hated what my sister and I had to endure. I loathed what he went through even more. My hand landed on the back of his head. His hair felt gross, but I stroked my fingers through the thin strands anyway.

"I already sucked cock and fucked for money. I didn't see any difference, and the website was nice. Flashy and sophisticated looking. The site and the kid with the BMW promised a fancy apartment in Vegas, a whole new wardrobe and the kind of money I only dreamed of making. It was all pretty upfront, or so I thought. It was clear their business was sex for money, besides being an escort, they also expected applicants to perform on camera. I was never quite desperate enough to get caught up in porn, but if it got me off the streets, I was willing to do just about anything. Once I filled out the application and uploaded a video, they would send someone to meet me for a face-to-face interview." The teen leaned into my touch like a kitten seeking warmth and comfort. "I heard back from them the same day I filled out the online form. They sent the guy in the RV the same week to pick me up from the fleabag motel I was camped out at in LA. He told me my interview was to have sex with him and if he decided I was good enough and he thought I would make the cut, he would take me to Vegas. I must have passed because I was in the RV later that day, only something wasn't right, and I knew it. Why would a company that promised a penthouse apartment and a designer wardrobe send a busted-up RV to take me to Vegas?" He turned his face, and I brushed my thumb over his banged-up cheekbone.

"I told the guy I wanted out, that I didn't want to go to Vegas anymore and he laughed at me. He told me his boss already had a buyer for me, and that scared the shit out of me. I tried to get away. We stopped at a McDonald's, and I tried to run. That's when he beat me up and locked me in the bathroom. I kept trying to get away, I almost did at the campsite in the desert, but I hadn't eaten anything in days. I ran out of steam, and he caught up to me. That's when I got this." He lifted his hand with the cigarette burn and let it fall. "Mikey just turned eighteen. He told me that he'd moved out and promised I could stay with him. I haven't seen him since I left home, but I have a few regular tricks who let me use their phones so I can contact him." A sad smile moved across the kid's face, but his eyes remained closed. It was the same expression I got when I thought about Opal.

Lane cleared his throat roughly, and the hand that wasn't resting on the steering wheel clenched into a fist. "Would you mind letting me talk to your brother, kid? I've got two older brothers myself, and I know they would do anything for me, so if your brother is the same way, I can drop you off in Denver with a clean conscience. It won't keep me up at night for the rest of my life."

Bauer nodded under my palm, and I could feel some of the tension drain out of him. "I don't have a phone. If you let me text him from your phone, I'll have him call you when we get wherever it is we're going."

I let go of my hold on his head and turned to look out the windshield. I exchanged a knowing look with Lane and shifted uncomfortably on the leather seat.

I tugged on the ends of my hair and told Bauer, "We're headed to Vegas. We're on our way home to Wyoming and were going to hit all the hot spots along the way. We already have a couple of rooms reserved, but we can skip staying in the city if it's going to be painful for you or if it freaks you out. We'll skip the Grand Canyon and power through to Colorado instead over the next few days."

He was quiet for what felt like a long time, and I could feel something that felt like anxiety practically vibrating off of him. "I'm not going to have to fuck either one of you or both of you if I let you take me to a hotel, am I?"

I gasped, and I was sure my face resembled a fish out of the water as I blustered and blundered to answer him in a way that would reassure him down to his bone. I didn't need to worry about it; Lane had it covered.

"Kid, this entire trip was her and me trying to figure out if we could still be friends while working together and sharing the same house if we ended up in bed together. That's complicated enough without dragging someone else into the mix. All we're interested in is helping you out. We're both familiar with what it feels like to end up backed into a corner with nowhere to go. I know it's probably hard for you to believe after all you've been through, but there are good people in the world." Lane sounded so ernest and sincere it was hard not to have faith in every single word he said.

The teen was silent again clearly trying to make a better decision than the last one that put him on the road to Sin City.

When he spoke, he sounded so young and wistful it cracked my already fragile heart into a million pieces.

"Is it a nice room? I can't tell you the last time I spent the night on clean sheets."

Lane coughed to cover a dirty word and nodded even though Bauer could only see the back of his head. "We got adjoining suites. Five-star all the way. You can have Brynn's room, and we'll bunk together. You can order anything you want from the room service menu, and we'll find a shop to get some clothes that fit you. Typically, I'd never let a teenager loose in a swanky hotel on the Vegas Strip, but you make me feel even more small-town than I am, kid."

"How can you trust me and want to do something nice for me after everything I told you? You know I don't deserve it. You know there's a good chance I'll be gone in the morning." He sounded so resigned, and I wondered if that was how I sounded every time I had to go back home to my mother and her mistakes.

Lane waited until the teenager met his gaze in the rearview mirror. "I told you there are good people in the world. I choose to believe you are one of them. Nothing you told us makes me think you're a bad kid, and none of it was anything you wanted to do. You did what you *had* to do to survive, and you did it when most kids are just figuring out who they are and who they want to be. What we do during desperate times isn't who we are, that's the worst version of us. What you do when you have the option to make better choices is the man you're going to be judged by."

Bauer seemed to process Lane's words. I could almost see him weighing the authenticity of the man before him against all the other men who had used and abused him in his young life. I wondered if Lane was ready to take his own advice. What I did when I had no other choices, wasn't who I was. That girl had nowhere else to go and nowhere else to turn. It was the woman I was now I needed him to see. I wanted desperately for him to understand now that I had choices, lots of them, many of them great and promising, that he was still the one I wanted. He would always be my first choice.

To break through some of the emotionally thick atmosphere that permeated the small space, I dug around on the floorboards by my feet until I found the bag of snacks I'd picked up at the gas station. I held up the bright yellow and green bag containing Lane's favorite junk food and offered it back.

Bauer screwed his thin face up into a look of utter disgust and flatly informed me that Funyuns were gross.

His reaction made me laugh and forced Lane to chuckle as well. It wasn't much, but it was enough to put us all on even footing and for me to feel like we'd gained some footing where this young man was concerned.

As soon as we got to the hotel, I was raiding the minibar and crying myself to sleep, so I didn't have to think about all the horrible things that brought the boy into my life. It made me wonder if Lane had to do the same thing when it came to me. Was every thought he had about me punctuated by the memories of *why* he couldn't separate his life from mine? Did he still see the little girl with bumps and bruises, or did he see the woman who had learned to take care of herself?

The thoughts twisted and turned until my head started to

pound in an insistent throb.

Screw the minibar, I was ordering a bottle of top-shelf whiskey from room service and passing out before I had to worry about spending another night within touching distance of my favorite blue-eyed cowboy.

CHAPTER 9

Hard or Soft

LANE

"I UNDERSTAND THAT YOU'RE JUST trying to help the kid out, but I don't think you've thought of all the ramifications of picking a runaway up and taking him across state lines."

Cy's voice was infinitely patient, but I could hear his concern for the teenager he hadn't met in his tone.

"And what if you get to Denver and the brother doesn't have his shit together. Eighteen is pretty young to take on raising someone else."

I closed my eyes and pressed my forehead to the glass window. Down below, the lights of Vegas glittered like a piece of gaudy jewelry. I was glad I was so high up and separated from the noise and chaos that spilled out onto the Strip. Vegas was the opposite of what I was used to, and I was man enough to admit that I found all the people and noise intimidating. This city moved at a pace I'd never seen before, and the rush of it all made my head hurt.

"I can't even put words to what this kid will do if he runs again, Cy. People have been taking advantage of him and using him for so long. He doesn't know anything else. I can't be the one to force him back to the streets. I just can't." Not to mention Brynn would rip my nuts off and feed them to me for breakfast if I so much as suggested going to the authorities behind the kid's back.

"I understand, Lane, but I think you're missing the big picture. What about whoever set the kid up?" Forever the big brother looking out for me. Of course, Cy didn't want me embroiled in something bigger than I could handle. "They sent out that other kid as bait. They have a fucking website to lure unsuspecting victims in. They sold that kid like he was property. This isn't one man in a beat-up old RV, this is a corporation and like any business, whoever is at the head of the table won't like losing money. I know you can watch your own back, but you've got Brynn and now this kid relying on you too. That's a lot for anyone to manage."

I didn't bother pointing out when he first met Leo he was guiding not only her but two other men unfamiliar with the Wyoming wilderness to safety with armed drug runners on his tail. I never doubted for a second that my older brother would get everyone out alive. I was a bit disappointed he didn't have the same faith in me.

"I'm not going to let anything happen to them. I'm going to get everyone home safe and sound." I wanted to sound as confident as I felt, but there was a waver in my voice and one in my self-confidence when the ramifications of what was at stake started to settle on my shoulders. I had no idea how Cyrus held the whole world up. I only had a portion of it, and I was already exhausted from keeping the weight from dragging me down.

"Lane." Cy swore, and I could practically see him dragging his hand over the salt and pepper scruff that covered his face. It was his signature move when he was stressed out, or when Sutton ended up in a situation no amount of brotherly love and concern could get us out of. "I know you would die to protect anyone who you think is your responsibility. I thought you were going to die in my arms waiting for the search and rescue copter when you got shot trying to protect Daye. What I don't want is you in a situation where you have to prove that. I'm getting married soon. I can't have a wedding without both of my brothers as my best men."

I didn't tell him about the guy with the RV pulling the knife on me in the parking lot, but it was like he already knew. He always seemed to know when I was in over my head.

"I'll be careful, and I'll give Webb's brother a call and see what he has to say about the website and whoever might be behind it." Webb had taken over Sutton's position on the ranch when my brother left for California. He was also one of the people Cy had led through the woods that fateful week he met Leo and when Em came into Sutton's life, in order to find his missing brother, an older brother who just happened to be a DEA agent. The Bryant brothers couldn't be any more different from one another if they tried, but the cop and the criminal were as close as us Warners were. "If things feel off once we get to Denver, I promise I'll get the authorities involved. I need this kid to feel safe. And Brynn really needs to be the one to give it to him." And I would stand between them both and whoever tried to stop that from happening.

"How is she?" Both of my brothers considered Brynn family and loved her in a different way than I did. It would devastate them if I made the wrong call and something happened to her. "How are you?"

I let out a bark of laughter and glanced over my shoulder to where Brynn was sprawled across the bed, her feet on the pillows where her head should be. On the floor near one of her limp hands was a half-empty bottle of Booker's Rye. The booze cost more than one of my truck payments, but Brynn seemed determined to lose touch with reality for the evening. She spent a good chunk of the afternoon putting Bauer back together in the privacy of the room I insisted he take for the night. When she came back to the suite we were sharing, I asked how the kid was doing and how extensive his injuries were. All she could do was shake her head and tell me it was too hard to talk about. She ordered the bottle of whiskey a few minutes later and proceeded to put a solid dent in it all by herself. I tried to get some dinner in her but was waved off. She didn't even offer to share, which told me whatever injuries I could see on the kid, was just the tip of the iceberg.

"We're both doing the best we can. We're finally being honest with each other about what we want and talking about how we got so far off track. The way I was hurting when she turned down my proposal was so big and took up so much room that I couldn't see around it. I had no idea the way she hurt felt as huge as mine did to me."

"It's amazing what you can learn when you take the time to talk things out." I rolled my eyes at the humor in his tone.

"It took me a while to figure out what I wanted to say." I also needed time to figure out how to say it without sounding pathetic and pitiful. No one wanted to admit they'd let their fears get the best of them, that they had been a coward.

"It's worth the time it takes to get it right. Keep me updated on your progress home and don't hesitate to call if you need anything. Keep your eyes open and don't let that soft heart of yours get you into trouble."

I promised him I would do my best to stay safe and assured him I had no illusions about what Bauer was capable of even though he was so young. The boy had lived a thousand lives already, and none of them were anything good.

I dropped my phone on the ornate desk and moved over toward the bed. I had pulled Brynn's boots off of her feet before she passed out, but there wasn't much more I could do to make her comfortable. Sighing, I ran my hand over the silky fall of her hair and wished there was more I could do to take care of her. She was going to have one hell of a hangover when she woke up, and none of that was going to do anything to erase the images she now had of what Bauer had been through.

I pulled my hand back when her dark eyes suddenly popped open. It was obvious she was still out of it by the way she squinted up at me and frowned in confusion. She flicked her tongue out to lick her lips and my dick instantly hardened. There was a steady throb that had been pulsing in my blood since our heated kiss. A taste of her was never going to be enough. It was a tease to my senses that had lust and desire threatening to overtake all the other things she forced me to feel. She pulled her hands up and folded them under the cheek that pressed to the mattress. She blew out a shaky breath and asked, "Do you know how easily it could have been me in that RV? I was so close to ending up exactly like that kid, Lane. So fucking close."

I put my hand on the back of her head and sifted my fingers through her hair. The coppery strands slid across my knuckles, and I felt the impact of that barely-there caress all along my cock. The sensitive flesh thickened behind my zipper and I lost myself in the image of what it would be like to have that soft, silky hair rubbing against the inside of my thighs and slithering across my balls.

It wasn't an appropriate reaction to what she was telling me, but there was no controlling the longing now that I had embraced it and called it what it was.

"But you didn't, and now you're giving him a fresh start. That's what you need to focus on." I brushed a thumb along her cheekbone and bit back a groan when she leaned lazily into the gentle touch like a cat stretching in the sunlight.

"Do you know why my mother stopped bringing her men home once I agreed to marry Boyd?" There was pain speared through every word of that question. It was more noticeable than usual because of the care she was taking to keep from slurring and sounding sloppy.

"No. I don't know much about what happened after Dad

asked you. I didn't like to think about why you told him yes when you had told me no. It was selfish and immature, but now I can see how much I missed by thinking that way." It was true. There was an entire chunk of her story I hadn't bothered to read. I loved the beginning where it was her and me against the world, but I skipped the entire middle part of the book when things got hard.

"She stopped bringing her mistakes home because your dad paid her off. Every single month like clockwork he gave her two thousand dollars. He threatened her. He tried to get Opal out of the house as well. He offered to double the amount if she would let my sister leave with us, but Mom refused. Partly because she didn't want to be alone in that musty trailer surrounded by people who were disgusted by her, but mostly because she gave Boyd an outrageous figure he refused to pay. He agreed to pay the protection money, and he told Mom that if Opal got so much as a hangnail the money would stop. He promised that he would be checking in on them and touching base with Opal's teachers once a week. He ordered her to keep her men away from the house or else he wouldn't pay anymore. All my mom ever wanted was someone to take care of her. She wanted to be kept. She stopped putting us in danger because she got paid to put us first for once. Not because she loved us, or cared about us. Your dad bought my freedom and my little sister's safety." Her eyes drifted closed, and her shoulders shook in such a way that I knew she was fighting to hold back her tears. "I keep paying her now that Boyd is gone, and I'll keep it up until my sister is eighteen and can get out of that house the way I did. Once Opal is an adult I'm writing my mother off. I won't have anything to do with her or her mistakes ever again."

It was so much worse than I imagined. My old man saved her life and put a lot on the line, including his reputation, to do so. All I could see was her rejection. I was blind to how badly she needed salvation from someone who could actually provide it. Even if she had accepted my proposal, there was no way I could do for her what my father had done. I didn't have the means, and truthfully, I was too young and full of myself back then to see that there was another way to fight back with anything but anger and violence.

Silently saying every dirty word I could think of, I tugged my boots off and climbed into the bed upside down so that I could lie down beside her. I pulled her into my arms and was struck again by how soft she felt, but there was no ignoring that she had a spine forged of steel. I rubbed a hand up and down her back, muttering useless words while she battled booze and ugly truths for control of her emotions.

I thought she was drifting back to sleep when she went limp in my hold. I rested my chin on the top of her head and told myself I was not going to screw this up. I promised both of us that I would figure out how to be whatever it was she needed me to be. I had my eyes closed and was concentrating hard on keeping my excited cock to myself when she whispered a question that pulled me from my reveries.

"What would you have said back then if I was the one who asked you to marry me?"

She rolled over so that we were face to face. Her gaze was darker than the rest of the room around us, and I couldn't tell what she was thinking. One of her hands fluttered until it landed in the center of my chest. My heart lurched at the contact. Every time this woman touched me, I felt something I'd never felt before. It was almost as if everyone who came before had to fight and claw their way through protective layers and never quite reached the unguarded core of the man beneath the smile and charm. There was none of that with Brynn. As soon as her fingers hit my skin, she was touching every raw and uncovered piece of me, and I felt that contact all the way down to my toes.

"I have no idea what I would have said. My parents' marriage was a nightmare, and that was all I had to go by when it came to relationships. You were the one thing in my life I never wanted to risk losing, so there's a good chance I would have said yes if it meant I got to keep you close by and tie you to me forever. I would have fucked up either way. I was so screwed up back then, so busy trying to prove I was good enough, strong enough, so that Dad didn't have to worry about me or the ranch when Mom left and with Cy going, then again when he got sick. I wouldn't have been able to give you what you needed back then regardless of who asked and who said yes." I was giving it all to the birthright my father was leaving behind, trying to show him I was the man he needed me to be. There was nothing left for anyone else.

She leaned forward and pressed her lips to the point of my chin. "What if I asked you now." One of her hands lifted and curled around the side of my neck. My pulse jumped to kiss her fingertips. She lifted one of those long, shapely legs and wrapped it around my hip. There was no hiding how hard I already was, and I nearly forgot my name when she slowly started to writhe and grind against me. It was languid and sensual and quickly made me forget she didn't have a handle on herself because of the whiskey.

I smoothed a hand down the elegant line of her back until it was resting on her ass. I allowed myself a squeeze of that delectable flesh before pulling back, so there was more than an inch of space between our bodies. I could feel the heat radiating from that spot high between her thighs, and combined with my aching dick was making it hard to think straight.

"You want to ask me to marry you, Brynn? You weren't even sure you liked me anymore when we started on this trip." A groan slipped out when she used the leg that was coiled around my waist to regain the space I'd put between us. She was hot enough that I was ready to stick my hand in the fire and let it burn.

"I just want to be the one to ask. I want to pick the time and the place. I don't even care if you say no. I want to be the one asking the person I choose to spend the rest of their life with me. I'm sick of being the one who gets asked and either I'm not ready, or the question doesn't mean what I want it to mean." Her lips ghosted over mine, and I tasted whiskey and want on her breath.

"I guess you'll have to ask me and we'll find out what I'd say." I honestly didn't know the answer. I never planned on getting married aside from marrying her to get her out of that house when she was younger. But if she wanted to spend the rest of her life with me, I couldn't deny that I liked the way that made me feel. I was settled and whole in a way I hadn't been since I pushed her out of my life.

She sealed her lips against mine, and I groaned when her tongue darted between my teeth. She was the headiest of flavors and intoxicating in a way that went right to my head. I kissed her back, taking my time and drinking up every drop of that smoky flavor. When she licked along the sensitive roof of my mouth, there was no stopping my hips from thrusting forward, or my cock from searching out her liquid warmth. I was so turned on it was hard to pull a coherent thought out of the haze of lust that was consuming me.

"As much as I like where all of this is going, you drank half a bottle of top-shelf whiskey. I think we need to put the brakes on and revisit this exact spot when we're both in a better frame of mind."

She pulled back and shot me a scowl. Her eyebrows dipped to form an angry V above her nose, and her obsidian eyes seemed to shift to an even darker shade of black as she glared hotly at me. Her words were sharp and pointed when she spoke. I could feel the way they pressed into my unprotected heart. "When are you going to trust me to know what I want, Lane? When are you going to believe that I know what's best for me? I'm a big girl, I don't need you to protect me anymore, and the last person I want to be saved from is you."

She started to wiggle away, but I locked my arms around her and used the hand I had on her butt to keep her in place. I lifted my eyebrows and watched her closely. "You want me, Brynn, or is this the booze and a broken heart talking?"

She blinked at me and studied me intently in the dark. "I want you, Lane. I've always wanted you, and it has nothing to do with the booze or the broken heart." She let me tug her body even closer to mine and didn't argue when I rolled her so that she was underneath me and I was hovering over her in an extended push-up. She reached up and pushed at a lock of hair that had fallen over my forehead and dangled into my eye. "You are the only thing that will make all the bad things we faced today go away. You are the only man who has ever been able to make the rest of the world disappear, even when it's falling down around me, and the wreckage is impossible to ignore."

I only had so much self-control and so much willpower. This woman and I connected on every single level except for one, and if she said she was ready to cross that bridge that took us from friends to lovers, then who was I to stop her. Especially when everything inside of me wanted nothing more than to meet her in the middle of that bridge. Hell, I would follow her over if she decided to jump off the damn thing.

With a feral sounding growl, I dropped my mouth to hers and lowered myself so that I was braced above her with a forearm over her head. It took no time at all to pop the buttons on her flannel shirt and even less time to get her jeans open, and a hand shoved down into the tight space. Her skin was so soft, but her wet, faltering folds and the silken skin hidden between them was even softer. She arched up against me making our teeth clash and driving the aroused points of her breasts into my chest. There were still too many clothes in the way, but I didn't have the wherewithal to do anything about it. Keeping my throbbing dick trapped behind my zipper was the only thing keeping me from coming all over her like an excited teenager before I got inside her sweet heat.

Her tongue twisted around mine and her hips lifted to ride my fingers, and I found her soaked opening and delicately protruding clit. The slip and slide as I worked my way inside her lithe body had a damp spot growing on the fly of my jeans. We were both wired and ready to blow. The anticipation of this moment, of how we would feel, and move, and the taste was almost too much to take. Brynn panted into the ravenous kiss as she frantically pulled on the hem of my shirt, wordlessly asking me to remove it. I had to pull my hand free of her grasping, pulling center to get the garment off. While I was up on my knees, I urged her to lift so I could pull her pants down her endless legs and ordered her to strip off the rest of her clothes while I was unveiling her creamy thighs and perfectly bare and pink pussy. She had a smattering of freckles that danced across her lower abdomen, and I couldn't stop the urge to lower my head and connect the dots, and I ran my fingers teasingly from the inside of her knee back up to her wet and willing center. I felt her muscles contract, and her thighs spread wider when I dipped the tip of my tongue into the tiny indent of her belly button.

Her fingers threaded through my hair, and I let her drag me up her torso until my mouth was hovering over the tip of one puckered nipple. I exhaled a deep sigh and watched as her pretty points contracted into even tighter peaks. They were a rosy, raspberry color that glowed against her golden skin. All the parts of her individually were perfect, stunning, flawless; when they were all together and splayed out before me, willing and waiting, I knew there would never be anything more beautiful. At that moment, all I wanted was to be worthy of that kind of beauty.

I pushed my fingers back into her damp opening and used the pad of my thumb to circle her clit. I swore I could feel that little bud of pleasure vibrating against my finger and I felt the way she reacted when her pussy clenched down tightly on my stroking and searching fingers. She let out a gasp that echoed through the big room, and her back bowed up off the bed when I lowered my head and encased her nipple in my mouth. I used my teeth to tug on the sensitive skin and rubbed the rough scruff of my chin across the satin surface of her breast. Brynn's fingers tightened in my hair, and her thighs quivered. Her chest was rising and falling with raspy breaths, and she was saying my name over and over again. Her eyes were only half open, and there was a pretty flush covering all of her naked skin.

She was so responsive. Her reactions were both sweet and wild with every touch, every stroke, every flick, and twirl. I kissed my way across her collarbone, stopping to leave a mark at the base of her throat. When I landed on the breast I'd neglected up to this point, I added another finger to the ones that were already inside of her and added more pressure to her pulsing clit. I could feel her arousal flowing hotly over my fingers and taste it on her skin. When she pulled her legs up and set her heels on the edge of the bed so she could move more fully against me, I almost lost it. My cock pressed painfully against the denim keeping it from her skin and hardened to the point I was worried any move I made was going to leave us both with a mess. I rumbled dirty words against the side of her neck and moved my fingers with more force.

She threw her head back, red hair fanning out like flames across the white comforter. She looked as close to the edge as I was, but she was coherent enough to tell me between moans, "I'm so close, Lane, but I want to feel you. I want you inside of me. I want you to take me."

Shit. I was planning on getting her off at least once before I got inside of her. This had been such a long time coming I didn't want to ruin the moment or have it end before it even began.

"I'm close. Too close. Once I feel you all wrapped around me,

I'm going to lose it. I want this to be good for you, Brynn. I want to be the best you've ever been with." I wanted to replace every guy I was unknowingly fighting with for her heart.

She huffed out an irritated sound and pushed against me until I was standing at the side of the bed shirtless, with the head of my cock poking out from the top of my jeans. The slit was shiny and almost angry looking with my arousal.

"It's you, so it's already better than it's ever been. I want you to fuck me. I don't care how long you last. Hopefully, we get to do this a couple million more times, and you can make it up to me then. Besides, I told you I'm right there. I won't last long either. I've waited my whole life for this moment."

I grunted when she put her hand on the button of my jeans and wrestled it open. The brush of her fingers against my overheated skin was enough to make my knees shake, and my balls lift and tighten. When she reached for the zipper, I had to wave her off. There was no way I was making it through her putting her hands on me and taking me out of my pants without blowing my load.

To distract her and to get rid of the pout on her face I handed her my wallet and told her to find the condom I had stashed in there.

When I shoved my jeans down to my knees, my dick bounced up toward my navel. The swollen tip left a trail of moisture in its wake, and I could feel the heavy vein that ran along the backside of my cock throb with each beat of my heart. Brynn's eyes widened at the sight, and her mouth dropped open in appreciation. Her gaze lifted to mine as she handed me the condom.

"That's the only part of you that's always been a mystery. I have to say the wait was worth it."

I wasn't about to be recruited for porn anytime soon, but I'd never had any complaints about what I was working with. I did feel a swell of masculine pride surge through me at the naked admiration in her eyes. I loved the way she looked with, and without, her clothes on; it was nice to know the feeling was mutual.

I rolled the latex down my shaft hissing through my teeth at the sensation. I usually had way more staying power than this, but something about her went right to the center of every desire and want I had. This was about so much more than getting in and getting off. I'd never fucked anyone I cared about before. I never went to bed with anyone I was desperate to keep in my life before. This was the first time I'd ever been with anyone my heart wanted as much as my cock did and it was wreaking havoc on my control.

Once my cock was sheathed, I shoved my pants the rest of the way down my legs and crawled up over her. Immediately her legs locked around my waist, her heels digging into my lower back. Her hips effortlessly lifted and my hardness met her softness with no resistance. Her fingernails dug into my shoulders, and I curved the hand I wasn't using for balance around the curve of her hip. Even with the condom on I could feel how hot and tight she was. Her body quivered and shook around mine as I pushed my way inside. That sexy slide had both of us swearing and closing our eyes as the push of my body gave way to the pull of hers. I was surrounded by velvet heat. I was encased in the kind of warmth I never wanted to leave. Being inside of her brought it all together for me. This was how happy was supposed to feel. She was the only one who ever gave me that feeling. This, more than a good time, this was something that glowed radiantly from the place that had always belonged to her inside of my heart.

"Fuck, Brynn . . . why did we wait so long to do this? You feel so damn good." I started to rock into her, hips pumping, my hand curling around the back of her leg and lifting so I could open her up even more. I loved the way she moved around me, taking whatever I had to give as I moved faster and got rougher.

"So do you. It feels perfect, and you didn't even have to try."

She ran one of her hands over her breast, and I swore again when she started to play with her nipple.

"Oh, I'm trying, believe me. It's taking everything I fucking have not to come before you."

She smiled up at me and lifted her head so our lips could touch. Her tongue flicked against mine, and I felt my orgasm swirl around the base of my spine and coil along my nerves. She made a noise that almost sounded like a purr, and her eyes got a dreamy, faraway look in them. "Come. I've dreamed for years about what you would look like when you let go. I know all your expressions except for that one."

Her teeth attacked my ear, and one of her hands skated down my spine and smoothed over my clenching ass. It was too much. She was too much. This moment collided with all of the feelings I was having, and I thrust inside of her hard enough to make myself see stars as I exploded inside of her. I felt her body ripple in approval around mine, her inner walls locking down on my still pulsing dick. I shifted into her a few more times even though I was empty and had nothing left to give. I let go of her thigh and reached between us to playfully pull on her clit, and that was all she needed to follow me over the edge. She might have imagined what I looked like when I came, but there was nothing that could have prepared me for how spectacular she looked when she let go and lost it. The way her mouth opened on my name and the way her eyes glittered with satisfaction would stay with me forever. I would risk everything and give anything I had to put that expression on her face as often as possible.

"You okay?" When I pulled out, we both groaned at the separation. She smelled like sex and whiskey, and on top of all of that, she smelled like me. I wanted to bottle the scent up so I could take a whiff whenever I wanted. Losing her after inhaling that intoxicating mixture wasn't an option for me now.

She gave me a sleepy smile and stretched languidly. "Best I've ever been."

I felt the same, and I told her as much when I kissed her and got up to deal with the condom.

I found myself wondering if there was even another answer besides yes if she ever did ask me to marry her.

CHAPTER 10

Float or Sink

BRYNN

I WASN'T EXPECTING BAUER TO still be in the room adjoining ours the next morning. He was skittish and nervous in a way that led me to believe he was absolutely going to bolt as soon as he was left to his own devices.

I'd taken him to one of the shops in the hotel and spent a mini-fortune on the basics for him. I tried to get him to eat dinner with Lane and me, but he flat out turned me down. He did use Lane's phone to send a flurry of text messages to his brother, but there hadn't been a response back. Lane let the kid keep his phone in case the brother was tied up and couldn't shoot a text back until later. That left Bauer with everything he needed to cut and run. He was so used to relying on only himself; he couldn't fathom two complete strangers honestly having his best interest at heart and worrying about him.

When the connecting door opened silently under my hand, I held my breath as I peeked into the still dark room. I thought for sure he would lock me out. I literally begged the teenager to let me look at his varied and extensive injuries. He tried to refuse the same way he had with dinner, but I pushed and pleaded until he caved. There wasn't much I could do for the old wounds, but the fresh ones and the wounds that looked raw and possibly infected I did my best to clean and bandage up. There wasn't a spot on his long, gangly frame that wasn't marked in some way. He'd been through hell in the back of that rusted out RV, and when I said as much, he quickly corrected me and told me that some of the bruises came from his time hustling. The poor kid hadn't seen kindness in so long he didn't recognize what it was anymore.

There was a lump under the covers in the center of the bed. I sucked in a surprised breath and put a hand on the center of my chest when my heart leaped in reaction. I couldn't believe he was still here. I couldn't believe he believed in us enough to stay.

I was backing out of the room as quietly as I could when a disembodied voice drifted up from the cocoon of covers. "I know you're there, Brynn."

I stopped and pushed a hand through my damp, shower-sex tangled hair. I'd done a lot more to get dirty than clean while soaping up and sucking off Lane this morning. I should be embarrassed by getting caught snooping on Bauer, but I wasn't. I wanted him to know someone cared, that he was worth checking on and fussing over.

I tugged on the belt of the fluffy bathrobe from the spa-like bathroom that I'd thrown on after my shower, twisting it around my hand. "I wanted to see if you were still around. I wasn't sure you were going to be here this morning."

The covers rustled, and suddenly his head appeared amidst all the white linen and cotton. His hair was clean, but the auburn strands were sticking up in a million directions indicating that he fell asleep when it was still wet, and it had dried crazy. The red in his hair made me smile, and so did the way he rubbed the sleep from his eyes with his fists like he was a little kid. There was still some youthful innocence buried inside of him. I wanted to give him the chance to let more of it out. He was young enough that there was still time for him to salvage his childhood.

"I wasn't sure I was going to be here either. I planned on taking off, but after you left, I took a shower, ordered some food and tried to get in touch with Mikey again. It's been years since I wasn't smelling my own stink and not fighting off hunger pains. I've been sleeping with one eye open and my hand on a switchblade for so long I think I forgot what it was like to sleep straight through the night. I told myself I was gonna close my eyes for a minute. I guess I needed more than a minute and having a full stomach didn't help my plans either." He reached for the phone that had dropped to the floor at some point in the night. I could tell from the glower on his bruised face that he didn't like whatever was on the display. He shoved a hand through his wild hair and looked up at me. "Thank you for last night."

I tugged on the terrycloth and nodded. "It was my pleasure." I motioned to the phone. "Any word from your brother?"

He shook his head and threw himself back against the mountain of pillows. "No, and that's not like him. Mikey always responds right away when I find a way to contact him."

I worried my lower lip with the edge of my teeth and tried to push down the apprehension that was rising in the center of my chest. "Did you tell the guy in the RV about Denver?" I didn't know how far the people who abducted Bauer would go to get him back, or if they even would try.

Bauer shifted his eyes toward the ceiling and tapped the phone against his palm. "No. I didn't tell that asshole anything other than I wanted him to let me go." His thin shoulders shifted, and he pulled at his hair in frustration again. "But I did tell the guy who picked me up in the BMW that I had an older brother. When we were exchanging sob stories, I told him all about Mikey trying to protect me from my dad and how he promised to take care of me once he was old enough."

That wasn't good. That meant the kid they sent in as bait knew more about Bauer than he did about the people who snatched him. His older brother not responding suddenly seemed even more alarming, but I didn't want to worry him any more than he already was. I forced a smile that I was sure he could see right through and offered a platitude that he met with a flat stare. "I'm sure we'll hear from him soon. Order something to eat, and after we pack up, we'll get on the road. If we drive straight through, we should hit Denver sometime after midnight."

He nodded and looked back at the phone. He tried to appear nonchalant, but I could see how anxious he was.

I told him, "Take your time."

Hoping I wouldn't freak him out or give him the wrong idea I walked over to the bed and sat down on the edge of the mattress. I reached out a hand and put it on his bony shoulder, giving him a reassuring squeeze. His eyes were so sad and filled with so many secrets that it was impossible not to get pulled into the darkness trapped inside of them. This kid got to me on so many levels it was nearly impossible to separate his hurt from mine. I was starting to understand why Lane had felt the need to put his entire future on the line for me when we were younger. All I wanted to do was put myself between this kid and everything in life that was going to hurt him.

I felt him shiver under my light touch and watched as he slapped a practiced but indifferent expression on his face. "It'll be okay, Bauer. Whatever is waiting for you, it will be okay. You don't have to face it alone." I knew how hard it was to have hope when it felt like every day brought some new, unmitigated horror with it.

"I don't want anyone else to get hurt because of me . . . because of who I am." The last part of his sentence dropped off and his face twisted into a mask of disgust.

It was so wrong that the people who were supposed to love him unconditionally didn't. It killed me that anyone would tell a child that who they were was somehow wrong and worthy of all the pain and suffering he's been through.

I squeezed his shoulder again and rose to my feet. I didn't want to crowd him, even though I wanted to stay close by if he needed me. He needed to know someone would show up for him, no questions asked.

"There is nothing wrong with who you are. You are exactly the way you were always meant to be, just like I was. When I was born with this red hair all I heard was how wrong it was, how ugly and against my heritage it was. I was an anomaly, a monster and my mother and her people never let me forget it. I thought something was wrong with me until my little sister came along. She looks just like my mom and just like all the other little girls on the reservation where I grew up, but she wasn't treated any better than I was. My mom still acts like she was an inconvenience and an abomination, and the people on the reservation still treated her like she was less than worthy because our dad is white. Some people hate because that's all they know how to do. That's their problem, not yours, and eventually, you will find someone who loves everything about you. Anything that happens from this point forward is not your fault, Bauer. That blame lands squarely on the shoulders of the people who only had one job, to take care of you, to raise you. They failed, not you."

Something I said erased the self-loathing that was creeping over his entire body. His head cocked to the side, and I bit back a smile because he reminded me of a curious puppy when he looked like that.

"You grew up on an actual reservation?"

I nodded. "I did. My mother belongs to the Crow Nation. My grandfather is one of the Crow tribe elders. Believe it or not, he used to be a rodeo star back in the day." If they had been better people, I would have taken so much pride in both those facts. I never took my heritage lightly, but it wasn't something that I used to define myself either. I couldn't, not when I heard over and over again I wasn't enough of anything to claim it. "He was very disappointed when my mother hooked up with a roughneck and had me when she was still a teenager. I don't know if he hated that my dad was white more than the way he beat on my mom when he could be bothered to be around." My dad was my mom's biggest mistake, and very much like Lydia Warner, he came and went like a bad rash we could never quite get rid of.

Bauer jerked his gaze away from mine once again and fiddled with the seam of the comforter. It was crazy that his mannerisms appeared so young and untried when his eyes seemed ancient and world-weary.

"I loved history when I was in school. Learning about cowboys and the Old West was my favorite. Is Lane a real cowboy? He looks and acts like one."

I couldn't hold back the laugh that bubbled out. "He's the real deal. If you ever make your way to Wyoming, he can show you how to rope and ride, how to herd cattle and catch fish. He can even teach you how to play sad country songs around a campfire. His family's ranch is pretty much my favorite place on the whole Earth."

A wistful look crossed Bauer's face, but he hid it when he looked back down at Lane's phone, swiping the screen and typing what I assumed was another message to his brother. "I would like that . . . a lot. Once I told my dad I was gay, he stopped trying to teach me anything besides how not to be gay anymore."

I could tell by the inflection that he didn't believe a trip to the ranch would ever happen, so I told myself that I would prove him wrong. I would show him that sometimes those of us who had

had to fight for every little thing we had, eventually got the things we wanted most because we deserved them.

"Eat something hearty for breakfast. I don't know when we're going to get a chance to eat lunch. Don't give up on your brother. He's probably just tied up with something." That got me an absent nod that felt like it came from any teenager who was done with an adult hovering over them. It made me smile.

When I got back to the suite I shared with Lane I was surprised to see our bags already packed and the room empty. When I left to check on Bauer, Lane was still in the shower weak-kneed and breathing hard from the blowjob. It appeared he had recovered and was getting us both ready to go. I couldn't help but feel a little swell of pride that it took him a few minutes to recover after I was done with him. I'd wondered how he would taste and feel in my mouth for a long time, so I made sure to draw the experience out and savor it for as long as possible. It was torment and temptation for both of us.

Out of the corner of my eye, I saw movement in the bathroom. The door was open halfway, and Lane was standing in front of the vanity, the lower part of his face covered in a thick slather of white foam. He was watching himself in the big mirror as he scraped a razor over the stubble that dotted his chin. Of the three Warner brothers, Lane was the only one who kept his face clean-shaven. I asked about it once, and Cy jokingly told me it was so that no one missed the sexy little divot in his youngest brother's chin. Like Lane Warner needed anything else to make him absolutely irresistible.

Wordlessly I moved around him, pushing him back a step, so I was between him and the sink. He lifted his dark eyebrows as I made a gimme motion with my hand, asking him to give me the razor. Under the robe, I wasn't wearing any clothes. Watching him watch me with those hooded and hot baby-blues, I suddenly felt every place on my body where that scruff he was getting rid of rubbed my skin raw the night before.

I wrapped my fingers around his jaw and moved his head, so I had a clear shot at his cheek. Slowly and carefully I pulled the blade across his skin and watched as smooth, tanned flesh was revealed.

He didn't flinch.

He didn't twitch.

He didn't tense.

He let me handle him like he was mine to do whatever I wanted with, and there was something so exciting and arousing about that that I felt my body start to throb and hum in response.

He stood perfectly still and trusted me to take care of him. He trusted me and more than that he believed that I wasn't going to hurt him now that I knew that I could. He watched me with those bright eyes of his, and I swore he saw all the things I'd tried to keep from him for so long. There were no secrets left, nothing left to hide.

When I had all the shaving cream removed, I dropped the razor in the sink behind me and found a washcloth that I could finish cleaning him up with. The burn in his eyes changed from something hot to something that bordered on the edge of dangerous. I let out a strangled yelp when his hands found their way under the heavy material of the robe and landed on my naked backside. His rough palms moved across my skin in a caress I felt right between my legs. My arms went around his neck as he pressed me harder into the marble behind me, dropping a heated, wet kiss on my mouth before lifting me up like I weighed nothing and setting me on the edge of the vanity.

It felt good to have his strong body pressed into mine. It was hard to ignore that rigid length that pulsed against my center behind the towel he loosely wore around his hips. Nevertheless, I felt obligated to warn him, "We don't have much time. Bauer can't get ahold of his brother, and he's worried. We need to get on the road soon."

His dark hair rubbed against my fingers, and the muscles in his shoulders flexed enticingly where I held him close.

That grin of his did what it always did, charmed the pants off me, not that it was hard since I was mostly naked.

"I'll be fast . . . in a good way."

It was hard to argue with that, and there was no denying the promise of pleasure in his eyes.

When he kissed me again, I kissed him back and arched into his touch as he pulled the belt of the robe apart. I obediently opened my legs to make room for him as his hands drifted up and down my thighs. His tongue teased mine, darting in, and out, and around. It felt like he was mapping out the way I tasted and all of his favorite spots in my mouth so he could revisit them over and over again. I submitted to his control, letting him handle me and take care of me the way he let me maneuver him.

He pushed the robe off my shoulders, and it pooled around my hips where we were pressed together. His hands worked their way across my chest. He took his time tracing the line of my collarbone, stopping to circle the mark he left at the base of my neck the night before. His palms skimmed over the swell of my breasts, his thumbs pausing to circle the swollen tips. My nipples pulled even tighter under his touch, throbbing with a pleasure so sharp it had me pulling in a pained breath.

He outlined my ribs and rolled his fingertip around the outside of my belly button, all while making love to my mouth. His lips never left mine, and his tongue never let up on its sexy exploration. When his hands reached the tops of my thighs, I had to pull back so I could catch my breath. Lane grinned at me again, and I was ready to hand my heart right on over to him then and there if he promised to never smile at anyone else that way ever again.

I couldn't get a single word out though because he used his

thumbs to trace the indent where my legs were wrapped around him. That curve led him right to the place that was already wet and waiting for him. Typically, I took a minute or two to get warmed up and into the swing of things. With Lane, I had a hair trigger, and it took nothing more than the flash of those blue eyes, or the hint of that lady-killer grin and I was ready to beg him to stick his cock inside of me. He wasn't the only one who was running hot and fast when we were together like this.

His fingers dipped between my legs, and I felt a rush of moisture follow. That grin of his turned wicked, and before I could get my thoughts in order, he dropped to his knees on the bathroom floor. My head fell back with a gasp, and my fingers clutched desperately at the edge of the countertop. I felt him use his fingers to lightly stroke the slick folds in the way of his target. He made a low sound of appreciation, and my heart tumbled when he dropped a sweet kiss on the inside of my thigh.

"When you blush, you blush all over, Brynn." He sounded like he liked the pink heat that was under my skin. "You are so pretty, everywhere."

His rough fingers carefully pulled me open. I'd never been this exposed to anyone before. I'd never let anyone study and examine me the way Lane was doing. While I sought out intimacy and the kind of connection I only felt with him, when it came time to let someone in who wasn't Lane, I couldn't do it. For him though, I let my legs fall open even more, letting him move me like I was liquid as he put my legs up on his wide shoulders. I gladly lost myself in the sensations he was creating. His breath was hot against my core, and I almost came right out of my skin when I felt the edge of his strong, white teeth on my clit. The almost bite made my spine stiffen and had my ankles digging into his back.

His tongue flicked at my entrance, lapping up the silken moisture he drew out of my body. When he moaned in satisfaction, it vibrated against my most sensitive parts and had my head spinning.

"I like the way you taste, Brynn. Doesn't matter where my mouth is on your body, it all tastes so good." He proved his point by licking his way inside of my body, making love to me with every part of his mouth.

I tossed my head from side to side as he curled that subtle appendage and sought out every place he could find that would make me scream. When I was panting his name, and begging him to hurry, he changed his focus so that his mouth was surrounding my clit and his fingers were pushing in and out and scissoring back and forth inside of me. He used his tongue and his teeth to relentlessly torture my clit, biting down on the hypersensitive spot and soothing the sexy sting with mind-numbing kisses. He curled his fingers with unerring accuracy and hit the place inside of me that made me a slave to his touch.

That steady pressure against that tender spot combined with the rougher, more aggressive attack on my clit pushed me into the oblivion of pleasure so quickly that I didn't even have time to tell Lane how close I was or how amazing what he was doing felt. All I could do was helplessly come apart under his hands and mouth as he continued to work me over, pulling every last pulse and shudder of my orgasm out of my body. When he pulled his thick fingers out of me, they left a wet trail across the insides of my thighs, a sight that was so erotic and satisfying I wanted him to paint my entire body with the proof of how good we were together.

I had no energy, so when he pulled me to him and cuddled me into his chest, I flopped into his embrace like a limp noodle. "Fast seems to work just fine for both of us."

He chuckled and I felt it rumble on the top of my head. It was such a simple, perfect moment that I wanted to freeze time and keep the way it felt forever. "We did everything else in slow motion. It took us years to get here, Brynn. Eventually, it won't feel like we have to rush through all the good we have together. Soon enough we'll know that this, what we have together, isn't going to go away."

I hoped he was right. I wanted the time and the space to savor this particular bend in the ever-winding road we were traveling together.

CHAPTER 11

Give or Take

LANE

THE KID LOOKED EVEN YOUNGER and more fragile in clothes that fit, all spit-shined and polished up. There was no way he was a day over sixteen, and that was probably pushing it. His eyes were locked on my phone, which he was holding in a death grip. Brynn wasn't exaggerating when she said he was freaking out over the radio silence from his brother. I would be in the same spot if I couldn't get ahold of Sutton or Cy for any length of time, so I was going to do my best to get Bauer to Denver as quickly as possible. Hoping against hope that Mikey was tied up in some typical garbage that came with being a new adult and on your own for the first time. Those were distractions that seemed so important at the time and could make him forget just how much his little brother relied on him. It happened to the best of us.

"Are you bummed that you didn't get to experience Vegas in all its glittery glory?" Brynn asked the question sounding somewhat worried about my answer. She was walking close to my side, but her eyes were locked on the young man we were following. She felt responsible for him. She had clearly taken on his pain as her own so that he wouldn't have to carry the burden alone. I admired her for it, but it also made me worry. There was no telling what was waiting for us in Denver and I wasn't going to throw the kid to the wolves. I promised her I wouldn't get anyone with a badge involved in Bauer's situation, but if the brother wasn't up to par, or if something *had* happened to him, I didn't have a choice. I wasn't going to put her in a dangerous situation because she was too blinded by her soft spot for the boy.

"I don't think I need anything Vegas has to offer. Everything I wanted was in my bed last night and this morning."

She blushed, and her head tilted to the side as she finally pulled her eyes off of Bauer and looked up in my direction. "I thought you were all for flashy and glitzy. That seems to be your thing."

I frowned down at her and used a fingertip to push back the brim of my ball cap. "What are you talking about? I'm a simple country boy through and through."

She snorted and rolled her dark eyes. "Except when it comes to women. The brighter they shine, the more you seem to notice them."

It was my turn to cock my head to the side and study her. "The only thing I notice about a woman is if she's noticing me. I've spent my entire life getting looked over for Cy and Sutton. I learned early on to pay attention to the women who weren't using me as a replacement cowboy."

She made a face, and I saw her jaw clench. "The clients from the ranch you spend time with, they all look like they stepped off the pages of a magazine or came from a reality TV show. There is nothing about them that is simple or country." She couldn't hide that my choice of recent bed partners rubbed her the wrong way.

"All those women have one important thing in common, Brynn." I reached out a hand and hooked our pinkie fingers together like I used to do when we were kids. "I knew each and every single one of them was leaving at the end of the week or in a couple of days. None of them were going to stick around, so it didn't matter that I had zero emotional investment in them. None of them could hurt me because none of them were the type of woman I could ever see by my side for the long haul. It was all fun and games. No risk and fleeting reward."

Except it wasn't always fun and rarely did it feel like a game that had any winner. I didn't want to be lonely any more than anyone else, but at some point, the endless one-night stands started to make me feel even more isolated than I did when I was alone. The type of women I was wasting my time with reminded me of my mother, all fantasy, and no substance. They were safe because I knew I would never love a woman like Lydia Warner which meant I would never end up a broken shell of a man like my father. No one would ever own me that way. Only it was starting to feel more and more like I belonged to the woman at my side all along.

"Is that what you're afraid of, Lane, being hurt?" Her shoulder brushed mine as we reached the elevator and Bauer violently jabbed at the little button.

I shrugged which shifted the weight of the duffle bag I was carrying. "I'm afraid of not being enough just like my old man. I've got a good life, and I like the man my father raised me to be, but all of that has to be enough for the girl who gets me. I've seen what happens when it isn't. I don't want to kill myself trying to give someone the whole world when my little part of it, the part of it that we occupy together, is all theirs. I will give the person who's mine all that I have . . . why shouldn't that be enough?"

"For the right person that's more than enough, that's more than they will probably ask for." It was more than she'd ever asked for considering she had never, not once since the very beginning asked for anything from me or from anyone else in my family.

The metal doors swished open, and Bauer gave me a look over his shoulder. "Be happy you have a piece of something to share with someone, dude. There are a lot of us out here that don't have anything to give to anyone."

That was a startling and heartbreaking bit of insight from someone too young to feel like they didn't have anything to give to anyone.

His eyebrows arched and a crooked grin split his banged-up face. He looked down at our hooked fingers and mumbled, "Looks like you decided to take the risk? Was it worth it?"

I couldn't suppress a chuckle. "The friendship was never really at risk. It's been through hell and back and survived things that definitely should have killed it. It's pretty damn resilient."

Brynn dug her elbow into my side and pressed the button to take us down to the lobby. "It was on life support for a while. Neither one of us was ever quite willing to pull the plug though."

Bauer shifted uncomfortably, his fingers tightening even more on my phone. "I've never had anyone like that except for Mikey. He was always there for me, always had my back. He never let anyone talk down to me or pick on me for being one of the only out kids in our town. If something happened to him because of me, I wouldn't be able to handle it." He was already on edge, one tiny push from any direction and he was going over. He wouldn't be headed back to the streets if something bad happened to his brother. No, if Mikey was hurt or worse, Bauer's next stop was six-feet under.

Brynn let out a breath and quietly assured the timid teenager. "You have us now. And you just heard how stubborn we both are when it comes letting go of someone we care about." I could see how badly she wanted to reach out to him, to pull him into her arms and offer him the comfort and security he's been robbed of his entire life. "You aren't alone."

The doors opened silently, and Bauer took the opportunity to escape the thick blanket of concern Brynn was trying to wrap around him. He pushed at his floppy auburn hair and fiddled with the phone in his other hand. Sensing he needed some space I tugged Brynn back to keep her a few paces behind the teenager as he zipped and buzzed his way along the busy carpet and past rows and rows of already hopping slot machines. Once again, I thought the sheer number of people and the noise level was overbearing. I also hated that every breath I took was clogged with cigarette smoke. How anyone ever thought of this madness as a way to get away from it all was beyond me. I was pretty certain my first trip to Vegas would also be my last.

I moved my hand to Brynn's lower back, and in my mind, I saw the way her spine dipped in right there and daydreamed about the way her delectable ass felt in my hands as I hammered into her. There was no comparison between Brynn and another woman. They were all forgettable and forgotten. Whereas every single part of her from the very start was imprinted on some part of my memory. Every word she spoke, every face she made, the way she moved, the way she felt, the way she tasted and turned in my arms, none of that would ever be forgotten regardless of where we ended up at the end of the road trip. She was so much a part of me that I was starting to suspect I wouldn't be the man I was without her. She taught me as much about love and loss as the old man taught me about breeding cattle and branding.

I was so distracted by my thoughts and my plans for the future, a future that definitely had her and I doing a whole lot more of what we were doing upstairs, that I didn't notice that Bauer had stopped abruptly. I stumbled a little, grabbing onto the kid to keep from sending him to the ugly carpet when I bumped into him. He looked over his shoulder at me, eyes twice as wide as normal and lower lip trembling.

I kept my hand on his shoulder and lowered my head so he could hear me over the din and ding of the casino. "What's up, kid?"

He blinked rapidly and gulped so loudly that I could hear him above the racket around us. "There are three guys at the front door. They're all looking at their phones and checking out every youngish looking guy who walks by. What if they're here for me?"

"How is that possible? How would the people who took you know you were with us in Vegas? Why wouldn't they just assume you went to the police back in California when Lane got you out of the RV?" Brynn sounded slightly shrill, but she purposely moved so that she was in front of Bauer, keeping his smaller frame trapped between the two of us. I snatched my camo hat off my head and plopped it down over his. I motioned for Brynn to hand me the black Ray-Bans she had hooked in the collar of her shirt and silently handed those to the teenager as well. It wasn't much in the way of disguises, but it was the best we could do in a pinch.

I leaned around the two of them so I could get a look at the men who had the kid so spooked. Sure enough, three hulking bodies that looked like they belonged as extras in a gangster movie were lurking at the front of the lobby near the doors. I'd left my truck with the valet the day before, so that was the only way out.

"I texted Mikey, and I sent him an email. I told him where I was going and I gave him your plate number just in case something happened. If I didn't make it to Denver, I wanted him to have some kind of clue to find me." He looked back at me and even though I couldn't see his eyes with those dark shades on I could clearly feel the panic pouring off of him. "That's why he isn't answering. They did something to him to get information about me."

"Hey," I squeezed his shoulder again. "You don't know that. We don't know anything yet." But I had to admit it was the only way they could know where we were. There were too many ho-tel/casinos on the Strip for them to randomly pick the one where Bauer just happened to be, not to mention the fact they seemed to know he was no longer alone in the desert. Three guys that size was overkill for an underfed street kid.

"My brother would never sell me out, not willingly. I have to get to Denver . . . NOW!" He moved as if he was going to go around Brynn, but she blocked him by extending her arms and stepping backward.

"I'll get you to Denver. But you need to use your head. There is no way you stayed alive on the streets as long as you did, doing what you did, without thinking smart." I pushed past both of them, turning to face Brynn. "Find a side exit. Make sure the men in black aren't watching it and slip out. Find a crowd of people and try and blend in as they move up the Strip. Make your way to the next casino, and I'll come pick you guys up at the entrance. Keep your heads down and move quickly." I motioned for Bauer to hand me my phone back and told Brynn to text me when they got somewhere safe.

Brynn gave me a sharp nod and reached back to grab Bauer's hand. His was shaking, but hers was rock steady. "How do you know they aren't looking for me and you as well? What if they know what you look like too, Lane?"

"I'll deal with it. You take care of the kid." She nodded stiffly and bit her lip. I bent my head so that I could soothe the abused flesh with a kiss. "Cy was right. This is so much bigger than we thought it was."

Bauer made a noise that sounded like he was choking as he reached forward to clutch at the back of Brynn's shirt. "Oh, my God . . . they want me because I accidentally overheard RV guy telling BMW guy who the client was. I know who they sold me to."

My head whipped around and I frowned at the cowering teenager. "What?"

Bauer nodded and pressed himself into Brynn's back. He was shaking like a leaf, and I was worried about him being able to stay on his feet. This conversation was killing valuable minutes, but this new revelation was eye-opening. Bauer was more than the property they bought and sold; with the knowledge he was carrying around in his brain, he was a goddamn liability.

"Who bought you, Bauer?" Who in their right mind thought that purchasing a child for sex, and lord only knew what else, was okay?

The kid shook his head at my question and started to pull Brynn back toward the busy casino. His head was down, and he looked like he was a split second away from bolting. "You wouldn't believe me if I told you. No one would. That's what RV guy told me when I told him that I overheard the name. We gotta go."

Brynn turned pleading eyes to mine, so I nodded at her. "Go. I'll be okay." At least this time the threat was right in front of me, and I was walking right at it instead of the ambush that took me out last time. Before she took off, she stepped into my space and threw her arms around my neck. She put her mouth on mine and kissed me as if it was her life that depended on it . . . because it kind of did. I kissed her back with just as much fervor, making sure she could feel my resolve to get us all out of this.

I let her go, and she immediately grabbed Bauer's hand and started to pull him through the crowds that were starting to gather in the bustling casino. She did what I told her to, kept her head down, and soon they were lost in the sea of strangers. Taking a deep breath and steeling myself for whatever was waiting, I shoved my hand through my flattened hair and started for the front doors. I called down for the truck before Brynn and I had left the room, so all I had to do was collect the keys and run like a bat out of hell.

As I approached, I kept my eyes on the toes of my boots and begrudgingly admitted Cy was right . . . as usual. I should have called Wyatt Bryant last night and asked him if he had any Fed buddies who were willing to get involved in this mess. It was all quickly spiraling out of control. When I got close to the first man, he gave me a thorough once over and looked back down at his phone. He let me pass without a word but the second guy, the one closest to the door stuck out a hand and forced me to stop or muscle my way past him. I paused and gave the goon my best good ol' boy grin.

"Can I help you?" I tucked my phone into my front pocket and hooked my thumb through my belt loop. I could do simple and country in my sleep. It was a role I was used to playing. I liked it when people underestimated me. It gave me the upper hand.

"Where are you visiting from, cowboy?" The guy in the suit was trying to appear friendly, but failing terribly.

I cocked my head to the side "Why? Do you work for the hotel? Did I win something? Hot damn! I never win nothing." I widened my grin and made sure I kept my posture relaxed when all I wanted to do was punch him in the face over and over again. I could see the screen of his phone the way he had it tilted. Sure enough, there was an image of Bauer looking terrified and so young on the device.

"Sorry, no. I'm looking for the owner of the black pickup out front. You look like the type to drive something like that. The plates are from Wyoming." He sneered at me. "Those boots look like they belong in Wyoming."

Shit. They were watching the truck. I hadn't factored not being able to get to Brynn and Bauer into my rushed plan.

I was silently sizing the guy up, wondering if I could take all three of them and how heavily armed they were when suddenly the chaos of the casino amped up to a thousand. A shrill alarm went off, sounding like an air raid siren and suddenly hotel and casino staff were ushering the packed casino floor in our direction, clearing everyone out as the fire alarm continued to blare. The guy in black reached for my arm, but I deftly maneuvered out of his grasp putting space and people between us as he lifted his phone to his ear. I waved a hand for the harried-looking valet. Keeping an eye on both the men dressed in black as the battle-scarred tourists began flooding out of every opening. The noise outside was worse than it was inside and the fear of the vacating people was tangible. They were the best distraction ever, and I sent up a silent thank you to the heavens. I was pretty sure Brynn was the one who pulled the alarm. She was always quick on her feet. I told her to find a crowd to move in, and she had gone one step further to create a mob to get lost in. Saving my ass in the process.

"Let me move my vehicle so the emergency trucks can get in." I pointed to the truck and waited impatiently for the guy to find my keys. A security guard was threading his way through the crowd, so I reached out and tapped his shoulder to get his attention. He seemed irritated but paused when I told him, "Three guys are walking around dressed head to toe in black. They were lurking at the front of the casino before the alarm was pulled. I don't know if they were armed, but it was suspicious as hell." There was no need to mention the tragedy that had befallen Vegas several months earlier. Anything that was even the slightest bit off was a threat, and those in charge took it as credible intel they had to investigate.

Once I had my keys in hand, I tore out of the entrance like I was driving a race car instead of a truck.

It was time to call for backup. There was too much at stake.

CHAPTER 12

Live or Die

BRYNN

BAUER WAS SHAKING SO BADLY that it was a mini-miracle he was still on his feet. The kid was holding onto his composure, barely, but he was doing it. The path out of the side door appeared to be clear, but I wasn't taking any chances. This entrance was far less populated and crowded than the main doors, and anyone looking for Bauer would have no trouble spotting him if we went out this way. I was scrambling to think of a good distraction when the red fire alarm mounted on the wall near the restrooms caught my eye. I knew there were a million cameras trained on the casino floor, but I had to take the chance that I was faster than security would be.

I nudged the teenager with my elbow and waited until he slowed enough that we were walking side by side. I tilted my head so I could whisper in his ear. "As soon as I move I want you to run for those doors." I indicated our escape with a lift of my chin. I pressed my phone into his clammy hand and ordered, "Don't wait for me and don't look back. Get somewhere safe and call Lane so he can come and pick you up. Understand?"

He took the phone reluctantly. He tugged the nose of my

sunglasses down so were eye to eye and muttered, "What about you? I can't show up without you. Lane will flip out."

Lane would flip, but he would also do the right thing and protect Bauer while getting him somewhere safe until he figured out what was going on with the kid's brother. He couldn't stop being a hero, even when things went absolutely wrong, and that was one of the things that I loved most about him.

"Lane will get you to Denver no matter what. I'll be right behind you, but if it looks like you're lingering and waiting around for something to happen, that makes us both look suspicious. Lane said we should find a crowd to blend into in case that exit is being watched. It's too early for there to be many people on the streets. If I can't find a crowd, I'm going to make one." I grabbed his hand and gave it a reassuring squeeze. "It's going to be okay. I know that it's hard for you to believe that since things have never ended up okay for you in the past, but your team is due for a win, Bauer. I'm not going to let you down, and I know for a fact Lane would rather die than let anything happen to either of us." I waited until I got the smallest nod of acknowledgment. He didn't know how to believe in anyone else, but he was willing to try for me. "Good. Now go!"

I gave him a gentle shove and waited until he was a few feet away with the exit in clear sight. Glancing around to make sure our little heart to heart hadn't attracted any unwanted attention I made sure the coast was clear and meandered toward the bathroom. I bent my head down, letting my long hair fall forward and cover my face. I was glad our rush this morning prevented me from pulling the thick mass up and out of the way like I normally did. I kept my eyes on that little white lever, fingers twitching where my hands swung loosely at my thighs.

"Excuse me, dear." I almost jumped when the door to the bathroom swung open, revealing an older woman dressed head to toe in contrasting neon colors. She smiled politely at me while fidgeting with her designer purse. I put a hand on my racing heart and forced myself to return her friendly expression. "You wouldn't happen to know if there is a Starbucks anywhere around here, would you? I'm dying for a frappuccino."

I shook my head in the negative and shifted a step closer to the alarm. "I have no idea. I just got in last night and haven't had much chance to explore."

She waved a heavily jeweled hand in the air and stepped around me. "No problem. I'm sure there's gotta be one close by." The woman cocked her head to the side and studied me for a painfully long moment. I could see Bauer shifting uncomfortably out of the corner of my eye. "You're quite lovely, my dear. That is some very unusual coloring you have. That red hair can't be natural. Your stylist deserves an award."

Any other time and place I would have had something smart to say to that, but right now there were more pressing matters at hand. I thanked the woman for her backhanded compliment, and once she was gone, I lunged for the alarm handle before anyone else could exit the restroom. Almost instantly an ear-splitting shriek and flashing lights filled the occasion. The gamblers glued to the slot machines barely flinched, but the rest of the hotel guests milling about the lobby immediately started muttering and looking for available exits.

Bauer bolted just like I instructed him to. I saw his thin frame delicately weaving between bodies as people surged toward the door. I kept the family camo hat in sight as I followed a hundred feet behind him. Security started filling the floor, guiding pedestrian traffic while talking into invisible microphones and scanning the increasingly nervous crowd. I moved swiftly and with purpose, keeping my eyes on the prize, refusing to be distracted by the mayhem I created.

As soon as Bauer was out the side door, I let myself breathe a sigh of relief. Unfortunately, that reprieve was short lived as my upper arm was grasped in a steely grip. I was mere inches from the door when a burly security guard with a bald head and mean eyes grabbed me.

"Ma'am, you'll have to come with me. Pulling the alarm with no cause is a crime." I blinked up at him and tried for an innocent expression, but his stern expression never wavered. "I'm sorry, but you're kind of hard to miss with those legs and that hair."

Fair enough. My hair did stand out like a beacon. I nodded and was getting ready to go quietly with the man and face my punishment when the guy suddenly put his fingers to his ear, straining to hear something coming over a radio hidden there. He dropped his hold on my arm and started to move the opposite direction of the crowd. I watched his retreating back as he yelled to another guard, "We have a problem at the front. Possible shooting, armed assailants. All hands on deck."

I refused to freak out over the fact that Lane was out there with those armed men. He was trusting me to do my part, and I had to have faith that he would do his. I ran through the door, rudely pushing past looky-loos and dawdlers. I almost knocked over the woman in neon, offering her a slight smile of apology, but didn't stop until I was outside. I kept to the middle of the milling crowd, moving slowly and methodically until I reached the fringe of the group. Once I had room to move, I jogged toward the closest casino. My frantic pace and wild-eyed look got me a few strange glances, but I slipped in mostly unnoticed due to the commotion next door.

I had no idea where to start looking for Bauer. Luckily, he found me instead. I was weaving through the slot machines and blackjack tables in the direction of the lobby when I was suddenly tackled from the side. Bony arms wrapped around me, and we nearly went to the ground in the aftermath of Bauer's enthusiasm.

"I'm so glad you made it. I thought it was all over when that security guard grabbed you."

I hugged him back briefly but urged him to keep moving. "Were you waiting for me? I told you not to do that. I almost didn't make it."

He pulled on my hand and forced me to change direction, guiding us away from the casino and the entrance of the hotel.

"This casino is attached to a mall. There's another entrance on the side of the building not facing the Strip. I already sent Lane a text and told him to meet us there. It'll be less busy than the main entrance." He started moving purposely in the opposite direction I was planning on going.

"How do you know that?" I followed him, casting furtive looks over my shoulder every few minutes to make sure no one was following us.

"I stopped to look at the directory while I was waiting for you." He turned to look at me, and I wished he didn't have the glasses on so I could see his eyes. The kid was hard to read without the dark shades offering him one more shield to hide behind. "It's habit. I always need to have more than one way out of a room." Of course, he did, because nine times out of ten when he was in a room, he was paid to be there by someone who wanted to use him and hurt him.

His words had me grinding my teeth together and hating every adult in his life who had failed him. I thought I hated the ones who had hurt me, but somehow my anger was twice as hot and doubly dangerous when it came to this lonely, abandoned kid.

When we got to the exit of the mall, Lane was already there in the idling truck. I wanted to cry seeing that he was in one piece and unharmed. His expression was fierce and focused as I hustled Bauer into the cab, following him up in a rush. I practically jumped across the center console in order to drop fevered kisses all over the side of Lane's handsome face. He let out a breath that had his shoulders shaking. His hands lifted off the steering wheel and tangled in my hair. His lips hit mine with reverence and so much relief that I felt it push against all the fear and adrenaline that was coursing through me.

I returned the kiss with a passionate one of my own, and when I pulled back, he was already moving the truck forward. None of us said anything as Lane navigated the complicated Vegas traffic. It was a snarled mess made even worse by the hectic goings-on at the casino we'd just fled.

It wasn't until we crossed into the tiny corner of Arizona that we had to get through on the way to Utah that Lane decided to break the silence. He told us that we needed to stop for gas. He didn't tell us that when we stopped, he was going to take a couple minutes and call for backup. I knew he didn't want to send Bauer running, but we were dealing with things neither one of us had any experience with, and our lack of knowledge could get everyone killed.

When he told me he was calling Ten to ask her to meet us in Denver, I didn't object. The woman was a forest ranger now, but at one point in time, she worked for the FBI. She was a badass, through and through. Tennyson was a bloodhound when it came to finding missing people. If anyone could track down the legendary Mikey, it was her. Lane also wanted to call Webb's brother Wyatt. I had no clue what a DEA agent could do for us, but I figured he might know someone who could help. As long as everyone agreed that the priority was keeping Bauer safe and out of the hands of the people who bought and sold him, I told him to call whomever he had to. I felt bad going behind the kid's back, but if the end result was Bauer being protected from the people who hurt him, I would deal with the guilt. After all, he was a child, and it was about time someone made some decisions that were in his best interests.

I distracted him with a mini shopping spree in the gas station. We grabbed what seemed to be one of everything off the junk food aisle including Lane's precious Funyuns. I also bought him a pair of cheap sunglasses so I could confiscate mine. He seemed so appreciative of the cheap gift that it twisted my already sideways heart into more knots.

He was quiet the entire time we were in the convenience store, and it took me a minute to realize his demure demeanor was due more to the truckers coming in and out than the events back at the casino. Bauer was no stranger to out of the way stops and long, lonely trips on the highway. It didn't occur to me that these types of places probably held some pretty shitty memories for him, just like every time I was forced to return to the reservation and to my mom's trailer did for me. It was a place I never wanted to visit, old ghosts found in haunts of places best left buried. I had to force myself to go when I wanted to check on my sister. I bet it was the same for Bauer.

Lane also dropped a quick call home to let Cy know what was going on. I could tell by Lane's side of the conversation that his older brother wasn't happy with the dangerous turn of events. From the sounds of things, Cy was trying to talk Lane into forgetting about Denver and head straight home. He wanted us back at the ranch, and he didn't care if we brought the kid with us. I could hear Lane explaining that he didn't want to betray Bauer, that he promised the kid he would help him get to his brother, but Cy didn't seem to be moved by his younger brother's dedication and loyalty. I understood where the oldest Warner brother was coming from. It had been Cy's responsibility to take over the ranch and his brother's care when Boyd died. He'd dropped everything, left his life behind to do what was expected of him, and the last thing he wanted was one of his younger siblings out there fighting this kind of battle alone. It was Cy's job to be the roadblock against all the bad shit that was bound to come looking for boys as wild and wicked as the Warners were.

Lane eventually told Cy he had to go. I heard the other man practically yelling as his little brother hung up on him. Bauer seemed amused by the exchange but his gratitude at knowing Lane wasn't going to change the plan and stop him from getting to Denver and his brother was palpable. Slowly but surely, he was letting us get around the walls he'd been forced to hide behind to keep his sanity and any remnants left of his soul alive.

I offered to drive for part of the way and was surprised when Lane took me up on the offer. Those Warner boys rarely let anyone near their precious trucks, even the women they loved. It was another move proving that he trusted me, that he was ready to give me all that he had. We were no longer former friends trying to pretend we hadn't turned into adversaries along the way. We were friends who turned into lovers—lovers who were going to do their very best to be each other's forever. We weren't shoulda, woulda, coulda. We were *happening* now. Finally, it was our time.

The drive through Utah was both beautiful and boring. There were some stunning rock formations the first part of the drive, but halfway, the road turned as long and blank as the drive out of the desert in California. Both Lane and Bauer dozed off leaving me alone with my thoughts. I tried my best to keep my mind off what we were walking into once we hit the Mile-High city. I wanted Bauer's brother to be everything he needed and the young hero he described, but I had my doubts. I was sure the young man loved his brother, after all, he'd put himself between Bauer and his father's misplaced anger time and time again. But the reality of helping someone who had been through the kinds of things Bauer had been through, I wasn't sure Mikey was ready for that. I didn't know how much he knew about his brother's past, but I was betting Bauer hadn't been completely honest with Mikey about what he'd done to simply survive.

I knew there were parts of my ordeal I refused to share with anyone. It was easier that way. I didn't want my old experiences to taint the way people saw me. I didn't want pity, I wanted a chance to prove that I was nothing like my mother. I wanted a shot to show the world I was the woman Boyd Warner allowed me the time and space to become.

And I wanted that same opportunity for Bauer.

The weather was gross when we got into Colorado. Windy as hell and raining so hard it was difficult to see out the windshield. I gladly handed driving responsibilities back to Lane and tried to catch a quick nap. The howling wind was noisy enough that I thought it was going to be impossible to rest, but the next thing I knew Lane was shaking me awake. It was dark outside, and the clock on the dashboard told me that it was closing in on midnight. The skyscrapers of downtown Denver were lit up all bright and shiny, and it was still raining out. Lane was asking Bauer for directions to his brother's place, and we both cringed when he rattled off an address that was recognizably in a less than desirable part of the city. Certain streets ran through parts of Denver that we all knew to avoid when we traveled to the big bad city . . . well, big and bad for those of us from small-town Wyoming.

"Is your family from Denver?" Lane asked the question innocently enough, but I could see him watching Bauer in the rearview mirror.

The teenager was closed in on himself, arms wrapped around his legs as he stared unseeingly out the window.

"No. I'm from the coast." It didn't go unnoticed that he didn't mention which coast he was from. "The city I'm from has a really nice part and a really, really bad part. I grew up on the dividing line between those two places. Sometimes it was scary. Most of the time it was a typical suburban upbringing complete with a white picket fence."

"Mikey always loved the mountains. He's an avid snowboarder. He always talked about going to college in Denver when he was old enough. It's so cool he managed to make that dream come true." He sounded so wistful I could practically feel the longing for something normal like the chance at college in his tone.

"Bauer"—Lane hesitated for a second before plowing on—"Are you sure your parents never reported you missing or as a runaway? Maybe your mother had a change of heart along the way."

The teenager snorted and shook his head violently back and forth. "No way. I got picked up for solicitation in San Francisco and again in LA. When they ran me through the system, nothing came up. They had to call my folks before dropping me in foster care over and over. My parents don't give a damn about what happens to me. The only person who cares about me is Mikey."

"Not the only person, kid. Try and remember that." Lane never raised his voice or sounded frustrated. He was the quiet re-assurance, the steady, unwavering strength that someone as skittish and gun shy as Bauer needed.

Bauer simply turned and looked out the window, a look of doubt laced with a sliver of hope on his face that spoke volumes. If he only knew the hell we'd both been through to get to this moment, he'd truly understand that someone can come out of the depths of hell and onto the other side if they had people worth fighting for on the other side.

We lapsed back into silence for the rest of the ride to the rundown apartment complex off of East Colfax. Lane took his time trying to find a place to park. It took me a minute to realize he was circling the block to make sure we weren't being followed. I was pretty sure the woman standing on the corner around from where Lane finally parked was a prostitute, and there was no question that the guy sitting on cracked concrete steps in front of the building was dealing drugs. He eyed us up and down as we moved in unison to the front door. There was no security door. There was a busted-up intercom that Bauer bypassed, pushing his way into the complex with Lane and me hot on his heels. I could feel the heat of Lane's hand on my lower back. It was reassuring when the situation was anything but. The elevator was broken, so we climbed three flights of stairs until we reached apartment 3F. Bauer took a deep breath before knocking, and I watched him deflate when there was no response. He knocked again, this time calling his brother's name and lifting a foot to kick the wood.

Lane reached around the redheaded teenager and put his hand on the knob. The cheap door swung open with barely a touch.

Bauer fell back a step, and I instinctively reached out to catch him. I heard Lane swear and held the teenager up as he started to collapse into my arms. I peeked around Lane's broad shoulders and couldn't stop my whispered "Oh, fuck" that slipped out.

The apartment was dingy and small. It was decorated like any straight, eighteen-year-old male would decorate with lots of posters of bands, beer, and breasts. The furniture was obviously second hand and mismatched in a way that made my head hurt. However, none of that held a candle to the fact that the place had been trashed. Absolutely demolished. It looked like everything Mikey owned had been shredded and dumped in a pile in the living room. It was a mess.

There was no sign of Mikey anywhere.

We were too late, and Bauer was going to break down.

I held onto him even tighter, determined to keep it and him together as Lane and I exchanged knowing looks.

We were standing right on the fault line as things shifted from bad to worse and the quake that rumbled under our feet was ominous and worrying.

CHAPTER 13

Freeze or Melt

LANE

THE STUNNING REDHEADED POLICEWOMAN WHO arrived to check out the apartment and to take the missing person report was watching me with sympathetic eyes that were almost as dark as Brynn's. She told me there wasn't much the police could do about the teenager being gone considering Mikey was eighteen, and it wasn't clear that he had been taken against his will. Even with all the destruction and mess in the apartment, his TV, MacBook, and video game console were all in pieces but present. Nothing was indicating that the disaster wasn't caused by a rowdy party or careless teenagers. And since I couldn't go into all the details of *why* I suspected someone had snatched the kid against his will, all I could do was watch as she was blown off by the neighbors and given the stink-eye by the other people she questioned at the apartment complex. Clearly, this was the kind of place where a police presence was unwelcome, no matter how attractive that presence may be.

She handed me a card that had Officer Cross printed on the front. She had jotted down a couple of numbers telling me how to reach her if any more information became available. I got the distinct impression that she had picked up that there was so much more at play here than I was admitting to, but I promised Bauer I wouldn't make him talk to the cops. It was the only way he'd agreed to go with Brynn to a hotel while I stayed behind and played upstanding citizen. The kid was frantic, ready to run off into the night, checking every alleyway and dumpster for his brother's body. He was concerned Mikey was dead, even though there were no signs of a struggle in the apartment. Nothing Brynn or I said could convince him otherwise and trying to get him to calm down had been nearly impossible.

It was only the appearance of Ten and Webb Bryant that eventually broke through Bauer's near hysteria. Ten had a no-nonsense demeanor and a way of making it seem like she had everything under complete control. As soon as he realized she wasn't there to arrest him or force him to go to the authorities, he relaxed. When she looked the distraught teenager in the eyes and promised him that she would find his older brother, it was almost as if Bauer was compelled to believe her. Or maybe it was nothing more than having a whole group of people on his side for once that finally had the kid believing in miracles. The kid had never had a shield to hide behind, and the world had fired shot after shot at him while he was unarmed. Now there was a virtual wall surrounding him, and we weren't going to let anything get through.

I wasn't surprised to see Webb with Ten. The former crook had taken to following the Ranger around like a lost puppy. He was Ten's opposite in pretty much every way, laid back and goofy where she was stern and serious. She barely tolerated the reformed criminal when we were back home, but here in a busy metropolitan area, she was differing to Webb's knowledge of where the bad guys liked to hide because he used to be one. Webb mentioned that he tagged along because his brother was catching a flight in tomorrow as well. Wyatt Bryant apparently had a personal connection in

Denver's FBI field office and thought he would get better results having a conversation face to face with this guy about what was going on with Bauer and the men who wanted him.

The cavalry had arrived full force and wasted no time in getting to work, which finally convinced Bauer to go with Brynn while I handled the mess at the apartment.

The very pretty cop gave my arm a little pat, and I caught sight of the simple wedding band on her finger. I wondered what kind of guy she was hitched to. It would take someone secure in themselves and in their woman to trust her out on the streets looking like she did and doing what she did for a living. I would spend every second Brynn was out of my sight with my heart in my throat if she wore a badge and carried a gun like this redhead did.

"Seriously, if you can think of anything else, please give me a call. We take missing persons very seriously, especially when the circumstances around their disappearance are highly question-able." She cocked her head to the side, taking in the mess in the apartment. "And if you find out that he did simply take off with his friends for a few days and resurfaces, please let me know."

I got the feeling that she was a very nice woman who proba-bly saw a lot of really bad things in her line of work and that she really did want to help. I wished I could get Bauer to talk to her, but the kid was adamant that he wasn't talking to the police. He seemed as frightened of law enforcement as he was of the men behind his abduction.

"I will. I hope that's all it is." I shook her hand and followed her out the door, casting one last look at the destruction left behind. It didn't make any sense. If they had Bauer's brother why not use him for leverage to get Bauer to do what they wanted? They didn't have anything to bargain with if Mikey was dead. There was noth-ing to hold over Bauer's head with his brother out of the picture.

"You said he was a snowboarder. I didn't see a board or any

other gear in any of the wreckage and Keystone opened their slopes early last weekend. He's eighteen. When you were that age did you stop and think about letting anyone know where you were going or did you just take off chasing a good time?" She said it with a smile but her sharp gaze missed nothing. It was clear she knew my angle was more than a family friend concerned about Mikey's whereabouts.

"When I was eighteen, my dad was dying, and me and my brothers were doing everything we could to keep our family's ranch afloat." I lifted an eyebrow at her. I softened my words with a tilted grin. "Plus, I never had to chase a good time, they always seemed to find me."

She returned the grin. "Oh, I have no trouble believing that. Keep me updated on the kid. If you haven't heard from him in a day or so, give me a call and we'll ramp up our efforts and put an alert out." The radio pinned to her shoulder squawked to life, and her friendly demeanor shifted to all business in the blink of an eye. She rattled off a bunch of words that made no sense and gave me one last sympathetic smile. "Protecting the people we care about is hard. Sometimes it puts us in a tough spot. You look like the kind of guy who can take care of his own, but keep in mind that it doesn't have to be you against the world. There are people who genuinely want to help."

I flashed her a genuine grin and lifted the brim of my hat up. "If you weren't married and if I didn't have my own redhead to go home to, I think I would have a mighty big crush on you, Officer Cross." She was something special. I could tell even in the short time we spent together.

"You would be surprised how often the wedding ring and the fact the other person has a woman at home get ignored when people talk to me on the job, Mr. Warner. I appreciate your restraint. Have a good evening." She slipped into her police cruiser and took off with the sirens blaring.

The guy who was dealing on the front steps when we first pulled up to the apartment came out of the shadows he'd been lurking in and gave me a furious look. He lifted the front of his baggy sweatshirt up to show me that he had a gun tucked into the waistband of his low riding jeans. His sneer was ugly, and his tone was serious as he told me, "We don't like narcs around here. I suggest you go back wherever you came from before you get hurt."

I held up my hands in a gesture of surrender. I wasn't the Warner who wasted time going head to head with thugs like this guy. That would be Sutton. The middle Warner brother was the one who couldn't walk away from a fight, I had more important things to worry about than overstepping on someone else's turf.

"I got no beef, buddy, just checking on a kid who lives here as I haven't heard from him in a few days is all." And with that, I turned and got out of that crime-infested neighborhood as quickly as I could.

I sent a text to Brynn, asking where Ten had dropped her and Bauer off. She shot back directions to a hotel located downtown. It was nice, not as nice as the one in Vegas, but I could sleep under the covers without worrying about bed bugs and guests renting rooms by the hour. She also told me she was currently in the room she got for me, Bauer, and Webb to share. She didn't get into much detail but indicated that Bauer was not handling the newest development well and she was hesitant to leave him alone. I asked her if she thought me showing up would hurt or help and it took a long time for her to respond. When she did, it didn't take a genius to figure out Bauer was having a moment and didn't want to seem weak or needy in front of prying eyes. I offered to hang in the bar until she gave the all clear even though I was exhausted, eyes gritty and grainy from the long drive.

It was minutes before the last call when I sat down at the

bar, so I ordered two beers and struggled to keep my eyes open. The guy sitting next to me started asking me about life insurance, and the bartender shot me a sympathetic look as he worked on shutting down the bar. I nodded politely in all the right places and mumbled vague responses as the guy kept talking. I was zoned out, thinking about all the things about Mikey's disappearance when a hand landed on my shoulder.

I turned my head just as Brynn was lowering her head to kiss my cheek. Our lips met in a surprise kiss that chased some of my sleepiness away. "Hey. How's the kid doing?"

I swiveled the bar stool around so I could pull her between my legs. Her back pressed against the bar as I handed her the extra beer. She took it gratefully and chugged a mouthful of it back before answering my question. "He finally fell asleep, but he's not all right. He's convinced his brother is dead and he's inconsolable. He's not listening to anything I have to say."

I took a drink of my beer and ran my hand up and down her thigh. "I'm not so sure anything happened to Mikey. The cop that showed up pointed out that nothing was taken. Everything was smashed to pieces, but nothing was missing, and there was no blood, no signs of a struggle. What if they showed up looking for Bauer's brother and found an empty apartment, but wanted to make it seem like they took the kid? They could have easily gotten into Mikey's messages on the computer if they synced to his iCloud account and figured out Bauer was coming here. None of it makes any sense."

She reached out a finger and dragged the tip of it over the bridge of my nose and down to my lips. She traced the top one with a gentle touch. "Ten said the same thing. She told Bauer that the men who took him had Mikey and would use him to lure Bauer out of hiding, but he didn't want to hear it. He's certain they would just as soon kill Mikey on the off-chance Bauer told him who the guy behind all of this is."

"He give you a name yet? That would go a long way toward getting the right people involved in stopping this from the bottom to the top." I couldn't keep the hope out of my voice even though I knew it was a long shot. The kid was determined to hold onto all his secrets. She finished her beer and reached up to wrap her arms around my neck.

Her breath was warm on the side of my neck as she traced my jaw with the tip of her nose. "No, but I have the feeling whoever it is, it's someone we would recognize. He keeps saying no one would believe him. We have to give him time. He's in fight or flight mode. Why don't you come take a shower and get a couple hours of sleep in my room? I'm worried that you'll wake Bauer up if you go into yours right now. He needs to rest. Maybe it will help him think a little more clearly in the morning."

Ten and Webb were still combing the streets and prowling through back alleyways looking for anyone that might have the whereabouts on the missing brother, so Bauer currently had a room to himself. Ten mentioned she didn't think they would be back until the sun came up.

"You think leaving him alone is a good idea?" The kid was twice as skittish as he had been when we left Vegas.

She brushed her lips across mine and pushed her fingers through the short hair at the back of my head. "I think we need to give him the benefit of the doubt. I want him to trust me, and I want to believe I can trust him."

I sighed into her kiss and couldn't deny that the idea of me and her alone in the same hotel room held a lot of appeal. "You're going to be heartbroken if he's gone in the morning." And that was the last thing I wanted when I'd started all the work it took to fix it.

She gave a tiny shrug and snuggled into my chest, the top of her head fitting perfectly underneath my chin. "I'm already heartbroken. If he's gone, then we go after him. Simple as that."

I felt her smile against the base of my throat, and her fingers got more possessive in my hair when she told me, "Webb told me to tell you that it was about time you got your head out of your ass and realized what was waiting for you at home. Ten also mentioned that she was happy we were done dancing around one another. She said she was getting tired of watching us two-step around each other."

I hummed in agreement and shoved my hands into the back pockets of her tight jeans. I gave a little tug and pulled her until all her softness was pressed right up against my hardness. I was going to have a permanent indent on the underside of my dick from my zipper by the time we got back to Wyoming.

So far it had just been Brynn and me trying to figure out the changes in our relationship. We were alone navigating these unknown waters, but the truth was, how we were together affected a lot of other people. Sure, our family and friends would want us both to be happy, and they all would say us being together had been a long time coming. But she had been married to my father, and we had the same last name. That made things awkward. People were going to talk, and I knew how much she hated that the first time she got tangled up with a Warner.

"This isn't going to be easy, you and me. People are going to have opinions and ideas, and when they offer them up without either of us asking, it's going to piss me off. I don't want you hurt anymore, Brynn." And I would do whatever I had to make sure she never felt that kind of hurt again. I was no stranger to fighting for what I believed in, but for her, I would burn the world down and take everyone who meant her any kind of harm with me. Not to mention she was going to run into Jack eventually. I was sure Sheridan, Wyoming, was already dissecting every which way Brynn had screwed up that seemingly perfect relationship, and when she showed back up hand in hand with me, there was going to be no end to the hell she was going to face.

"Oh, Lane." She wrapped her arms around my shoulders and pulled back so she could look me in the eye. I always thought her eyes were so dark and mysterious, so hard to read, but there in the dim light of this hotel bar, I could see everything. I could see every step of the arduous journey she had traveled, mostly on her own, to get to this point. "Those people can't hurt me. Not anymore. They don't have that power. I refuse to let them matter. The only person who can hurt me when it comes to you and me . . . is you."

That was a heavy responsibility, one that I took as seriously as keeping my father's dream alive. I hated that I didn't realize that I could wound her as easily as she wounded me before I almost lost her.

I clutched the firm flesh I was caressing in my hands and gave her a crooked grin and a heavy-lidded leer. "Oh . . . I'm gonna hurt you sometimes, Brynn. But trust me, you're gonna like it and ask me to do it again and again . . . and again."

Her eyes widened and the insurance salesman I'd forgotten about up until that point choked on the last of his drink that he was nursing while he obviously eavesdropped. I barked out a laugh and slid off the barstool, clasping her hand in mine and leading her through the bar to the elevators.

Once I had her inside the elevator, I backed her against the mirrored wall, held her flawless face between my hands and attacked her mouth like it had been years rather than minutes since I'd had a taste of her. She opened her lips obediently and wrapped her arms around my waist. She parted her legs in invitation, and I inserted my knee. Rubbing it along the inside of her thighs until it was pressing against the seam of her jeans right where she was already warm, and I would bet, wet. She was so beautifully responsive. She came alive with the touch of my hands and mouth. I always thought she looked like fire and now that I knew how she could burn and how sweet her heat was, I couldn't wait to play in the flames.

She moaned into my mouth, and the blunt edge of her teeth bit into the curve of my lower lip. She chased the tiny sting with her tongue and arched her back so that her torso was rubbing impatiently against mine. Even through the layers of clothing separating us I could feel how hard her nipples were and the rapid pounding of her heart. I used my thumbs to gently caress the line of her jaw and twisted my head so I could lick my way around the delicate shell of her ear. She made a whimpering noise that I made a note of. That was good information to have for later. I wanted to memorize all her hot buttons and most sensitive places, so I could use them and torture her with them later. I wasn't kidding about hurting her sometimes. She made me lose my mind a little and keeping all that lust and desire in check took every ounce of self-control I had. I could only hope that I got to her the same way and there would come a time that she got as lost as I was and hurt me right back.

I was working my hands under the hem of her shirt when there was a soft ding, and the elevator stopped on our floor. I was still kissing her when the doors opened. I was still kissing her as I walked her back down the hall. I kissed her up to the doorway, pressing her back against the door and stealing each and every breath as she scrambled to find the room key. Her fingers were shaking as she touched the little plastic card to the sensor. We fell into the dark room in a tangle of arms and legs. My hat went flying. I twisted at the last minute so she would land on top of me instead of the other way around. I wanted to fuck her, not crush her.

She hovered over me, long hair hanging down around my face. She kissed me and then used her hands on my chest to push herself to her feet. She stood over me like a goddess, like an ancient warrior ready to take what was hers. She started pulling off her clothes, dark eyes locked on mine as she ordered, "Strip, cowboy." All I could do was obey.

I lifted so that I could pull my shirt off and went to work on my belt and jeans. I had the denim open and the zipper down when Brynn's naked body landed back in my lap. Every working brain cell I had short-circuited, and all the blood in my body felt like it rushed to fill my cock. The wet tip dragged against the soft skin of her inner leg, marking her with my arousal and seeking out her heat.

"I hope you picked up protection at one of those gas stations we stopped at because I'm out." We'd used up my stash in Vegas.

She curled her arms around my neck and tilted back, putting her puckered nipples right in line with my mouth. I took the offered treat between my teeth and gave a hearty suck. I swirled my tongue around the pebbled flesh until she was squirming on my lap, her pussy rubbing erotically along the length of my rigid cock. It was her turn to mark me with her wetness, and all I wanted to do was drown myself in the evidence of her passion.

"I did, but they're across the room in my bag, and I don't want to get up." She blinked at me and suddenly looked shy which was hard considering she was straddling me naked as the day she was born and practically riding my dick. "I'm squeaky clean. I got tested for everything so I could donate blood when you were shot." She blushed and looked away. "I haven't been with anyone since then either. I couldn't seem to get in the mood with you lying in the hospital fighting for your life."

I reached up and cupped her precious face in my hands. "I'm good to go as well. They ran a million tests while I was in ICU and I haven't been with anyone except you since then either. Are we really going to do this?" I hadn't gone bare, ever. That was one thing Dad had drilled into all of us, wrap it up because the consequences were lifelong if you didn't. Sutton was the only one of us who hadn't taken that advice to heart.

"I want to. There have always been so many things keeping us from each other. I don't want there to be any barriers between us of any kind."

Holy shit. If she didn't already have a hold on my heart, I would have handed it over to her right then and there.

"All right, Brynn. No more barriers between us. It's you and me and whatever comes our way." I tangled my hands in her hair and pulled her down for a kiss.

She only offered a quick peck before her mouth moved to my throat. Her teeth dragged across my Adam's apple and worried the throbbing vein on the side of my neck. The wet tip of her tongue licked across my collarbone, and I nearly dumped her off of me when she took my nipple into the moist heat of her mouth. She flicked her tongue back and forth across the sensitive nub until I dug my fingers into her scalp and forcibly removed her mouth. She let the tortured peak go with a pop and moved her lips down the center of my chest until she reached my stomach. She took her time outlining each abdominal, tracing every dip and divot. She skated her fingers along the sharply defined V that narrowed down to my happy trail on either side of my hips. I got that definition throwing bales of hay and tossing saddles around. I was glad she appreciated what all that manual labor had done for my body.

Her nose brushed along the dark fuzz of my happy trail and when the very tip of her tongue slid across the swollen, aching head of my erection, I came up off the floor. My back bent, and my hands clasped her head in a death grip like she might suddenly change her mind and stop doing what she was doing. I opened my legs as far they could go while they were still encased in my jeans and moaned as she teased the leaking slit, chasing the proof of how much I wanted this, wanted her, as it slid down my cock. She wrapped her hand around the base of my dick and shifted so she could take the rest of my length into the smoldering cavern of her mouth.

I throbbed against her tongue, hips lifting involuntarily. She hummed a satisfied response and bobbed her head lower until her lips were touching her twisting and burning fingers. I was in her mouth so deep I was hitting the back of her throat every time she lowered her head. She sucked until her cheeks were hollow and it made my head spin. She squeezed the base of my cock and started sliding her hand up and down to meet the rise and fall of her mouth. I felt consumed by her like she was claiming every single part of me and it felt divine. She seemed to know exactly how I liked to be touched, and she wasn't afraid to be a little rough. I felt the edge of her teeth more than once as she licked and nibbled on the underside of my cock.

When she shifted so that she could maneuver her free hand between my legs I had to pull her off. As soon as her fingers touched my balls, her touch delicate and light on that sensitive place, I lost it. I was so wound up that her whispering touch over that tightly drawn sac and pressing in on that magically hidden spot right behind it had me ready to go off like a rocket.

With a growl, I lifted her up and wrapped my arms around her waist. I pulled her back to the top of my straining erection, now shiny and glossy from her mouth. I used a thumb to bend the stiff shaft toward her entrance, seating her on my rigid cock and frantically thrusting up to meet her damp entrance. I slid into her heat with no resistance, Brynn's body sucking me in as she fell to meet my lifted hips.

She threw her head back on a gasp and curled her hands into fists on my chest as she started to ride. Her undulating hips moved in my hands, and her perfect breasts swayed in my face. I was too caught up in the moment to do anything more than revel the way she clamped down around me. The clutch of her body bare against mine was mind-numbingly good. It felt like we were melting together, fusing as one and becoming stronger together than we were apart. "God, Brynn, you feel so fucking good. I never want my dick back. You can keep it, it's yours."

She laughed, and I felt the vibration move through my throbbing dick. "That's exactly what I always wanted. You sure know the way to a girl's heart, Lane."

She bent at the waist so she could touch her lips to mine. She was flexible on top of everything else. I was an idiot for wasting so much time being afraid of things I was never going to be able to control when I should have focused on what I could. Things like making her moan my name and writhe on top of me like she currently was. I let her kiss me breathless while working a hand between her legs so I could touch her in a way that was bound to drive her wild.

As soon as I brushed her clit, she went stiff above me and lost her perfect rhythm. She started panting and grinding on top of me, unashamed of how good she was feeling and letting me know loud and clear that I was hitting all the right spots.

With a grunt, I rolled us over and braced myself above her with an arm on the carpet above her head. I was going to have rug burn on my knees and on my ass, but I didn't care. I hammered into the woman below me like I was trying to fuck her through the floor. It was raw, primal and messy. I loved it. Loved feeling the way she got wetter and hotter the harder I thrust into her, and the more primal I tried to take her.

My orgasm struck like lightning. One second I was growling into the damp skin under her ear, the next I was shaking all over and emptying inside of her in a furious rush. Luckily my release triggered hers, and she met me thrust for thrust and surge of pleasure for surge of pleasure. We were a wet sticky mess, but I refused to move or to let her go. This was how we were always supposed to be, stripped down to our very basic selves, exposed and uncovered. This is who we really were to each other, lovers who had loved and lost each other too many times to take this moment for granted. From here on out we would let nothing, *nothing*, come between us.

"I'm pretty sure you're my forever, Brynn." The words were whispered in the darkness, but I knew she heard them. "And I'll always be thankful that I was your first."

Her lips landed on my jaw, and I felt rather than heard her sigh. "You're my only, Lane Warner. My only one." It wasn't a proposal, but it was pretty damn close.

CHAPTER 14

High or Low

BRYNN

WHEN I CRAWLED OUT OF bed the next morning I had to shift Lane's arm off my chest. After rolling around on the floor and then on the bed, he'd taken a shower and practically fell asleep standing up. Instead of sending him back to his own room I let him crash in my bed. I couldn't resist checking to make sure Bauer was still tucked in safe and sound. There was a bump under the covers, so I left him alone, even though I wanted to tiptoe into the room to make sure it really was him in the bed and not a pile of pillows. Ten stumbled into the room sometime around dawn. She looked exhausted and frustrated. She waved me off when I sleepily asked her if she had any luck tracking down Mikey's friends or someone who might know where the kid was. She told me we could talk in the morning—she was too tired to even realize it was already morning—and then gave me a wink and told me that Lane looked good in my bed. I silently agreed. It had taken long enough for him to get there that I doubted I would ever get tired of watching him sleep.

Once I was free of the heavy muscle that was caging me in, I stumbled into the bathroom and made my way through my morning ritual. I was finishing up brushing my teeth when a light tap on the door caught my attention. Not wanting to wake Lane or Ten if it wasn't necessary I rushed to the door before whoever was on the other side could knock again. Webb had his forearm braced on the doorframe above his head, and his attractive face was set in worried lines. I knew what brought him by this early without having to ask, but I did anyway.

Pulling the toothbrush out of my mouth I sighed and muttered, "He's gone, isn't he?"

Webb nodded and ran a hand through the hair on the back of his neck. He had dark circles under his vibrant blue eyes, and white lines of tension were radiating out from the corners. He looked younger than he was, with an air of mischief that perpetually hung around him. It wasn't hard to picture him getting in and finding all kinds of trouble. He reminded me a lot of Lane that way.

"Yep. My phone rang this morning. I put in a few calls seeing if anyone from back in the day knows anything about this website and who might be behind it. I got a call back, and when there wasn't any movement, not so much as a flinch from the other bed, I got up to check it out. The bed was ice cold, and there were pillows under the sheets. I don't know if Bauer left before or after I got in last night. I was too tired to check things out. He left this." Webb handed me my cell phone. "Bet he was smart enough to know we could track him if he held onto it."

I took the phone and felt my heart sink to my toes. I was right when I told Lane my heart was already broken for Bauer. What I didn't know was that all those shattered pieces were going to throb so painfully, amplifying how badly the teenager's disappearance hurt. The ache ricocheted through my body, leaving no place untouched.

"I can't believe he left." I rested my forehead on the edge of the door and held my phone in a death grip. "He isn't going to make it out there on his own. He's not thinking straight. His brother's dis-appearance has him reacting instead of evaluating all his options."

"That kid isn't used to having options, Rosy." I was never sure where the nickname came from that he'd started using once Cy hired him to help out on the ranch. I thought it was cute, and I'd never had a nickname before so I always let it slide. "All he knows is acting on his instinct, and right now they're screaming for him to do something, to do anything. He thinks those dudes who snatched him killed his brother, and now all he wants is revenge." He pushed off the door and gave me a knowing look. "I've been in his shoes."

When Webb first came around, he was lying about who he was. His brother was missing and presumed dead in an undercover drug bust that went horribly wrong. Webb convinced his brother's partner at the DEA to come with him to the ranch after signing both of them up for a week-long wilderness retreat. He was bound and determined to find his brother's body and the people who he thought had killed him. Webb was going to take every bad guy on that mountain out as payback. He was living and breathing revenge; it was the only thing keeping him going when he thought Wyatt was dead. Luckily Wyatt hadn't been harmed, and Webb's grand revenge scheme hadn't been necessary. Not so lucky, Webb was shot and nearly died on that mountain for his efforts. So really, he did understand where Bauer's head was at.

"How would he even know where to find those people? They sent someone to him. They recruited him off the streets and then abducted him in broad daylight." I thumped my fist on the door and turned my head as a rustling sound came from where the beds were. Lane was sitting up, watching us with narrowed eyes, his arms crossed over his wide chest. Ten had the covers pulled up over her head, but I could tell she was awake by the way she kept shifting under the cotton.

"Check your phone. Look at whatever website he last visited.

I bet you he used the same one he filled out the application for to get in touch with them." Lane's voice was rough with sleep and residual sexiness.

I scrolled through my browser, and sure enough, the website that had gotten the kid into so much trouble in the first place was the last one that someone visited. I poked at the different icons and tabs until I got a page for contacting the company. The box was blank, but it would take absolutely no effort to fill it in and fire off a message to the people Bauer believed were behind his brother's demise. He wasn't only walking into the lion's den, he was doing it waving a big, fat juicy steak and taunting the monster to come and get him.

"We have to do something." I pushed my hair off my face and started to pace back and forth in front of the bed where Lane was struggling to wake up. Still holding my toothbrush in my hand, I waved it around like a wand. "We can't let him go out there and wage war on these people all by himself. He's a baby, for Christ's sake."

I was tapping my phone on my hand when I noticed there was a notification on the text message icon. Pausing mid-step, I clicked it open and looked at a mile-long string of words that had been typed in the ongoing conversation thread I had with Lane. Clearly, Bauer had something to say before he bounced and left his goodbye in the one place he knew I was bound to look.

Thank you for all that you did for me.

I'm so sorry I'm leaving without telling you in person how much your help meant to me.

I told you that I didn't deserve someone good like you or a hero like Lane.

I'll never forget everything you did for me. You made me believe that there really ARE decent people in the world. People who care about strangers, and about doing the right thing.

Since you'll never see me again, I want to tell you the name of the man who bought me from the creeps running the website. I know I said you would never believe me, but I think you will, and I don't want him to have the chance to buy or sell anyone else. I'm tired of kids like me getting used and thrown away like we're garbage. I'm not trash. I'm just a kid who wanted to be loved by his family. I don't want to be punished for loving who I want to love.

Look into a man named Jonathan Goddard.

He's a big deal back where I come from. He's rich and powerful, so be careful. Rumor has it he's going to be the president one day. It's a terribly kept secret that he likes little girls, but apparently, he doesn't mind a pretty boy when he's been bought and paid for. He liked that he was bringing me back to the place I tried so hard to run away from. The guy in the RV told me his boss charged extra for finding a kid from the Point for Goddard.

You and Lane take care of each other. You both deserve to be happy.

All my best . . . Cameron Bauer

I was openly crying by the time I got to the end of the note. I collapsed at the end of the bed and let Lane fold me in his arms. I put my face on his shoulder and let the tears fall as he read the note out loud. By the time he got to the end, he sounded as emotional as I was and I could feel the way his big frame stiffened.

"Goddard? Why does that name sound familiar?" Lane asked the question while he was stroking a hand over my hair and doing his best to comfort me, but all I could do was picture skinny, battered Bauer back on the streets, outnumbered and seriously outgunned.

"Bigwig politician out on the West Coast. Guy has more money than God. He made the news a few weeks ago because his stepdaughter came up missing. There have been rumblings about corruption in his camp and all kinds of underhanded dealings for years, but he's tough on crime and comes from a long-standing political family and old money, so people tend to look the other way. He's got the job of cleaning up one of the dirtiest cities in America, so the press and media tend to give him a pass. I'm not surprised the guy is dirty, or that the kid didn't think anyone would listen to him." Webb's tone was dry, but I could see that this new development bothered him quite a lot.

"How do you know so much about this Goddard guy?" Ten pushed the covers off her head and sat up as she snapped the question in Webb's direction. Webb's gaze immediately rolled over her naked shoulders and sleep-rumpled hair.

He gave her a flirty wink and leaned back against the door. "I passed through that part of the country a time or two in my old life. When you're a career criminal, the place that makes or breaks you is the Point."

Lane and I exchanged a confused look. "The Point?" We asked the question in unison which had Webb grinning at us.

"The Point is what they call the place where good goes to die. My time there is not a part of my life I like to think about. The guy I had to be when I was there is not someone any of you would want to be acquainted with. Bauer is lucky he got out of there alive, and now we gotta do something to make sure these assholes don't drag him back there or put him in the ground." I always thought of Webb as the kind of guy who was flirtatious and fun. He didn't seem to take much seriously, and sort of drifted wherever the wind decided to take him. After his revelation, I was starting to see there was a lot more going on underneath his crooked grin and twinkling eyes. Again, he reminded me a lot of the youngest Warner that way.

Ten was peering at the younger man like she had never seen him before, but she quickly shoved away her bemusement and looked around the room where we were all watching her and waiting for some kind of instruction. She sighed and ran a hand over her face, trying to physically push the sleep away.

"Bauer doesn't know his way around Denver. He's got no one to turn to, and no place here where he's going to feel like he has the higher ground. The kid's been living on the streets for years, so his survival instincts have to be good. Where would he go where he feels comfortable? What kind of place does he know inside and out?"

Lane rested his cheek on the top of my head as I leaned into his touch. "He was hustling street corners and working cheap no-tell-motels in LA before they picked him up and tried to move him to Vegas."

Everyone in the room cringed at the bleak description of Bauer's life on the streets.

I cleared my throat and lifted my hands to wipe the wetness on my face. Crying wasn't going to do anyone any good. I needed to get it together. There would be plenty of time to be sad that Bauer didn't trust me enough to take care of him after we got him somewhere safe and had the men responsible for luring him into this situation dealt with. I wanted them all behind bars, and I wanted Jonathan Goddard to suffer. The man didn't deserve to see another sunrise as far as I was concerned. As soon as Wyatt made an appearance I was going to demand that he have his friend in the Bureau do something about the crooked politician.

"He also knows his way around a truck stop. He told us that was how he got out of his town when his parents first kicked him out for being gay." I plucked at the comforter and stared at the ceiling. "He seemed really uneasy whenever we stopped at one when we were driving here from Vegas."

Ten made a noise of disgust as she pushed the covers off her long legs and swung them around to the floor. Webb let out a sound that he quickly covered with a cough when he caught sight of the fact that the blonde Ranger was wearing nothing more than a tank top and panties. I could have sworn I saw Ten smirk, but the expression was gone before she rose lightly to her feet.

"Well, my guess is he wouldn't go too far. I say we split up. Lane and I can check the closest truck stop. Brynn, you and Webb hit up the closest hotels and motels that rent rooms by the hour." She lifted her arms above her head in a stretch that exposed the bottom part of her stomach. This time Webb didn't bother to hold back his groan of appreciation. Ten just rolled her eyes and made her way to the bathroom. "Call your brother and leave a message. Tell him the kid is missing and that he's trying to use himself as bait. Get Wyatt moving on this thing before he touches down."

Lane yawned and slowly started to crawl out of bed. His voice was raspy when he mumbled, "I met a cop yesterday when she came to check out the brother's apartment. She seemed nice and like she genuinely cared about what was going on. I think she could tell it was more than a ransacked apartment. I think I should give her a call. We're past the point of letting Bauer call all the shots. I walked the line to keep him from running, and he ran anyway."

"Considering we have no idea where we should even be looking I think reporting him missing or calling him in as a runaway might be a good idea. We need as many eyes as we can find on the streets looking for him." Ten yawned and turned her back to the room. "I need a shower and about one hundred cups of coffee. Let's wrestle up some grub before we get going. Who knows how long we'll be pounding the pavement or what we'll turn up."

"I'm a little sad you don't want to spend the day with me, Ten." Webb lifted his eyebrows at her as he headed to the door. "I thought you couldn't get enough of me."

Lane chuckled as Ten whipped around, eyes blazing with furious green fire. I didn't think it was funny at all. I knew the younger man liked to needle her and poke at her thick skin, trying to find a weak spot, but now was not the time or the place for those games.

"I don't want Lane and Brynn distracted by one another when

they're out there walking into Lord knows what. They'll be too busy trying to keep each other safe; they'll forget to watch their own backs. I told you yesterday on the drive down, you aren't nearly as cute or as charming as you think you are, Webb. I used to put guys like you behind bars for a living. You don't fool me in the slightest. The guy you were back then is still part of the guy standing right here in front of me now, and I don't want anything to do with either of them." She enunciated her point with a dramatic flip of her long blonde hair and the slamming of the bathroom door. I could hear a long stream of swear words coming through the wood.

Sighing I got to my feet and gave him a reproachful look. "You shouldn't antagonize Ten like that. One day she's going to shoot you, and she never misses."

Webb stuck his hands in his back pockets and rocked back on his heels. "She can hate me all she wants. As long as she's feeling some kind of way about me, I'll take it. It means I'm on her mind. Anything is better than the freeze-out she's so good at." He headed for the door saying he saw a Starbucks a couple blocks over so he would handle rounding up a quick breakfast for everyone.

When he was gone, Lane made his way over to me and wrapped me up in a rib-cracking hug. I squeezed him back, so grateful I had his unwavering strength to pull from and lean against. "All I wanted to do was get you to come home. How did we end up here?" I sounded as lost as I felt.

He kissed my forehead which had me shivering all the way to my toes and told me, "Our journey has never been a straight shot. We're always taking the wrong turn or running out of gas along the way. This is just another bump in the road, but we'll make it home, and we'll make sure the kid finds his way. Home isn't going anywhere, and it doesn't mean anything without us there."

"He's never had a home, Lane." And I knew how lonely and horrible that felt.

"We'll find him one, Brynn."

I hoped he was right because my heart couldn't take him being wrong.

CHAPTER 15

Win or Lose

LANE

"**Y**OU'RE PRETTY HARD ON WEBB. Don't you think you can cut him some slack?"

Ten and I were pulling up to our fifth truck stop on the outskirts of Denver. We'd been at it all morning, and so far we'd come across nothing while looking everywhere we could think of for the missing teenager. There was no sign of Bauer, and none of the people we asked had seen anyone fitting his description. I was starting to lose hope, thinking the kid may very well have outsmarted us all. The gun was missing from the glovebox of my truck which only served to add an extra air of urgency to our search. Ten had been fairly quiet most of the day, not that she was ever very chatty. She tended to be hyper-focused when she was working. Apparently, that meant in the city as well as the wilderness.

She shot me a narrow-eyed look. Green eyes sharp as polished glass. "He's annoying, and he always has some kind of agenda which he doesn't bother to share. I wish Cy had never offered him that job. Webb Bryant does not belong in Wyoming."

I rubbed my thumb along the side of my mouth and pulled the brim of my ball cap down lower on my forehead. "He seems to like it there. Where do you think he belongs?"

She shook her head, a frown tugging at her pale eyebrows. "Somewhere where all his reckless behavior won't impact anyone I care about. He's trouble, Lane. I don't know what kind, but I can see it in his eyes. He's nothing but bad news."

I sighed and rubbed my tired eyes. "He was, but he's changed. You don't think people are capable of turning things around? Look at my brothers. Sutton was two steps away from being a junkie, and now he won't even have a beer. Cy was dead set on spending the rest of his life alone and lonely, now he's getting ready to marry the love of his life. And what about me?" I poked myself in the center of my chest. "I've been walking around blind for years, thinking I could never have the one woman I've always loved. I was going to fill the void with random women until the day I died. That was the plan. But now I realize I don't have to be alone, that the fear of being left and being hurt my mother instilled in all her boys was ruining the best thing to ever happen to me. I can see it all so clearly now, but not before Jack proposing to Brynn right in front of me opened my eyes. I don't think Webb is destined to always be the bad guy."

Ten gave a very unladylike grunt in response and purposely turned her head so that she was looking out the passenger window as I pulled into the truck stop off of I-70. It was a massive building that was painted yellow. The chain was unmistakable, and so was the crush of semis and big rigs filling the lot. In this situation, Bauer was the needle, and a busy trucking complex with hundreds of long-haul drivers coming and going was the haystack.

"I can't figure out what Webb wants. I don't understand why he won't walk away when I've made it perfectly clear I'm not interested in him in any way. He's too young, too unpredictable. I don't trust him." She said it as if she was trying to convince herself of her reasons for being so harsh with the younger man. I didn't believe her. The reason she was so standoffish and argumentative toward Webb was that he got to her. Somehow and someway the slick, city boy who walked the edge of being law abiding had broken through the icy shell Ten wrapped herself in.

"He's willing to put himself right back in the center of a life he worked really hard to leave behind to help out some kid he doesn't even know. From where I'm standing, the good in him outweighs whatever bad that might still be hanging around. I think you should lighten up a bit, is all. You don't need to keep everyone at arm's length, Ten."

I'd grown up with Ten hanging around. Her family's ranch bordered ours, and she and Cyrus had always had a friends with benefits arrangement, one they picked right back up with when both returned home from the East Coast. When Cy meet Leo everything with Ten was put on ice, and neither seemed to mind, even though they had spent years as convenient lovers. Even with a lifetime of having her as part of the Warner's inner circle, Ten was still practically a stranger. I had no idea what brought her home after she left the FBI. I had no clue how she was fairing in her life now. I couldn't tell if she was happy or sad, fulfilled or just going through the motions. The only thing that was crystal clear was her animosity and aggravation where Webb was concerned. The blond, newly minted cowboy was the one person who forced her to react.

We climbed out of the truck, and I shifted my shirt to cover the revolver I borrowed from Webb. They brought a small arsenal with them from Wyoming, and since Bauer lifted my gun, I was grateful for the forethought. Ten pulled a hat similar to mine on her head and tucked her long, blonde ponytail through the hole in the back. She pointedly changed the subject by asking, "Have you heard from the cop you called this morning?"

Officer Cross had been incredibly helpful when I called and explained that on top of the trashed apartment building I was now dealing with a missing teenager. I told her I believed the two incidents were connected and she responded that she would do her best to get an Amber Alert going for Bauer. She told me that she would hit up several of the shelters that took in runaways and some of the special services that were specifically designed to help displaced LGBT youth to see if Bauer had reached out for help. She asked that I keep her updated if I came across a description of whoever it was that I suspected of abducting the teen. There still wasn't much she could do, but she was doing all that she could to help.

"They got the Amber Alert up and going, and they posted the plea for information on the Denver Police Department's social media feeds. No one on the streets has seen him, but that doesn't surprise me since he isn't from Denver. Bauer had a pretty sizable head start, who knows if he's even in Colorado still. The people who took him in the first place move really fast. They had him seduced, scammed and scooped up all within a couple of days. They know what they're doing."

She nodded in agreement and inclined her head in the direction of the parking lot. "I'm going to go check out the RV section and see if anything looks suspicious."

That was how we had divided each stop. She took the outside, and I scouted the inside since she couldn't exactly stroll into a men's restroom without causing a riot. I dipped my chin in acknowledgment, silently hoping that Brynn and Webb were having better luck than we were. When Brynn called for her last check-in they weren't turning up anything either. All in all, it was an entirely frustrating day.

I pushed my way into the convenience store part of the complex and wound my way through all the different aisles. There was no sign of Bauer, but there was an endless line of truckers and road weary tourists browsing. It was busy, so I ended up getting jostled from side to side and bumped every time I tried to turn around. Grumbling in annoyance, I prowled through the diner attached to the building, still coming up empty just like I had at every stop before this one. The bathroom was my last stop. I figured there was little chance Bauer was hiding out in the first place anyone would look for him, and I knew from my various visits to truck stops today that highway patrol officers were often found making a quick stop to make sure things were on the up and up in places like this. Bauer wasn't the only one who figured out trolling truck stops was a good way to find a ride and quick buck. Apparently, it was common practice.

The bathroom was as busy as the rest of the truck stop. Every sink and urinal had someone at it, and there was a steady stream of men coming and going from the shower section of the bathroom. Nothing seemed off or suspicious, so I was turning to leave when one of the chipped metal doors to the bathroom stalls opened and a shockingly familiar figure stepped out. We stood to face each other, each blinking in surprise. The guy from the RV didn't seem any worse for wear. His eyes still looked beady and mean. He was still the size of a small truck, and his ugly face didn't look any happier to see me than I was to see him. We both knew there was only one reason he was in Denver.

"Where is he?" I crossed my arms over my chest and watched him watch me in the mirror. I wanted to knock his smug look through the back of his skull.

"I don't know what you're talking about. Just passing through." He shook his hands off, making sure some of the water landed on me. I gritted my teeth together and tried to keep my annoyance in check.

"You're the golden retriever, the lapdog they send out to bring back their prey. I know they sent you for the kid. I bet they made you pay for losing him in the first place." I smiled at him, making sure it had a lot of teeth and sharp edges. "I hope they did every-thing to you that you did to the kid when you had him, and worse."

The RV guy narrowed his eyes and put his hands on his hips. We faced off, the other men in the restroom who didn't leave at the first signs of trouble were giving us a wide berth and curious glances.

"I'm sure that little shit told you what he overheard, so you know who he was sold to. What I did to that little shit won't even rank once he gets shipped back home and handed off to that old pervert. That rich asshole has a sadistic streak a mile wide and no one's willing to stop him. The kid will be lucky if he lasts a week in that bastard's dungeon." He made it sound like it was a done deal. "Can't believe that kid was dumb enough to think they would go easy on him and his brother if he handed himself over. These people don't like to have their business disrupted." It sounded like RV guy wasn't any more certain of Mikey's fate than I was. He really was nothing more than the delivery man.

"You fucked with his family. Of course, he was going to sac-rifice himself for his brother." That's what anyone who loved someone else would do.

The RV guy snorted and rocked back on his heels. "In this world, it's every man for himself. If the kid lives, that's a lesson he's going to learn the hard way. Get out of my way, cowboy. I have business to attend to. A high-value package to collect."

I shook my head and stepped into the other man's personal space. "I'm not going anywhere until you tell me where you're supposed to meet the kid."

RV guy lifted his hands and put all his weight behind his shove as he tried to move me out of his way. A couple of the other men milling about the restroom mumbled in concern, and one older man barked for us to knock it off.

"Not happening. I don't care how big your balls are, or how

many guns you pull on me, you won't ever be as scary as the guys who pay me to move those kids across the country. I'm not telling you shit, and even if I don't get my hands on the kid, they'll send someone else who will. They won't stop." I hated the certainty in his voice and his cocksure attitude. It also irked that he didn't seem to be bothered by the consequences of his horrific actions. He was playing roulette with people's lives, and he didn't care.

It would have been so easy to throw a punch, even easier to shove the barrel of my gun between his teeth and threaten to pull the trigger, but none of that was going to get me the information I needed. I had to find Bauer, that was the endgame, nothing else. Thinking about Brynn's story, and the way my dad finally managed to control her selfish, thoughtless mother, I dragged my hands over my face and let my shoulders fall dejectedly. The last thing I wanted to do was barter with this human garbage, but I didn't see any other option.

"How much would it cost me for you to give up the meeting point. I'll pay you. It'll be enough that you can disappear." There was no concealing the desperation in my voice. He held all the cards, and I had to play whatever hand he dealt me.

"There isn't enough money in the world to get those ass-holes in check. I'm gonna do my job, deliver the kid and keep on breathing." He nodded his head, and I should have seen the way he was winding himself up, but I was too preoccupied trying to figure out what my next move should be. "Nothing is standing in my way this time."

When he lowered his head and charged I was taken off guard. The top of his skull plowed into my unprotected gut like a bowling ball and when I hit the sink behind me, I felt the impact rattle all the way up my spine. I grunted and tried to wiggle free as heavy fists started pummeling my kidneys. I laced my fingers together and lifted them above my head so I could bring them down like a hammer on my attacker's back. A couple of guys moved to separate us, one calling out that he was going to call the cops, but none of it distracted RV guy from his mission to put me on the ground.

He got a solid hook to my jaw and an elbow to my ribs that made me swear and had stars popping in my vision. Those tender ribs were really starting to be a pain in my ass. I managed to land an uppercut that made his head snap back, and I shoved my fist in his face, mashing his lips into his teeth when he tried to regain his footing. Blood and spit spewed in every direction, and my knuckles split open. It had been a while since I'd been in a fist fight and I had a moment where I wished I was more of a brawler like Sutton.

I took a kick to my knee that almost dropped me to the ground but I was able to push back when he tried to body slam me into the wall.

"Watch out! He's got a knife!" The warning came as I was struggling to push his bulk off of me where he had me pinned. I felt the burn of the blade slicing through my shirt and cutting into the skin right before the heavy weight of his struggling form was suddenly jerked off of me by a helpful bystander. The stranger was forced to jump back as that knife waved wildly in the air, slashing at anyone who dared to get too close. I wiped my sweaty face and took a deep breath trying to assess the situation. There were too many people in the room to pull the gun from where it was stashed, and there were too many innocent people milling about for the guy to keep flinging that razor-sharp blade back and forth. I really hoped the man who had threatened to call the cops had followed through.

A brave trucker got sliced as he tried to jump the RV guy from the back. Blood flowed freely and had most of the remaining witnesses pushing out of the bathroom. I faced my adversary, hand on my side, feeling the sticky warmth of blood flood through my fingers as I covered my new wound. The bathroom was empty enough now that I could pull my weapon, but I wasn't sure my dominant hand was going to be steady enough to aim and pull the trigger. I wasn't trained for this kind of thing. My good intentions only took me so far.

"I'm walking out of here. Don't worry, I'll tell the kid how you tried to save him and failed. I'll make sure he knows it was all his fault, same with whatever ends up happening to the brother, because if they don't have him now, they will. No one who knows Goddard's name is going to make it out of this alive." The guy tossed back his head and laughed like a maniac.

I was running out of options. I slumped against the wall and tried to steady my breathing as I continued to bleed.

A voice hollered from outside, "Hey, you can't go in there! That's the men's room!"

The door swung open, and Ten marched in like she owned the place. She already had a weapon drawn, and the flinty look in her eye indicated she wouldn't hesitate to use it. She shot me a look and glanced down at the other man on the floor bleeding as profusely as I was. Her jaw tightened, and a muscle in her cheek twitched as she ordered, "Drop the knife."

The RV guy stopped laughing and shifted his gaze to me and the fierce blonde. She reminded me of a Valkyrie.

"Fuck you." He waved the knife in front of him with more vigor and narrowed his eyes on Ten. "I will go through you, bitch."

Ten scoffed. "You can try, but I will shoot you . . . bitch."

The man let out a roar that wasn't even close to sounding human and lunged for the former FBI agent. Luckily Ten was blessed with nerves of steel and years of training. She didn't flinch in the slightest as she pulled the trigger and dropped the charging man with a single shot to the shoulder. He fell to the ground in a heap, wailing and writhing in pain.

She kept her weapon trained on him as she approached

cautiously, pulling a pair of handcuffs out of her back pocket. It was easy to forget that even though her main objective was to protect the national parks that surrounded our home, she was still a law enforcement officer. Her eyes lifted to mine and flashed with concern. "You okay? Your brothers are going to kill me if I bring you home full of more holes that need stitches."

I nodded. "I'll live." My wince turned into a scowl as I pointed at the man on the ground. "He won't tell me where Bauer is. He was supposed to pick him up somewhere, so he's still out there on his own. The bad guys don't have him yet."

She made a face as she bent to lock the man's hands together behind his back. "The cops are on their way. He's going to jail for kidnapping, taking a minor over state lines and aggravated assault at the very least. He'll talk as soon as someone offers him a deal."

"I don't know if we can wait that long. He says they'll send someone else after Bauer and Mikey if he's not already in their hands." Frustration made every word jagged and sharp.

"Gotta work with what we have. We need to patch you up before you bleed out." She lifted her chin in the direction of my crimson-soaked shirt.

I nodded in agreement and pushed off the wall, wincing as the smallest movement sent shards of pain slicing through my body.

My phone rang, and while I wanted to ignore it, I didn't want to give Brynn a reason to worry if I missed her hourly check-in. Using my good hand, I fished the device out of my pocket and tried to keep the screen relatively blood-free as I swiped to answer her call.

"Hey." I didn't bother to look at who was calling before I answered, so when the voice on the other end replied, I was surprised when it wasn't Brynn.

"Mr. Warner?" The woman on the other end of the phone sounded confused by my breathless greeting.

"" Oh, Officer Cross. Sorry. I was expecting a call from some-one else. What can I do for you?"

"I have some good news actually. I handed my card to one of the neighbors the other night when I was at the apartment. I asked her to give me a call if she noticed anything odd happening next door. I didn't expect much, but I just received a call from her . . . the brother is home, and he's not alone. Your missing teenager appears to be with him."

I let my head drop and exhaled long and loud. "Of course, he went to his brother's place. Why didn't we think of that?" We'd been too focused on his old life to consider he may very well be running toward his new one instead.

She let loose a tinkling laugh. "Well, teenagers are unpredict-able. I'm headed over there to talk to both of them, but I thought you should know."

I sighed again. "Go easy on Bauer. The kid has been through hell and back. He might try and run when he catches sight of you."

"Don't worry, I'm good at handling men who have something to hide. I'll be in touch."

I hung up the phone and let myself collapse on the bathroom floor, it was kind of gross, but I didn't care.

I met the eyes of the man cuffed on the floor. It was my turn to smirk. "You lose, you piece of shit."

CHAPTER 16

All or Nothing

BRYNN

"**T**HIS IS BULLSHIT. I'M NEVER going to be able to afford to replace all of this stuff."

The agitated young man was the spitting image of his younger brother. However, he was filled out and carried more bulk than Bauer since he wasn't living on the streets. The older teen was alternating between kicking around the remnants of his belongings and pulling on his reddish-brown hair in aggravation. He appeared oblivious to how his actions were affecting his younger brother. Bauer was practically cowering in a corner, repeatedly apologizing to Mikey for bringing trouble his way, and shooting contrite looks in my direction. The kid was awash in guilt and regret, and the older boy's exaggerated mourning for his MacBook wasn't doing anything to soothe the younger boy's ragged edges. So far, I was unimpressed with his display of brotherly concern. In fact, the teenager seemed more interested in checking out me and the pretty cop who showed up to talk to both of them than reuniting with his younger sibling. It was a typical reaction from an eighteen-year-old, but I was disappointed that he didn't come across as the altruistic hero Bauer had built him up to be.

"I'll help you replace everything. It's my fault it all got broken." Bauer's voice was shaky and thin. He looked like he hadn't slept in a week, and he was jumping out of his skin every time the police officer directed a question at him. She assured him she wasn't going to haul him in as a runaway. She only wanted information on the men who had taken him. She explained that they had the man from the RV in custody and they wanted to coax him to lead them to the men behind the website and abduction. She promised him that Jonathan Goddard was never going to get his *filthy* hands on him.

Wyatt Bryant finally landed, so Webb took off a little while ago to pick him up from the airport. The DEA agent was already in touch with his contact in the FBI looking into what they could do about Goddard's involvement. Apparently, the politician was in the middle of a shit storm back home already. His stepdaughter had come forward with irrefutable proof of sexual assault, and an anonymous source had to uncover the fact that Goddard was using a nonprofit funded entirely by donations for nefarious deeds. The man was a slimeball, and he was going away for a long time, and Wyatt wanted to see if they could get federal charges thrown at him as well. They wanted the wheels of justice to grind the crooked politician up and leave nothing but corrupt dust behind. Right now, the scumbag was in custody back in his hometown, and his downfall was slowly starting to hit the media.

Officer Cross explained gently that Bauer was going to have to be a witness against the RV guy, which made him balk. He didn't want to see the man who had spent days violating him, and abusing him again. I thought he was going to break down in tears when he explained to the officer just how awful his time locked in the RV had been. He seemed embarrassed for his brother to know the intimate details of the last few months of his life, but the tall young man, still seething about his trashed apartment, seemed oblivious to his brother's discomfort and suffering.

Unable to stomach the dejected look on Bauer's face anymore, I moved across the room and pulled him into my arms. I kept my back to the rest of the room, blocking everyone else out as I tried to pour every ounce of relief and support I could into him. I rested my cheek on the top of his head and whispered, "None of this is your fault. They're just things. They can be replaced . . . you can't. When he has a second to calm down, he'll remember that." At least I hoped he would.

I turned my head when the other woman in the room asked, "Why didn't you respond to any of the messages Cameron sent you, Mikey?" The cop was scribbling notes and watching the scene between the brothers play out with a sharp eye. It was clear she wasn't any more impressed by Mikey Bauer than I was. "You had a lot of people worried about you."

The redheaded young man pouted and crossed his arms over his chest in a purely petulant pose. "A friend hooked me up with free lift passes. I hitched a ride up to the mountains so service was spotty and I don't have very many minutes. Mom and Dad cut me off when I moved out of the house because I told them I was going to find Cam and let him live with me now that I'm eighteen. They aren't speaking to me which means I'm on my own for everything. Money is tight."

I gritted my teeth to keep from snapping that he had been on his own for a few months, while his younger brother had been on his own for years at a much younger age. It wasn't fair to gloss over that making it on your own at whatever age was a struggle, but I was feeling fiercely protective over the emotionally fragile boy in my arms. All he wanted was to be loved by his family, to be cared for by the people who were supposed to do so without question, and yet, there was no mistaking his older brother was alluding to the fact that Bauer was going to be a burden on his already limited means.

The thin body shook against me, and I heard him sniff noisily. "I'll help you with the bills." His voice was barely above a whisper.

Finally, Mikey shook himself out of his shock and anger, looking over at where his brother was huddled against me like a wounded animal. "You're too young to get a job, Cam. And there is no way in hell Mom or Dad would sign off on a work permit. But thank you for the offer." He shoved his hand through his hair again and shifted his gaze over to the cop. "We'll figure something out. We can make this work. Hey, if he's going to be your main witness against some big sex trafficking ring shouldn't he be compensated for that? Isn't there some kind of reward in it for him?"

The policewoman lifted one of her rust-colored eyebrows, and her dark eyes flashed in annoyance. It was amazing how similar our coloring was. Everything about how she looked was a shade or two lighter than how I looked. Her hair more strawberry than fire, her skin more honey than gold, and her eyes were a warm, chocolate brown instead of nearly black like mine. Aside from those small differences, we could almost pass for sisters. The way she was clearly frustrated with Mikey also mirrored my current emotional state. I liked her instantly, and I was so relieved she was the one who had shown up to handle Bauer's case. I didn't get the impression she was willing to throw the disaffected youth to the wolves in favor of her career.

"I think your brother's reward will be in making sure these bastards can't do what they did to him to anyone else. By testifying against these guys, Cameron is taking a stand against anyone victimizing children for profit. He's going to be a hero." I rubbed a hand up and down Bauer's arm as he shook violently at the policewoman's words. "I think I have what I need from you boys for now. We'll need to be able to contact you both as we move forward with charges. If you're going to change locations, please be sure you inform me, and if you need anything, please don't hesitate to get in touch with me. You're a very brave young man, Cameron Bauer."

She gave me a grin as she walked to the door. "It sounds like you have yourself the kind of guy who finds himself in trouble even when he isn't looking for it, Ms. Warner. I have one of those myself, complete with a southern accent that makes everyone who gets near him act stupid and goofy. Keep an eye on your man. Your cowboy seems like a good guy."

A surprised laugh tumbled over my lips. "He's the best. I've had my eyes on him since I was five years old. He just now started looking back." I couldn't imagine the kind of effect Lane Warner would have on the unsuspecting female population if he had a southern twang. He was already dangerous, that would make him deadly.

The cop chuckled, and we shared the kind of smile that only women who loved difficult, shortsighted men could share. "I wish you all the best. It's a good thing you stumbled across that kid out there in the desert. This story could have had a much sadder ending. He needed you so badly."

She slipped out the door as her radio went off. Once she was out of the room, Bauer seemed to relax marginally. He shyly returned my hug and took a moment to pull himself together while I was still acting as a shield between him and his brother.

"Is Lane okay?" It didn't take a genius to know he was blaming himself for the injuries Lane had sustained in the truck stop bathroom as well as the wreckage of his brother's belongings.

I nodded. "He'll be fine. He needed a couple of stitches, and the fight didn't do his cracked ribs any favors, but he's okay. Ten said he didn't even want to go to the hospital, but the police made him so they could get his statement and take pictures of his wounds for evidence. He's more worried about you than he is about a little ol' knife wound." That was glossing over the damage my cowboy sustained but Bauer didn't need to know the grisly details of Lane's wound.

I got a wobbly smile for my efforts to lighten the mood and moved back as the teenager stepped around me. His brother was watching our interaction with open curiosity but for once remained silent, which was a good thing. I already wanted to scream and yell at him to have some compassion for everything he's learned about his little brother's past today.

The older Bauer boy cocked his head to the side and asked, "You're still gay, right?"

I gasped as Bauer blustered and tripped over his words. "What? Of course I am. Why would you even ask me that?" He stalked to the middle of the room and started absently moving piles of junk around in a futile effort to return order to some of the trashed belongings. "It's not something you randomly grow out of, Mike."

The older boy shrugged. "I was just wondering. If you suddenly decided that you liked girls, it would make things a lot easier. Dad might not ever get over himself, but I bet Mom would lighten up a little. It's hard to do this day in and out every day without any help from anyone."

I saw Bauer's jaw clench and watched as his hands curled into fists at his sides. "I know that. I've been on my own since the night Dad put you in the hospital. I haven't had anyone to ask for help in over two years."

His hopeless words were like an arrow that pierced through all the pieces of my shattered heart. I remembered how despondent I was when I thought there was nowhere to turn to for help for Opal and me. I could feel the weight of the world pressing down on me from every direction back then. My circumstances were a cage I was sure I was going to be trapped in forever. No way out was the reality I pushed against every minute of every day. When Boyd Warner stepped in and offered me an escape, it was the first time in my entire existence I felt free. There was no way I couldn't at least offer Bauer the same kind of key so that he could escape his very familiar prison.

I walked over to him and nudged his shoulder with mine. "Hey. I want to talk to you about something important." I looked over at Mikey who was openly staring at my ass. I rolled my eyes and snapped my fingers to get his attention. "Can you give us a minute? I want to talk to your brother alone. I'll help you clean up this mess when we're done, and I'll have Ten and Lane bring us all something to eat when they're released from the hospital."

The surly young man begrudgingly agreed, disappearing down a short hallway and into what I assumed was his bedroom.

I tugged Bauer over to the slashed couch and searched around for a place that seemed like it still had enough stuffing in it for us to sit. Perching gingerly on the edge, I pulled him down next to me and gave him a smile that I was sure had my heart, and my intentions stamped all over it. He'd finally fessed up and told the pretty police officer that he was only fourteen. Knowing how young he was, yet seeing how ancient and tired his eyes looked, it was a struggle to find the words to describe how heavy the pain from my past was. I didn't want to weigh him down with more than he already had on his plate, but he needed to know there was another door he could walk through, and that there was so much more than what he was used to waiting on the other side of it.

"When I was seventeen my mother had a boyfriend who liked to gamble. He was a drunk and mean, but he left me and my little sister alone for the most part as long as we stayed out of his way. All I wanted to do was turn eighteen so I could get out of that trailer that was rusting away on the reservation. I was kind of like Mikey because I was convinced that once I was the legal age, I could get my sister out of there and take care of her as well. I had so many plans, but they all fell apart."

I twisted some of my hair around my finger and let the memories drag me back to a place I swore I would never revisit. "I had no idea how powerless I really was. The boyfriend lost more than he could afford to lose on the Super Bowl and made a deal with his bookie. He sold me, promised me to the man he owed money to like I was currency. He drugged me and was handing me off for payment when social services showed up to check on my sister. Someone at her school finally noticed something wasn't right. They saved my life that night, but if they had been five minutes later, I would have been in the exact same situation as you just were."

Bauer was watching me with wide eyes and his mouth hanging open. I nodded to show him that I understood how similar we really were. "The problem was that I knew there was little anyone could do to keep the system from giving us back to my mother. Where I come from they want Native kids with Native parents, even if those parents are entirely unfit. That boyfriend went to jail, but what about the next one, and the one after that? I had no idea what I was going to do, and I was terrified."

"What happened?" His voice was breathless and scared for me.

"The Warner's happened. Lane and I were best friends, but I was deeply, madly in love with him. I always have been. When he heard what happened, he showed up at the hospital where they were pumping my stomach to try and get rid of the drugs in my system. He had a cheap gumball machine ring he got from a gas station. He asked me to marry him. He told me I never had to go back to the trailer, that I could come live with him and he would make sure my mother never got anywhere near me again."

Bauer gasped and looked pointedly at my ringless finger. "But you're not married? When you picked me up, you were just friends." His confusion was evident.

My smile wavered slightly, and I felt all those old feelings start to swirl around under the surface. "No, we're not. Lane wanted to take care of me, but he didn't love me, or at least he didn't know he loved me back then. We were so young, and my family was such a mess there was no way I wanted to drag him into all of that. I was trapped, I didn't want him stuck with me. And I had my sister to think about. Even if I married Lane and got everything I ever wanted, what was I going to do about her? I couldn't leave her behind."

He nodded and started to chew on his lower lip. "You're a good sister."

"I try to be. Anyway, when I was getting ready to give up all hope, when I was resigned to spending another year stuck in my own personal hell, Lane's dad approached me and offered me a way out. He told me that he was sick. His doctors only gave him a couple years max to live. He knew what was going on at home and he knew Lane had been willing to sacrifice his entire future to get me out of that situation. He also knew how worried I was about my sister, so he made me a deal. He told me I could marry him and take his name. I could live on the ranch, and he would make sure my mother no longer put my sister in danger. I remember asking him what in the world he got out of the situation, and all he said was 'I want my last days on this Earth to matter.' He gave me a way out, and he changed my life. I knew it was going to hurt Lane and change our relationship forever, but I couldn't walk away from everything his father offered. If Lane's dad hadn't stepped in, I would be dead, Bauer. I have no doubt about it, and I don't even want to think about what would have happened to my sister."

"That's amazing. I never knew there were people like that in the world until I met you and Lane." His wonder and amazement were clear in both his voice and his expression. I hated that basic human decency was so foreign to him.

"The whole Warner clan is pretty special, and I'm so lucky I get to call them my family. The point is I wouldn't be here if someone who could help, hadn't. I want to help you, Bauer. I want to give you a way out like someone gave to me. I want you to see that you have options, and people willing to make sure you succeed. I know you love your brother and that he sacrificed a lot for you, but he's still so young. He's going to have his hands full making it on his own, add in caring for someone else and that might be enough to break him. He loves you, but loving and taking care of are two very different things." I reached for his hand and gave it a squeeze. "I can do both in my sleep. I can love you and care for you without even thinking twice about it. I also understand where you're coming from, I know how hard it is to move on from everything you've been through. I would love for you to come home with me, Bauer. Come to Wyoming. Come to the ranch. Come be part of my family. Let me show you how good it feels to be safe, how amazing it is when you don't go to bed afraid that you might not wake up. I promise you will be surrounded by people you can count on. You will have so many adults trying to help you that you'll have to remind them you're more than capable of doing things for yourself. It's your turn to escape."

The more I talked, the wider his eyes got and the faster his breathing became. His face alternated between blushing bright red and leeching to an almost gray color. His unreadable eyes were flashing too many emotions for me to name and when his lower lip started to tremble, I knew what his answer was going to be before he said a word.

He ripped his sullen gaze away, fastening his eyes on the floor. Slowly and deliberately he turned his body away from mine, and I could see him shutting down. His thin shoulders hunched over and he wrapped his trembling arms around his middle like he was giving himself a hug.

"I can't go with you, Brynn. My brother gave up everything so I could be here. He's the only person who's always come through for me." His loyalty was admirable but wholly misplaced.

"I don't doubt that Mikey wants to give you a fresh start. What I question is his ability to provide that not only for you but for himself as well. He seems like a decent kid, but he's still just a kid. The last thing I want is for you to fall back on the one way you know you can get by if times get hard. I don't want you to have to make desperate choices anymore, Bauer. I want you to have the time and space to grow up, to learn to be the man you were always meant to be before your parents robbed you of that opportunity." I was pleading with him, but I could tell it wasn't getting me anywhere. He felt that he owed it to Mikey to stick around. He was taking on the responsibility of getting his older brother on his feet, considering he'd already been forced to figure out surviving on his own.

"I'll be okay. It means a lot that you offered everything you have to me, Brynn. You saved my life, and a bunch of other kids too. Lane's dad did more than just turn your life around when he made that deal with you, he put the wheels in motion so that you could be a lot of other kids' guardian angel the way he was for you." He shrugged and climbed to his feet. I watched as he shoved his hands down into his front pockets, still refusing to meet my gaze. "We've only known each other a handful of days. You think I'm worth saving, that I deserve a better kind of life, but you don't know me very well. I told you when we first met that I wasn't a good person, if I were I would have found another way to get by all these years. I've stolen things, I've lied and cheated. I've stood by silently while people I cared about were hurt and did nothing to stop it. I'm not like you, Brynn. You worried and sacrificed for your sister, you've put yourself in danger for my safety, and the only person I tried to take care of when I was out on the streets, is me." He looked away as he chewed on his lower lip so violently I was worried he was going to draw blood. "If I went home with you, eventually you would figure out I'm not worth the effort of trying to save. I think you should help someone who deserves it, someone who earned it, who earned you."

I climbed to my feet ready to keep fighting with him, but I could see how close he was to breaking. He wasn't telling me no because he *wanted* to. He was turning me down because he *had* to. At least that was what he believed.

"Find one of the good people Lane keeps telling me about. I know they're out there now. Offer them a chance to start over. They'll appreciate it and won't screw it up like I would. I'll never forget you, Brynn. I mean that."

He turned to walk away, but I wasn't ready to let him go yet. I captured him in a hug so tight that it made him squeak. When I let him go, I pointed a shaking finger at him and told him flatly, "I'm having Lane bring you a phone before we go. I'll be checking in on you every week. If you need help with anything, you will ask. If you and your brother are struggling financially, you will ask for help. I pay my mother every single month to make sure she keeps her nose clean and all her garbage boyfriends away from my sister, I'll do the same for you. No more turning tricks in truck stops. You're going to school and acting like a normal teenager. Do you understand me?"

I fully intended to give Mikey the same lecture. Where Bauer would never want to take advantage of my kindness, I had no doubt his squirrely, immature brother would.

"I'm not abandoning you. Not now, not ever. Okay?" After everything, he had to believe I wouldn't walk away . . . didn't he?

Finally, after what felt like forever, I got the tiniest nod in response.

"Okay." He sounded as broken as my heart felt. We were in so many pieces I had no clue how either of us was ever expected to be put back together again. There wasn't enough glue in the world for a project that big. Luckily love seemed to do the trick. It held all those sharp, jagged shards in place and filled up all the gaps where thoughtless, cruel people had stolen chunks of our souls.

I was going to have to work extra hard to let this lonely, stubborn boy know I had an endless supply to give to him.

There was no giving up on anyone I loved. If I had done that I never would have ended up where I was always meant to be—by Lane Warner's side.

CHAPTER 17

Fast or Slow

LANE

I HAD BRYNN'S LONG HAIR wrapped around my fist like a rope, and I was using it to pull her head back. The arch of her spine as I powered into her from behind was erotic as hell and the sexiest thing I'd ever seen. She was on her hands and knees on the edge of the bed in front of me, panting my name in time to each hard thrust. She had fingerprints on her hips from my other hand holding her in place as I made sure she knew she was mine over and over again. It was a good thing we were no longer sharing this wing of the house with Sutton and Daye, because I was making it my mission in life to make sure her screams and moans could be heard through the thick, wooden walls.

She turned her head on a gasp and looked at me over her shoulder with passion-glazed eyes as I hit the spot inside of her that made her entire body quiver beneath mine. I felt the happy vibrations rock through my cock, and the pleasure made my balls tighten and had the stirrings of my impending orgasm swirling along my spine. Since she was looking at me, I bent over her back and dropped a quick, sloppy kiss on the corner of her open mouth. The move had her giggling, which tightened her sweet, slippery center around the unbelievably hard length of my cock. I spent as much time inside of her as I could since we got back to the ranch. I took my time with her, learning every inch of her body, searching out all her most sensitive and responsive places, but some days all I wanted to do was get inside of her and get us both off as quickly as possible. It was a heady rush making her eyes roll back in her head, and getting her body to go pliant and soft under mine within minutes.

This morning was one of the times we were in a hurry not because we wanted to be, but because we had to be. Cy put me back to work the minute I had my boots back on the ranch. Business was backed up with both Sutton and me being gone, and with Webb taking off to help with Bauer, my older brother was so deep in rebooking and rescheduling rides before the winter, he couldn't see daylight. While I wanted time to bask in the new relationship glow and to savor the rightness of finally having the only woman I'd wanted to keep forever in my bed every single night, I couldn't ignore my responsibilities anymore. I was scheduled for three back-to-back, overnight rides and one that would take me through the weekend. I was going to be out on the range with tourists, teaching them how to fish and showing them all the wonders of the Wyoming wilderness, which I typically loved. It was less appealing than it always had been now that I had someone I was so wrapped up in waiting back at the main house for me.

Brynn needed to get up so she could get breakfast going for the guests and take care of packing the lunch I was taking with us to eat down by the river, but I wasn't done with her until we were both sweaty and satisfied. I wanted her too weak to move when this was over.

I dragged my bristly chin across her smooth shoulder and kissed the top of her spine. Standing back up, I let go of my hold on her hair and moved my hands to either side of her perfectly rounded ass. I loved the way it moved and bounced against my hammering hips. She had the prettiest skin, and it looked so good a little red and slightly marked from my hands and mouth. I slipped my thumbs along the delicate crease in front of me and grinned when she swore under her breath, body jerking in surprise. She was soaked, moisture coating my cock and making every glide in and out slippery and slick. She had to be close, I could feel it. I hoped she was because I wasn't going to last longer with those noises she was making filling the early morning. I was such a sucker for this woman. The littlest things she did turned me inside out. She was my ultimate weakness. She always had been, but now that I knew exactly what it was that I was missing, I knew she was the one person in the world who could undo me. I also knew that each and every time she forced me to unravel she would put me back together with the utmost care.

She muttered my name and started to move back against my thrusts with more urgency as I dipped my thumbs into that sweet, secret valley and used the pads to gently trace the super sensitive spot hidden there. Brynn wasn't shy when it came to sex, something that was initially surprising considering all of her negative experiences around the subject in her youth. She was open to most anything, and yes, she liked it when I hurt her just a little bit. She also didn't question me when I wanted to play with other parts of her besides the glorious spot between the center of her centerfold legs.

"No better way to wake up, Brynn." I groaned as she rotated her hips in such a way that made me practically swallow my tongue.

"Gives new meaning to rise and shine." She let out a garbled laugh and let her arms collapse, taking her upper half to the bed and driving my dick even deeper inside of her. I felt her break around me, body tightening and pulsing where we were joined. My dick kicked happily, and I swore it hardened even more as her release triggered mine. My orgasm burned quick and bright. Sending hot sparks of satisfaction popping along my skin. Nothing would ever compare to being inside this woman with nothing between us. It didn't matter how long it had taken me to get here, it was the place I knew I was meant to be.

I rolled to the side, so I didn't crush Brynn as I collapsed on the bed beside her. We were both shiny with sweat and covered in the scent of sex and lingering sleep. She blinked heavy eyes, as her slow, satisfied grin imprinted itself on my mind. The way she looked at this moment was going to be one of my favorite memories, one I pulled out when I wondered why someone as special and resilient as she was, tied herself to someone as foolish and scared as me.

"I missed seeing you smile." I reached out a finger so I could move a piece of hair out of her face. Leaving Denver without Bauer had been incredibly hard for both of us. When she told me that she offered to bring him with us, I couldn't say I was surprised. She knew the kid for less than a week, but there was so much of her history in his story, it seemed like they were cut from the exact same cloth. She knew him, and he knew her in a way that transcended time. Watching her already fragile heart try and find room for this new pain felt like it was going to kill me. I wanted to make it better for her because that was my job, it always had been, but there was no way to do that.

"I just want to know he's okay. I want to make sure he's not alone and that he's getting everything he needs. You didn't see him with his brother, Lane. They're just kids. They have no idea what they're doing."

She mentioned more than once she was worried Bauer was going to turn to hustling again if money got tight. To combat that possibility, she sent him a loaded Visa gift card once a week with a handwritten letter, telling him to use it for whatever he and Mikey might need. She was pretty sure Bauer was handing the cards over to his brother, but there was nothing she could do about it. She was stuck in an endless cycle, just like she was with her mother and sister. Luckily, Opal was turning eighteen in a few months, and my girl wouldn't have to worry about paying for her sister's wellbeing anymore. As soon as the younger Fox was of age, she was coming to live with us on the ranch until she started college in the fall. Opal had gotten a full ride to the University of Wyoming, so she was well on her way to freedom, relatively unscathed thanks to her older sister's sacrifice and the generosity of Boyd Warner. Brynn was counting down the days till she no longer had to engage with her mother and her painful past in any way.

Since coming home, the sisters were spending a lot of time together. They were always close, and Opal wasn't a stranger by any means, but I silently wondered if Brynn was trying to fill the void left behind when Bauer refused to let her save him.

"I think Bauer and even Mikey know more than most kids their age. You're doing what you can, Brynn. You can't force him to accept your help, all you can do is let him know that you are there and not going anywhere. I'm proud of you. You gave that kid something no one else ever did . . . you gave him hope. You changed his life forever. Because of you, he now knows what he could have if he's willing to reach for it and that is a very powerful incentive for him to continue to make good choices." I rubbed my hands over my face and rolled so I could prop myself on my elbow. "I need to shower and get down to the barn so I can get the horses ready."

I pulled her to her feet and guided her into the shower with me. I loved the way she looked as the water turned her hair dark and her skin into a slick honey-colored surface. Normally I would take advantage of her being naked and soft from our previous round of sex, but there was no time. All I could do was kiss her as she soaped me up and scrubbed me down. I returned the favor, lingering longer than I should have on her breasts and between her legs, after all, I was only human, and I'd wasted too much time pushing her away instead of pulling her close.

I was watching Brynn braid her hair when her eyes met mine in the mirror. "You know that Cy asked Jack to help out with a couple of the rides to get all the canceled trips caught up. There's a good chance you're going to run into him sometime this week."

I wandered over to where she was sitting so I could bend down and drop a kiss on the top of her head. I knew Jack was still a sore subject with her. As soon as we got back to the ranch, she'd gone over to Ten's property to properly apologize for the disastrous way she handled the proposal. She wanted to mend fences the best she could, but Jack told her that she should never have led him on. He accused her of being in love with someone else the entire time they were together, a charge she couldn't refute. He made her feel like crap and sent her back to me in tears. Cy had to physically restrain me. Everything inside of me was screaming that I had to hurt the person who caused her any kind of pain. I was ready to throw down, ready to defend her honor even though I was still healing from the knife wound and rocking over fifty stitches on my side.

My older brother pointed out that the reason Brynn and I went our separate ways so long ago was because I tried to fight her battles for her instead of standing by her and helping her battle through them. She was more than capable of handling not only Jack but anyone else who dared to question her motivations or the fact that the two of us belonged together. My older brother talked me off the ledge like he always did, and then informed me that Jack was sticking around despite having his heart broken and losing his woman to another man. In Cy's eyes that said something about the other man's character. I thought it made him annoying and problematic, but I was willing to look the other way when we had to work with one another.

"I'm not scared of Jack." I squeezed her shoulders and slapped my Stetson over my dark hair. The black strands were getting a little long and shaggy, but I liked the way Brynn tugged on them when she kissed me, so I was in no rush to cut it.

"I know you aren't scared of him, but I don't think you realize how badly I hurt him and how much being around you is going to suck for him. Remember, you stopped talking to me and couldn't even look at me for years when I turned down your proposal, and you didn't even love me. Keep those memories in mind if he tries to push your buttons, Lane." Strain made her voice raspy and thick. "I don't want to be the reason two good men go after one another."

It was something she was clearly worried about, so I nodded and gave her my best reassuring grin. "You're wrong, I did love you, I was too scared to admit it back then. I'm not now. I love you, Brynn, and I know what it's like to lose you. I'll be good." As long as he didn't talk shit about her, I would be a perfect gentleman. If he said so much as one disparaging word about the woman who was the center of my life, I would make no promises, other than the one where I would rip his tongue out and choke him with it.

She gave me a knowing look as I followed her down the hallway to the massive kitchen that served as the heart of the house as well as the starting point for most of our guests. Cy and Leo were already getting ready for their rides today. My older brother had grown up in a saddle the same way Sutton and I had, but he much preferred sitting behind a desk. The fact he was dressed to be out on the trail was a testament to how busy we were.

His sassy bride-to-be was a born and bred city girl, but she had taken to ranch life like a duck to water. She left the boardroom and never looked back. From the minute she committed to Cy, she was all in, meaning all of us had taken turns teaching her what she needed to know to be a fully invested part of the business Cy built from the ground up to save our ranch. She was dressed to take her own group on a ride, and she looked cute as hell in a tilted straw cowboy hat sitting on top of her twin pigtails. She was the perfect match for my brother's chilly and reserved demeanor. I loved having her around, and I loved how readily she accepted Brynn and me as a couple.

Cy was more reserved. He knew all about the challenges we would face when we decided to be together with the muddied history between us. He was also worried about what would happen if we couldn't make it work. Brynn was an integral part of the ranch and the retreat business. She was the one who made this remote property feel like home for our guests from all over the world. Cy wanted both of us to be happy, but he didn't want his family fractured. I tried to reassure him that Brynn and I were going to make this thing between us last forever, but we both knew that was a vow I had no control over. Anything could happen, and Brynn and I may very well fall apart. All I could do was work my ass off to make sure that didn't happen.

I kissed Brynn and gave Leo a good morning squeeze. I exchanged a rushed greeting with Cy as I hurried out the door to get ready for the day. The barn was already buzzing with activity. Webb had a family mounted up and was getting ready to ride them off into the mountains. We exchanged a friendly fist bump, and I shook my head when he asked if Brynn had heard from Bauer recently. He seemed as worried about the kid as we were.

Jack was in the corral surrounded by a group of horses. He turned back when he saw me enter the enclosure. Luckily there weren't any guests nearby to witness the tension between the two of us. It would have made for an awkward start to their adventure and with all the new competition cropping up at the neighboring ranches that wouldn't be good for business.

I brushed my horse down and spoke softly to her. She was going to work hard over the next week and needed some calm before the storm. I was snapping her bridle into place and rubbing down her strong neck when I felt a furious glare burning into the back of my head. Turning, I used a finger to tip the brim of my cowboy hat back and meet Jack's angry eyes.

We were dressed almost identically. His hat was tan where mine was dark gray. We both wore jeans, boots and thermal shirts under open flannels. Mine was black, his was white, which I guess was kind of fitting. I could see how I was the bad guy in his eyes. I stole his girl, even though she had been mine all along.

"Thanks for helping out. We all really appreciate it." I kept my eyes on his so there was no missing the unchecked dislike flooding his gaze.

"Ten asked me to do it. I respect the hell out of that woman, and I like my job. I didn't want to disappoint her. You, I owe nothing." He crossed his arms over his chest and continued to glare at me.

I sighed and used my forearm to wipe the sweat that had collected on my forehead. "You're right. You don't owe me anything, and I don't owe you a damn thing either. I'm sorry you got hurt while Brynn and I were trying to figure our shit out. It's not cool, but it can't be undone either. If you're gonna stick around, you need to get used to the way things are now, hell, the way they've always been. I was just too stupid to see it. We're a pretty tight-knit group, so you're gonna see us together, and you're going to have to watch her love someone who isn't you. I get that it sucks, and it's not what you wanted, but it is what it is."

He growled low in his throat and took a threatening step toward me which made the horse at my back twitch nervously.

"I wanted her the first minute I saw her. I could tell she was special, that she was good and kind, that she was made for this kind of life. I would have given her everything, and I never would have asked her to jump through hoops. You don't deserve her." He spat the last words out but fell back a step when my horse let out a high-pitched whinny and stamped her front hoof.

Her horseshoe tapped the dirt in aggravation as I sighed and reached up to try and soothe her. My voice was calm and steady when I replied, even though my insides were raging and roaring to go toe to toe with the heartbroken cowboy. "You're right, I don't, but that never stopped her from picking me. I'm going to marry her one day."

Jack snorted and tossed back his head with an ugly laugh. "Good luck with that, Warner. She doesn't want a ring." The bite of her rejection obviously still stung. I knew that feeling intimately and understood his candor and his bitterness.

I nodded in agreement. "You're right she doesn't want one, but she does want to give someone one, so when she asks me to marry her, I'm going to say yes and then I'm going to spend the rest of my life making up for lost time. It's been me and Brynn from the beginning, and it's going to be me and her at the end. It's the middle that got all screwed up because I couldn't recognize a good thing when I had it."

Jack watched me for a minute before grunting and taking another step away as he turned to face his mount.

"You better hold onto the good thing you got, Warner. If you don't, someone else will be waiting in the wings to snatch it up. Because if you fail this time, there won't be another second chance." I knew that. I was the only Warner who was going to get love right the first time around. I had to be because my first love was also my forever love . . . and I knew now that I was hers.

I didn't need to tell him I was never going to let Brynn go again because we both knew I wasn't that stupid. She was mine. We belonged together, and that was the way it was always supposed to be. She was nothing like my mother, she loved this ranch, and she loved me.

She wasn't going anywhere, and I would make sure I gave her a new reason to stay with me every single day.

CHAPTER 18

Heaven or Hell

BRYNN

I USED TO LOOK FORWARD to Lane going out on rides with the guests. It meant we didn't have to tiptoe around each other and I was able to breathe because there was a break in the suffocating awkwardness that always seemed to surround us. It also meant I wouldn't have to hear his current bed partner calling his name as his headboard slammed against our shared wall, and I didn't have to pretend not to notice them sneaking out the next morning. Those were the only nights I managed to sleep soundly. But now that he was mine and I spent every night since we returned home wrapped around him, leaving no room for anyone else, I missed him. I missed that naughty grin and the way his bright blue eyes twinkled with mischief. I missed his low laugh and the way his hands always seemed to be drifting over my ass inappropriately. I missed him riling Cy up and his joking around with Leo as she worked to calm her grouchy man down. Everything felt too quiet and still without him around. It made me restless and gave me way too much time to think.

I tried not to obsess that I hadn't heard from Bauer in over a week. He was pretty good about answering my calls and checking in with me regularly. He always sounded happy to hear from me, even though I could tell he wasn't exactly thrilled with his circumstances. His brother was working two part-time jobs and going to school. Mikey was also an eighteen-year-old on his own for the first time, so there was a fair amount of partying and hooking up going on. There was no way Bauer would ever say a disparaging thing against his older brother, but I got the impression Mikey's lifestyle wasn't exactly conducive to giving his younger brother a stable, secure home life. I could hear the longing in his voice when he talked about having a quiet place to sit and think.

The fact he hadn't answered the phone or returned any of my messages was making me anxious and without Lane around to talk me down, I imagined every worst-case scenario possible. The last thing I wanted was Bauer back on the streets. I didn't want him to run again. I might not like the fact he picked what his brother had to offer over the opportunity I presented to him, but at least I knew where he was and could normally get a hold of him. If he took off again, there would be no end to the ways I would worry, and I would sink every dime I had into trying to find him. I refused to let him disappear into the wind again. My sister told me I was obsessing over his safety the same way I worried myself sick over hers. I couldn't argue with her, and I couldn't stop the feelings from consuming me.

I looked up from the dough I was kneading as Leo walked into the kitchen. Her freckled nose was sunburned, and her strawberry-blonde hair was pulled up in a curly mess on the top of her head. She was a solid five inches shorter than I was, but she carried herself with such confidence and poise that she often seemed larger than life. When she first showed up at the ranch with Emrys, I figured they were nothing more than the typical rich-bitch city girls looking for an adventure and a roll in the hay with a hot cowboy. There were photos of Cy, Sutton, and Lane on the ranch's website, and their pictures were also plastered all over the vacation literature. The Warner brothers and their rugged good looks did more for business than the wild Wyoming landscape ever could. When Leo turned out to be just as prickly and stubborn as Cy, it was a refreshing change of pace. She refused to let the stoic, sarcastic cowboy roll over her and gave as good as she got. The fact she was able to melt some of Cy's icy walls he kept around his heart was a miracle, and I would be forever grateful she had given one of the greatest men I'd ever known reason to smile again.

"How was your tour?" Leo only went out on the range with families and all-girl groups. Cy insisted. We were too isolated, and the property was too large and remote for anyone to react quickly if a problem arose. He refused to let her go out with a group of men when she could so easily be outnumbered and overtaken. At first, Leo's feminist instincts had bristled at the demand, but eventually, she gave in, realizing it wasn't worth the fight when Cy had a point, and making him worry would mean he wasn't concentrating on his end of the business. He merely had to remind Leo of their own clusterfuck they'd barely survived out in the wilderness the first time she stepped foot on the ranch.

The petite redhead pointed at her face and wrinkled her nose. "Good except I forgot sunscreen. I'm going to turn into one giant freckle at this point." She was as fair as most redheads were and already had a liberal smattering of freckles across her nose and cheeks. It was a good look for her.

"They're cute. I bet Cy likes them." I tossed the dough into a bowl and set it aside, moving to the sink to wash the flour off my hands. She gave the concoction a curious look and lifted her eyebrows in question. "I'm making chicken pot pie for dinner tonight. That's the crust."

She hummed and rubbed her tummy with an exaggerated motion. "I'll need to order a wedding dress a size bigger than I usually wear now that you're back home. I can't believe I used to live on takeout and delivery. Home cooking is so much better."

I laughed and felt a blush rising in reaction to her praise. "Did you already find a dress?" There was no way she was going to find what she was looking for in Sheridan. She was going to have to go down to Casper, or Cheyenne, or even farther down to Denver to get something special.

She shrugged letting her shoulder drop carelessly. "I've looked around online, but nothing is jumping out at me. I want to make sure everything about this wedding is as different from Cy's first wedding as possible. I don't want him to have flashbacks." She wrinkled her nose again and rolled her eyes. "Plus, we have time." They weren't having the wedding until well after Emrys gave birth, and she was only six months along at the moment.

"This wedding won't be anything like the last one. You're doing it here at the ranch, right?" I felt guilty that I wasn't more involved. I'd been so caught up in my own drama that I hadn't been a very good friend, which made me cringe. Leo and Emrys were the first women who had accepted me with open arms even after hearing all the terrible rumors about me and in Leo's case, after mistakenly thinking I was Cy's wife. They both had been wonderful to me and showed me what real female friendship was all about. I should have been more invested in both the wedding and the baby.

She nodded and took the lemon poppy seed muffin I handed her. I'd made them for breakfast this morning, and there were several left over. "We are. We're going to keep it pretty small. You know how much Cy hates being the center of attention."

He did hate it. Having all eyes on him was more Lane's thing, and I found myself wondering if we ever got to that point if I would have to put up with a giant production. I would be happy with a courthouse wedding in front of a justice of the peace, something quick and easy, but I doubted the youngest Warner would let me get away with that. He was too proud that we'd finally found our way to each other. He would want to show us off, to flaunt our love for the naysayers and detractors to see. I sighed at the thought and turned to lean against the counter.

"It's going to be beautiful, and the only people who matter are the two of you. His first wedding was in an old, fancy church in Boston. I remember Sutton and Lane griping because they had to wear tuxes and Boyd fretting over how much everything cost. His first wife was all about the show and display, kind of like Lydia Warner was. She didn't give a single shit if the wedding had any part of Cy, or his life before her, in it. The fact that you're having it here already makes it a thousand times better."

She smiled at me as she broke off the piece of her muffin and handed it to me. I popped it into my mouth as she asked, "What about you and Lane?" She lifted her eyebrows as I started to choke on the flavorful pastry. "What's next for the two of you? You sort of skipped over the whole dating, boyfriend/girlfriend phase and went right to spending every single night together. I know you have a lifetime of love between the two of you, but do you want something more than that? Do you want to marry him?"

If it were coming from anyone else, it would have been invasive and annoying. Since it was Leo and she had been nothing but supportive I answered her honestly. "I would marry him tomorrow if it wouldn't look so bad. He's the only man who's asked me that I really wanted to say yes to, Leo. Telling him no when we were teenagers was the hardest thing I've ever done. Telling his dad yes was the second hardest. I can't tell one guy no, especially a good guy like Jack, and turn around and marry another one with barely any time between the two. People in this town already think the worst of me and say terrible things about how I became a Warner. I don't want to add fuel to the fire and drag Lane into that. He's given me so much."

She shook her head and reached out a hand so she could pat me on the arm. "You wouldn't be dragging Lane anywhere. He would walk willingly through any fire for you. That's the thing about asking someone to marry you, you both have to decide it's what you want. You can wait to ask him, and he'll say yes. Or you can ask him tomorrow and get the same answer. That's the thing, you're both finally ready and the time is right. You're deciding to do this together. No one else matters, Brynn. Not now and not ever."

I didn't have a response to her spot-on observation. I didn't want anyone else to define me by the choices I had to make in the past, and here I was using my choices to dictate what I could and couldn't do in the eyes of people that never wanted anything good for me. Sighing, I looked toward the front door and wished Lane was back from his weekend trip. I wanted to hold him. I wanted to kiss him. I wanted to lose myself in his pretty eyes and listen to him sing me to sleep. I wanted him inside of me.

I wanted to ask him to marry me. I did. I really did.

Almost as if I had conjured someone up with the force of my longing, there was a hesitant knock on the massive, wooden front door. The sound made Leo jump and we exchanged a confused glance as the noise sounded again.

"Are you expecting someone?" I asked the question as I started moving toward the door. All the guests were out with the boys, and the mail carrier had already delivered for the day. Opal was spending the night at a friend's house so they could cram for midterms, so it wasn't her either. Every now and then one of the ranchers from a nearby property would drop in and let us know about a lost cow or a broken fence, but we were too far outside the city for random visitors which meant we were cautious when we moved toward the door.

She shook her head which sent her curls bouncing. "No. It could be Ten." The forest ranger did stop by unannounced occasionally. She was usually looking for a free meal though, and it was still hours before I typically had dinner on the table.

I pulled the door open and didn't bother to stifle the scream of delight when I saw who was standing on the other side. I stepped onto the rustic front porch, pulling the still frail looking teenager into my arms as I did so. I couldn't believe Cameron Bauer was standing at my front door in the middle of nowhere Wyoming, but I'd never seen a better sight. I squeezed him so tightly that he started to struggle so he could breathe.

"Hey, Brynn. Long time, no see." His smile was crooked and a little shy. His hair was cut and styled in a trendy undercut that resembled the way Cy wore his. His face was void of the bruises that decorated it when we met, and his clothes looked new and fitting for a fourteen-year-old. He was still too skinny and fragile looking, but his eyes were bright, and he looked as happy to see me as I was to see him.

I couldn't stop myself from giving him another squeeze and dropping a hurried kiss on his forehead. "How on Earth did you get here?" I didn't mean Wyoming, I meant the ranch. There was no easy way here from Sheridan, and all the back roads were dirt. They looked the same, and many were unmarked. If you didn't know exactly where it was you were going, it was super easy to get lost.

"I took a bus to Casper and then caught another one that dropped me off in Sheridan. I was hitchhiking out this way when a cop stopped and asked me where I was going." He hooked a thumb over his shoulder, and I noticed the sheriff of Sheridan, Rodie Collins, was waiting in his Blazer. He touched his fingers to his forehead in a salute as I waved and pulled Bauer into the house.

"That wasn't very safe. This isn't the city, but hitchhiking is never a good idea. You never know who's going to stop and pick you up." I couldn't keep the concern from bleeding out. All I wanted to do was take care of him. I felt it inside every pore. "I'm so happy to see you. Surprised, but so happy. I was worried when I didn't hear from you all week."

He shuffled into the house in front of me, stopping when he caught sight of Leo standing in the hallway, watching us with unvarnished curiosity. She tilted her head to the side and offered him a welcoming smile. "Well, hello there. Who are you?"

Bauer looked over his shoulder at me and then back at Leo with wide eyes. "I'm Cameron Bauer."

Leo threw her head back and laughed so loudly it made the teenager jump. "Silly. Of course, I know who you are. Brynn and Lane wouldn't shut up about this wonderful kid they met on their road trip home. You left quite an impression, young man. It's lovely to meet you. Make yourself at home while you're here. You picked a good day to visit. Brynn is making pot pie for dinner, yum." She gave me a wink and moved toward Cy's office. "I'll let the two of you catch up."

I turned Bauer toward the living room and guided him to sit on the comfy, overstuffed leather couch. I reached out for his hand, thrilled that he let me pull the delicate appendage into my own. "As glad as I am that you're here, I need to know why you just showed up out of the blue, Bauer. What brought you to Wyoming? And why haven't you answered any of my calls this last week?"

His thin fingers twitched in mine as I ran my thumb over the thick scar that now decorated the back of his hand. His gaze darted around the room landing anywhere but on mine as he softly replied, "Mikey has my phone. His kept running out of data and minutes. He took mine since you gave me unlimited services."

I gritted my teeth and told myself I had to remain calm. I wasn't going to get anywhere with him by telling him how selfish and immature I thought his brother was. "Okay. I'll talk to Lane about adding another phone line onto the plan for your brother. Not being able to get in touch with you doesn't sit well with me. It makes me worry. I need to know that you're doing okay. Did you talk to the school about getting enrolled? Are you eating enough? Did you go buy yourself some stuff for your room like I told you to?"

He tugged his hand free and used it to push at his hair. Finally, he lifted his eyes to mine, and I could see so many familiar shadows darkening them. "I can't enroll without my parents' permission. They refuse to sign legal guardianship over to Mikey, not that he really wants that responsibility. I can't do anything without them; work, school, drive. Even with them out of my life they are still controlling everything." He sounded so defeated it made all the broken pieces of my heart shutter.

"Oh, honey, I'm so sorry. That isn't fair to you. Let's look at what other options you might have while you're here. I know in some cases you can ask to be legally emancipated from your parents. It's like getting a divorce from them. You don't need them to sign off on anything then."

His face twisted up in a look of disbelief and then sort of wilted right before my eyes. His head dropped, and his shoulders fell. He put his face in his hands and shook his head back and forth.

"It's so hard, Brynn. I thought it would be easy, well, easier, but it's not. The cops are all over me about testifying and being part of the trial. They want me to make statements about RV guy and Goddard. They want me to identify the kid with the BMW. It's all overwhelming, and Mikey is no help. He keeps telling me not to cooperate unless I get paid. He's never home, and when he is, all he does is party. He brings home the kind of people I tried to avoid while I was on the streets. It's nothing like I thought it would be. I'm still all alone, and now I feel even more alone than I did before." He lifted his head, and I could see twin tracks of moisture on his cheeks as tears rolled down his face. "Talking to you when you called every week is the only time I didn't feel like

I was forgotten about. Knowing you still cared is the only thing getting me by. I missed you, Brynn. So, so much."

He threw himself across my lap, shoulders trembling as he started to cry. I stroked the soft hair at the back of his head and patted him on the back. "I missed you, too, Cameron. Do you care if I call you that sometimes?" He nodded his head. "Good. Bauer was the boy on the run, Cameron is the young man with so many options in front of him. I've been worried about you since the minute we left Denver." He swallowed so hard I could hear it. "Tell me what you need from me, and I'll give it to you." I would give him anything if it made him feel like he wasn't alone anymore.

"I want to go to school. I want to get through this trial without feeling like every move I make is wrong. It's so scary every time the police show up to talk to me. I don't want to face the guy with the RV again, I don't want to tell a courtroom full of people what he did to me. I want to go to bed and not have to push my dresser in front of the door. I want to like my brother again because right now I kind of hate him. I want to prove you can trust me and show you that I won't take off every time something gets hard." He lifted his head, and his eyes were shiny with unshed tears as he finally met my gaze. "I want to be the version of me you and Lane see. I want to be the guy who's worthy of having people like you in my life. I want to be someone worth saving, Brynn."

I cupped his cheeks in my hands, wiping away his tears with my thumbs as I offered him a wobbly smile. This kid hit right at the center of my heart without even trying. "You already are that guy, Cameron. You just need to see it."

He nodded slowly. "I want to see it. Do you . . . uh . . . do you think . . . is the offer to stay with you while I figure my shit out still open? Do you think Lane will mind having me around?" Shyly, he asked, "Do you think he still wants to teach me how to ride a horse, and maybe he could teach me to play the guitar?"

"Oh, Cameron," I leaned forward and touched my forehead to his. I closed my eyes and exhaled all the worry and concern I'd been carrying around for this young man since leaving him on his own. "Welcome home, kid."

CHAPTER 19

More or Less

LANE

"HE'S A GOOD KID." IT wasn't the first time Cy said that about Cam since the troubled teenager had taken up residence at the ranch, but it was the first time he sounded like he really, truly believed it. Slowly but surely, Cameron Bauer was finding his way on the Warner ranch. Webb was the one who taught him to ride, Cy was the one who helped him with his homework because they were both good at math and I sucked at it. I took him with me on weekend rides and shoved a fishing pole in his hands before he could argue with me. The kid was also a natural at playing the guitar, so there were quiet hours that I sat with him and taught him all my favorite songs—yes, even Taylor Swift.

We all wanted to give him something he could take away from this place that would stay with him long after he left to find his own way in the world. We were determined, as a whole, to give the kid everything he'd missed out on before he became ours, and then some. Every time he learned something new, got a piece of the people who were determined to teach him all about what home and family was, he got emotional. His old man hadn't taught him anything but to hurt and to feel shame for who he was. He deserved so much better than that. We were all doing our best to prove that to him. The exact same way Boyd Warner did for Brynn Fox all those years ago. It was sort of ironic how full circle this whole thing had come.

It had taken some getting used to, having a streetwise, still skittish kid around the house. Cy watched the newcomer with careful eyes, but eventually, Cam won him over. It took a lot less work to get Leo on board. She was already hovering over the teen and fretting as much as Brynn did. The kid was smothered in affection and love, and it was obvious he couldn't be any happier about it.

"The brother, though, he needs a boot up his ass." Cy tipped the rocks glass he was holding up to his lips and finished the whiskey he was sipping on throughout dinner. Mikey Bauer was enough to drive anyone to drink. It was clear to see when the two brothers were together, that even though Cam was the one with the checkered past and questionable reputation, he was the Bauer who had been blessed with a kind heart and an endless well of consideration.

I nodded in agreement and took a pull from the beer I was holding. When Brynn mentioned she arranged for Mikey to come up and visit his brother for the weekend, I could see the apprehension in her eyes. The older Bauer boy was a bit of a disappointment across the board, but he was the only family Bauer had, so she didn't want to drive a wedge between them. I didn't think visiting a place with terrible cell phone service, and spotty WIFI was a good idea for a kid who couldn't handle being out of touch with his friends for even a second, but Mikey seemed excited about the prospect of seeing a real-life ranch, so I kept my opinion to myself. The fact that Opal was also around for the weekend had proved to be a good distraction for the older teen as well. Brynn's sister was pretty, soft-spoken and smart as hell. It was clear Mikey was interested, but every single time he said something shitty to his brother or made a snide remark about the ranch, she shut him down cold. There was a lot of her older sister in her, and that would serve her well when she got out into the big bad world. If I was being honest, I got a chuckle every time I witnessed the verbal beatdown Opal gave to the little shit. He deserved it for being an ass.

"He's not all bad, just a little clueless." I was thinking about all the times he put himself between his father and his little brother. And how he really did want Cam to have a safe place to go, even if he wasn't the best at providing it. He tried, and that was more than their parents did. "I think he needs to do some serious growing up. I've been there, blind to how my actions are affecting those who cared about me the most. One day he's going to get a wake-up call he can't ignore." I pointed the beer bottle in the direction of the kitchen where the brothers were playing a board game with Brynn, her sister, and Leo. The ladies were winning and having a great time lording it over the teenage boys.

"If I catch him trying to look down Leo's shirt one more time he's going to get more than a wake-up call. He needs to learn some goddamn respect for women." Cy's deep voice was low and thunderous. He could tolerate a lot, but anyone disrespecting his woman was a no-go.

I nodded in agreement and sighed. "I'll talk to him about it." The "again" hung in the air unsaid because I'd already knocked the teenager upside the head once for openly ogling Brynn's ass when she was serving dinner, and for the way he accidentally walked in on Opal when she was finishing her shower.

"It's crazy how different they are. I mean for all our differences, me, you, and Sutton are still pretty similar at our core. None of us are night and day like those two." He shook his head in bewilderment.

"Cam had to face a lot of obstacles Mikey didn't. I think that changes you. For instance, maybe all of us would have had better luck in love if we hadn't grown up with a mother who used it as a weapon against us." All three of us still bore the scars from Lydia Warner's version of love.

"I don't know about you, but I feel pretty fucking lucky in love now. Doesn't matter that I needed a couple of tries to get it right. All that matters is that I did." He gave me a cocky grin and pushed to his feet. "Speaking of getting lucky," he wiggled his black and silver eyebrows and moved toward the kitchen. "I'm going to collect my girl and take a peek at what's under her shirt because I'm the only one who's allowed to do that. I'll see you in the morning."

I waved him off, climbing to my feet as I heard Leo squeal and scream at Cy to put her down. Opal and Brynn's laughter followed as I made it to the kitchen just as he was carrying his woman off toward their private wing of the house. I gave Leo a wink as she kicked her feet and swatted good-naturedly at my brother's backside. I took her empty seat at the table, reaching out to swipe a finger through the frosting on the cupcake sitting untouched in front of Cam. He gave me a glare, but it was tempered by the grin on his face. Brynn had done a good job putting some meat on his bones, and he was slowly starting to relax and settle in. For the first week he was under our roof, he acted like any second he said or did anything wrong we were going to kick him out on his ass. I tried to explain over and over again that Brynn had worked so hard to get him here, that he was never going anywhere, but couldn't seem to get through to him. Eventually, I learned that I was going to have to show him that he was home. Every day I made an effort to include him in some part of the ranch. I wanted him to feel like he earned his place here and then maybe he wouldn't be so worried about someone taking it away from him.

"What are you all in here giggling about?" I took another scoop of frosting and swatted at Mikey's hand when he subtly reached for my unfinished beer. The kid was a menace, but in a way, he reminded me of myself at that age. I remember being wild and free when my mom was finally gone, all while making my own rules, and being thoughtless to how my actions affected everyone around me. Opal was purposely leaning away from the handsome young man, watching him out of the corner of her eye. She was used to thoughtless men from being raised in her mother's house, and she wasn't about to tolerate that kind of behavior now. It would have been so easy for Brynn to step in and defend her like she always had, but she was letting her little sister learn how to protect herself.

Cam started packing up the parts of the board game and gave me a narrowed-eyed look. "Did you know that Webb's older brother was gay?"

I paused with my frosting covered finger halfway to my mouth and gave him a startled look. "Wyatt? No, that's never come up. Did Webb tell you that?" Cam spent a lot of time with the former criminal. At first, Brynn was leery of their connection, but Webb was the only one on the property who knew what it was like to survive on the streets. Sometimes Cam needed a sympathetic ear to bend when life at the ranch got monotonous and boring. They had a connection that I would never be able to have with either of them.

"No, Wyatt told me when he came up with that FBI agent to question me about the conversation I overheard about Goddard. I told him I was trying to get back to school and how the emancipation was taking forever and how my parents were purposely dragging their feet on every damn thing. I may have been whining about the lack of future job prospects for a former gay hustler, and he told me that he was gay and had no problem getting a good paying job. He told me once I got back to school to take it seriously and work hard. He said my past doesn't have to define my future and that no one needs to know that I used to turn tricks unless I wanted them to."

Opal pushed away from the table and flicked her long black

hair over her shoulder. Mikey watched the motion with rapt attention, but the pretty, dark-haired girl seemed oblivious to the attention. "He's right. I'm not telling anyone about where I come from when I get to college. I want the chance to decide who I'm going to be and I'm not giving anyone the opportunity to tell me anything different." She walked around the table so she could hug her sister goodnight and stopped by to drop a quick kiss on my cheek. She pointed at Cam and told him in a stern voice, "You get to be whoever you want to be now, Cameron. Don't forget that, and don't forget to be someone who will make the people who gave you that opportunity proud." Clearly, she was talking about everything Brynn had given up for her to get to this point. Both of those girls were something else. How they managed to be so good and pure considering they came from somewhere so toxic and foul was a true testament to how strong their hearts were.

I told Opal goodnight as she swept out of the room. I turned to look at Cam and told him, "That's all really good advice, from both of them. Wyatt is a smart, successful guy, and Opal knows a thing or two about where you're coming from." I chuckled as Cam gave up trying to protect his cupcake, handing the entire thing over to me.

"You don't want to be a Fed or a cop though, right? You don't want a job where you make no money and get no thanks for risking your life, do you?" Mikey chimed in, and as usual, his thoughtless words had me wanting to kick him under the table. Would it be so hard to be supportive of anything that his brother was interested in?

He made a strangled sound and reached down to rub his shin. I laughed again because apparently, Brynn had given him a good thump under the table when all I did was think about it. She was getting more and more aggressive about putting the older Bauer brother in his place. She reached out and clasped Cam's hand. "You can be whatever you want to be. Who you love has zero bearing on your ability to go out there and be the best whatever it is you decide to be. Remember that."

He gave her a shy grin that he seemed to reserve only for her, and nodded his head. "I will. I think it's cool that he's openly gay and in the DEA. That's pretty badass. He must be pretty tough."

She dipped her head in agreement. "It is. He's also a good brother and a very nice man, which is also very badass."

Mikey made a gagging noise and pushed his chair back from the table. "I know you missed getting all the mushy, lovey-dovey stuff from Mom and Dad growing up, but now you're drowning in it, kid. I know you're gay and all, but damn, you still need your balls."

Without thinking, I plunked my beer down on the table and rose to my feet. I heard Brynn say my name and felt Cam scramble to his feet on his side of the table as well, but none of it slowed the furious rush of anger that was crashing through my veins.

I reached out and clasped the teenager on the back of the neck. He sputtered and struggled, and I frog-marched him out of the kitchen and out of the front door. My boots kicked up dust as I kept moving him against his protests and objections toward the barn. He was a well-built kid, but I had four or five inches on him and months of unaddressed aggravation to deal with. I would never raise a hand to someone I knew I could really injure, and I would never hurt someone without a really good reason. I knew both the Bauer boys had been knocked around by their old man, and it hadn't done either one any kind of favor, but Mikey needed some kind of discipline. He was out of control. I was going to put him to work the way my dad did when I mouthed off and overstepped the bounds he had set for me. All three Warner brothers were familiar with what happened in the barn when someone acted out.

Shoving into the massive building, I flicked on the lights and was immediately greeted with a round of snickers and whinnies from the horses. I dragged Mikey into the tack room and handed him the first shovel I came across. I lifted my arms and arched my eyebrows at the petulant teenager.

"When you talk shit, it's only fitting that you spend the rest of the night cleaning it up. There are thirty stalls. They all need to be mucked and then relined with hay. I'm going to stand here and watch you do each and every single one of them. Every time you bitch about it, I'm going to find another chore for you to do."

He looked at me and then down at the shovel. With a sneer, he threw it on the ground. "You can't make me do anything. I'm out of here."

He started to push past me, but I grabbed his arm and looked at him with a lifted eyebrow. "It's over fifty miles to the next main road and then twenty more from that road into town. There is no Uber out here, no cab you can call. This is your only option. Clean the stalls. The quicker you're done, the quicker you can get back up to the house."

"And if I don't?" Defiance was clear in every line of his body.

"If you don't, you're leaving tomorrow, and the free ride you've had because your brother loves you without question dries up. You are not going to disrespect him any longer, and you are not going to walk all over his generosity. You're that kid's hero, he risked his life when he thought you were in danger and you've done nothing but shit on him since you were reunited." I told Brynn to stop sending the gift cards, but she insisted that she couldn't. Even though he was a royal brat, Mikey Bauer was still one of her people.

He reached up to rub the back of his neck while looking down at the tips of his white sneakers. "You don't understand."

I scoffed. "You're right, I don't. I have two brothers I would die for, and who I know would die for me. You can't even be bothered to spare yours a kind word. He blames himself for everything that happened to you, including what your dad put you through. You might be a lot of things, but you aren't stupid. You know what your dad did has nothing to do with Cam and everything to do with him being sick and evil."

He shuffled his feet and looked up at me under his eyelashes. "I wanted things to be better with Cam gone. What kind of brother does that make me? When I woke up in the hospital and they told me he took off all I could think was 'thank God.' I don't have to be the guy with the gay brother anymore. I don't have to dodge Dad's fist anymore. I thought it would all stop." I could tell by his tone that it didn't. "I thought the same thing when he came back. Maybe it would be better. I wouldn't have to worry about where he was and what he was doing anymore. But then he told that cop how he survived, and all I could think about was how I wanted him gone so it would go easier for me. It's all fucked up. I can't get it straight in my head. I'm jealous he got away from Dad, but horrified at what he had to do to make that happen. I say dumb shit I don't mean because I can't find the right words to apologize, and I do mean stuff because I don't want him to look up to me anymore. I let him down in so many ways. I'm not a hero, I don't want to be one either."

I clasped the kid on the shoulder and gave him a little shake. "He will forgive you pretty much anything, right now. Keep it up, and you are going to push him so far away you'll never be able to reach him. You need to talk to him, explain all of this, and you need to learn some respect. I get that you haven't had it easy, none of us have. That's no excuse to be a little asshole, and if you check out my brother's girl one more time, I can guarantee you'll be eating all your meals through a straw. He's more territorial than a bear. And I'm pretty sure if you keep pushing your luck with Opal she's going to neuter you." I gave him a little push and nudged the shovel with my boot. "Now get to work. You're already looking at a long night." I could see he was debating pushing his luck and refusing, but he picked up the shovel and made his way into the first stall. I swore I could feel my dad reaching down from the heavens and patting me on the back for a job well done. Never had I felt more like the man he raised me to be than in that moment.

It was late when Mikey got done. About halfway through I felt bad for the kid and helped him finish the labor-intensive job. He was dragging ass and covered in all kinds of filth as we stumbled into the main house. All the lights were off except for the one in the kitchen. I could hear someone banging around in there and figured Brynn had seen us coming back from the barn. Sure enough, she came out of the arched doorway with a mug of hot cocoa, complete with a mountain of whipped cream on the top and a still warm chocolate chip cookie she handed over to the sleepy teenager.

In response to Mikey's outburst which had earned him long hours shoveling shit, Brynn addressed him with as much love as she would've addressed Cam. "You're right. We do have a lot of love to give around here. There's plenty for you if you decide you want some of it for yourself, Mikey. We're happy to share." She gave him a lopsided smile which he returned before slowly limping his way off toward the guest room where he was staying.

Brynn grabbed my hand and pulled me after her into the kitchen. I shook my head, telling her that I was tired. All I wanted was a shower and to pass out in my nice soft bed with her beside me.

I shut up when she backed me into the counter, reaching around for something behind me, before getting on her knees in front of me. I blinked at her in surprise and lifted an eyebrow. "Uh, I'm never going to say no to a blowjob from that pretty mouth of yours, but are you sure you want to start that here? Not to mention I'm all dirty and I stink." The entire lower part of the house was wide open, the only room on this level that had four walls and a door was Cy's office. Anyone could walk in on us at any time even though it was the middle of the night.

I laughed when she handed me a familiar yellow and green bag. I had no idea where she managed to find me Funyuns at this time of night, but I would take them. The laughter died when instead of reaching for my belt and zipper so she could free my rapidly thickening cock, she reached for my hand. Looking up at me with those dark eyes shining she held up one of the smaller round chips and asked me, "Lane Warner, will you marry me?"

I looked at her and then at the chip and back again. I felt the way my jaw fell open, and I could sense the way surprise had frozen my features. I blinked at her again, before bursting into a laugh that was loud enough to wake the entire house as I sank to my knees in front of her. "Of course I will. How could I turn down my favorite girl asking for my hand in marriage with my favorite kind of ring?" I kissed her forehead and the tip of her nose. I kissed her lips and felt them tremble beneath mine.

She sniffed a little and rubbed her cheek against mine. "I've wanted to ask you since we got back from Denver. I even had Leo and Em help me look at rings. I had a plan, I wanted to do something special, but after watching you handle Mikey in just the right way, I couldn't wait anymore, so I had to improvise. Luckily, I found your stash. You are such a good man, Lane. You are kind and patient. You love with no restraint. You take care of those who need it most, but you don't try to overtake them. You take care of me and Cam, and now Mikey. You are exactly what I've always needed." She wrapped her arms around my neck and kissed me like she never wanted to stop. "I really do want to marry you, Lane. You're the only person I would ever ask."

I let her put the chip on my finger and spun it around with my thumb before popping it into my mouth. She wrinkled her nose at the crunch. "Since you asked, I get to be in charge of the rings." She sighed and gave a reluctant nod. "And I get to get on one knee and tell you that you are my forever when I give you yours. You don't have to say yes or no, you just have to agree to be mine for all time."

She gave a little laugh and snuggled into my chest. "I already am so that won't be a problem."

I kissed her again and slid my hands under the hem of her tank top. Her skin was so warm and soft against my palms that I couldn't get enough of it. Before she could protest, I had her shirt over her head, her bra popped open, and my mouth was all over her breasts. I covered one with my hand and worked the other with my mouth. Her nipple pulled taut immediately against my tongue and the other one puckered and poked at the center of my palm. I kneaded the supple skin as I kissed my way up the long line of her throat.

"Not here. Anyone can come in." She sounded breathless, and her protest was weak.

"I'll be fast." I pulled back and wiggled my eyebrows at her. "You were the one who got on your knees. It gave me all kinds of ideas." I put my hands under her armpits and hoisted her up. Once she had those endless legs wrapped around my waist, I walked her back to the counter so I could set her down. Her pajama bottoms were easy to remove and much to my dick's delight she wasn't wearing anything underneath. I feasted my eyes on naked, gold skin and that perfectly pink and pouty place between her legs. Even her pussy was flawless, and I couldn't wait to get inside of her.

"I got on my knees to propose." She laughed as I pulled my shirt open and frantically worked on getting my pants unfastened. She took pity on me when I got an arm stuck and helped me strip down so that my jeans were on my ass and my shirt was a tangled mess on the floor near her pajamas. Cy would kill me if he knew what I was doing in here, but what a way to go.

I stepped into the V of Brynn's legs, my cock immediately

pressing into her soft, wet heat. My stomach contracted in pleasure, and my hands started to shake as I pushed her hair back from her shoulders. I kissed her cheeks, her eyelids, the tip of her nose. I kissed her forehead and the curve of her jaw and traced the sexy shell of her ear with my tongue. I worshiped the face that meant so much to me. Memorized every laugh line and curve. When I finally touched my lips to hers, I could feel the way she loved me in that kiss. Her heart was pouring out of her, her love caught in every breath. It was a special kiss, the first one we shared after agreeing to spend the rest of our lives together. It was the first one of many.

Her naked thighs clenched around me and her damp folds dragged along the underside of my cock, soaking me in her desire. We both shuddered as my tongue dueled with hers. So far none of this was going fast, which was perfect. The pleasure was drawn out, prolonged, lengthy. It forced pinpricks of anticipation to needle our skin and made our breaths choppy and rapid.

I curled my fingers around her jaw and held her head still as I ravished her mouth. She tilted her head back with total compliance and melted into me as I started to rock against her soft center. My dick dragged through her velvety folds, the tip tapping against her sensitive clit with every thrust. I felt my cock swell when she whimpered at the contact. Her arms laced around my neck and she started to move in a slow grind against me.

I ghosted a hand down her spine and got a hand on her backside. I used it to pull her closer to the edge of the counter, so I had better leverage to move against her. Her heels were digging into my ass, and my belt buckle was jangling distractedly where it dangled from my belt loop. I just knew the noise would awaken someone and I didn't care.

I dragged a thumb over her lower lip and down her throat. I rested my fingers on the base of her neck, not squeezing, but pressing down so she could feel me there. Her eyes drifted closed, and she went limp against me as I found her tight opening and pushed my way inside. Her muscles fluttered around my length, and she pulsed around me. My very happy dick kicked in response and thickened even more. Her pleasure pushed mine to new heights.

"Look at me, Brynn. I want to see my fiancée's eyes while I make love to her." I sounded like I'd been eating sandpaper, but she got the hint and pulled those midnight eyes open and locked them on mine. "That's it. There's my girl."

I started to move inside of her. A slow, steady rhythm that made both of us pant.

"Always been yours, Lane. Always." Her voice didn't sound any better than mine, but the roughness and unsteadiness were sexy as hell. We made each other unravel. It was glorious. There was nothing like coming undone with the person you trusted to put you back together when they were done with you.

I pounded into her, the counter digging into my thighs and sweat starting to trickle down my hairline. Her fingers were digging into the back of my neck, and she was whispering my name over and over again like a broken prayer. I put a little more pressure on her neck where I was holding her and tightened my grip on her ass. I kissed her until I couldn't breathe and pushed into her harder and faster as her body quickened and her inner walls started to vibrate and quake around my length. The sounds of sex echoed off the tiled walls, and I hoped like hell my brother wasn't about to walk in and get a close up of my 'o' face. We were close, but not that close.

Brynn's legs quivered where they were clamped around me, and her pussy tightened like a vise. Her orgasm tugged and pulled my cock, milking mine out of me. I threw my head back and gritted my teeth, giving myself over to the sensation of filling her up and being surrounded by her satisfaction. Sex with her was always something else, but knowing it was sex with the person who was mine and had been mine forever, added another layer to it. There was a possessive, primal part of me that wanted to parade her around looking so blissed out and content so everyone who dared to look at her like she belonged to them could see that I was the only one who was going to get her off from here on out. I owned her pleasure. Her body, and more importantly, her heart was all mine. I'd never been given a greater gift.

"Thank you for coming after me and bringing me home, Brynn." Neither one of us would be here, tangled up in one another if she hadn't been brave enough to go after what she wanted.

She laughed as she collapsed against my chest, her heart racing against mine. "Thank you for giving me a home to bring you back to, Lane."

Home. It's where my heart . . . and hers . . . had always been.

EPILOGUE

War or Peace

"**H**E IS SO ADORABLE."

For a second I thought the woman was talking about the baby I was holding.

I'd hijacked Emrys and Sutton's son shortly after the reception started. Gentry Warner was a great baby. He didn't fuss at all through Cyrus and Leo's wedding, and he didn't seem to mind being passed around from cooing adult to cooing adult. He was turning seven months old soon, and he was starting to look more and more like his mother. He had her inky dark hair and her beautiful, tawny complexion. However, when he opened his eyes and blinked his incredibly long lashes, it was Sutton Warner's glowing green gaze that looked up at you. Both his babies got their daddy's eyes, and they were lucky for it.

I kissed the baby on the head and smiled at the woman. Her name was Meghan Harlow, and she had come to the wedding with her two kids, Evan and Ethan. The family had been on the ride that went so wrong that ended with Leo and Cy falling in love. Her teenagers were frequent visitors to the ranch. Her son, Ethan, had even asked about coming to work on the ranch during the summer. He was a cute kid, around the same age as Cam. The two boys had been inseparable since the Harlow's showed for the wedding. I could tell Cam's interest was a little more than friendly, but Ethan didn't seem to mind. I had no clue if the gamer boy from New York swung the same way Cam did, and I figured it wasn't my place to pry. Cam had to learn how to navigate normal relationships with regular teenagers, and Ethan was a good kid. If he wasn't interested, he had the social tools and training to let Cam down gently.

It took me a minute to realize Meghan was talking about the teenager and not the baby. Cam and Ethan were standing in a circle with the rest of the groomsman. All of them looking sharp in black buttoned shirts, western cut jackets, black jeans, and boots. It was a good look for the Warners and for Cam. He cried when Cy asked him to stand up with his brothers during the wedding, and he'd nearly had a heart attack when Lane asked him to learn a song so they could play it together for Cy and Leo's first dance. I could have kissed the grumpy older man, and I did kiss the life out of my much more easy-going man. Including him in something as personal and permanent as Cy and Leo's wedding had finally gotten it through Cam's head that he belonged.

"He is. He's also a really good kid." One who was trying so hard every day to do the right thing. The baby started to fuss, so I gave him a little jiggle and made soothing sounds. "I'm glad he and Ethan are getting along so well."

The other woman nodded and gave me a sly smile. "I'm pretty sure your boy is the reason my boy is so insistent on coming to visit this summer. I've never seen him that excited about anything that involved work and getting dirty. Evan is my drama queen. She's over the top with everything. Ethan is usually caught up on his phone or one of his game things. He hasn't looked at either since he met Cameron."

Cam seemed equally as smitten, and I'd be hard-pressed to do anything to discourage the crush. The kid had so many adult decisions to make day in and day out that I wanted him to enjoy the experience of something innocent and pure. Ethan Harlow was a perfect distraction from the fact that the trial for the man who abducted him was getting closer and closer. The FBI rounded up a couple more kids taken in by the website, but Cam was still the main witness. Jonathan Goddard was no longer a threat. He hadn't been in prison for a week before the guards found him hanging in his cell, his bed sheet wrapped around his neck like a noose. It was a relief. For a while, Lane and I wondered if we should be worried about the people with the money behind Cam's abduction coming after him. But not long after Goddard's death, an anonymous file with all of the secret transactions Goddard made through the website was delivered into the hands of the FBI. They shut down the website that lured Cam in and managed to bring charges against the couple behind it. They were also getting ready to stand trial, with both RV guy and BMW guy willing to roll over and testify against them for lighter sentences. It was a lot to process for anyone, but Cam was doing his best, and we all made sure he never had to deal with any of it alone.

I hummed and lifted my eyebrows in a silent question. Meghan lifted hers back with a grin. "We should probably let them figure that out on their own." I tended to err on the side of caution when it came to introducing anyone new in Cam's life. I was a mama bear through and through where he was concerned. I was just now loosening up when it came to having Mikey around on a more regular basis.

The older Bauer boy had dialed back the attitude after his heart to heart with Lane. He was still kind of a punk, but it was tempered with genuine care and concern toward his little brother. He was still struggling to make ends meet in Denver, but more often than not he popped up on the ranch for holiday weekends and whenever he had free time. I was pretty sure it had as much to do with the fact my sister was coming around on those same holidays as it was him wanting to see his brother, but as long as he behaved I was getting used to having him around. Where I related to Cam and saw so much of my pain in his, Lane seemed to understand the way Mikey Bauer was struggling to live up to the exhausted image his younger brother had of him. Those two were thick as thieves these days, and all I could hope for was that Mikey figured out how to be half the man his brother, and Lane, believed him to be.

Meghan waved a hand, the sunlight catching on her diamond ring. "Nothing wrong with pointing them in the right direction. I haven't seen my boy smile like that since the last time we were here. That makes my heart happy."

We were interrupted when Wyatt's former partner, Grady, swooped in with a flute of champagne that he handed off to the elegant older woman. He dropped a kiss on her made-up cheek and gave me a wink. Grady had also been along for that fateful ride, so it was nice to see him again, and it was also wonderful to see him and Meghan together and happy. She'd dropped her abusive, cheating husband shortly after the trip and Grady had made his move not long after.

"Is my lovely bride planning Ethan's wedding already? I recognize that gleam in her eye."

I smiled at the distinguished looking man and handed the baby back to Emrys when she popped up at my side. Daye was hot on her heels, demanding her turn to hold her little brother. I was glad to see the little princess had settled down, and that her jealousy over not being the baby anymore had waned. She was a phenomenal big sister and took amazing care of her little brother. She didn't even seem to mind that she was no longer the center of attention all the time. Though today in her frilly, flouncy dress as she walked down the aisle dropping wildflowers before Leo, she'd certainly stolen every heart in the place.

"They make an attractive couple." Emrys chimed in with a grin as all four of us watched the two boys bend their heads together to look at something on Ethan's phone.

I groaned and dropped my face into my hands. "I'm not ready for my baby to start dating!" I ignored the laughter that broke out around me and lifted my head when I felt Lane's eyes on me. He smiled at me from across the space separating us and inclined his head where the two boys were standing with lifted eyebrows. I gave him a small nod, and he winked at me. Lane was all for our boy getting out there and living his life to the fullest. He wanted Cam to love and be loved in all the ways he had never been before. I shook my head at him, and his laugh had both Sutton and the boys turning to look between the two of us.

"The wedding was beautiful. Leo was stunning, and Cyrus looked so happy. I'm so glad they invited us. It's like witnessing the end of a romance novel in real life and seeing happily ever after play out for real." The older woman looked up at the former DEA agent and batted her eyes at him. "So romantic. Is it any wonder I have wedding fever? Evan burns through boys so fast, who knows if she'll ever settle on one. Ethan is my only hope for a big, beautiful day like this."

The boys did look cute together, but I was nowhere near the point where I was ready to think about Cam falling in love and leaving the ranch. I just got him, I wasn't quite ready to share him with anyone outside of family just yet.

I was getting ready to tell Meghan that when there was suddenly a commotion at the front of the tent. The wedding and reception were outside, and Cy had ordered a giant party tent in case the weather went south.

"What's going on?" Emrys put a hand on Daye's shoulder and pulled her close and clutching her baby protectively against her chest. Sutton immediately made his way over to her, and Lane followed until he was standing by my side. Leo and Cy were mingling with guests, so they missed the guys in black with FBI scrawled across their jackets pouring into the entrance of the tent. For a furious second, I thought they might have been there for my boy, and every instinct I had was telling me to run across the space dividing us and put my body between him and whoever thought they were going to take him away from his family and his home.

"What the hell?" Lane and Sutton started to move toward the uninvited guests as rumbles of unease and curiosity started to filter through the crowd. Silently, I made my way to where Cam and Evan were standing. I put my hand on his thin shoulder and realized he was shaking but trying to hide it.

Before I could assure him that everything was going to be okay, an authoritative voice barked out, "Sorry to interrupt, but we're here for Webb Bryant." The guy at the front of the group of intruders held up a badge that had his ID in it and pushed dark sunglasses to the top of his head. He didn't sound apologetic about the interruption in the slightest.

"Webb?" That was Wyatt asking what the feds wanted with his younger brother. He stepped up to the man who appeared to be the leader and asked him if he had a warrant.

Silently Webb broke away from the conversation he was having with Rodie about the Denver Broncos and made his way to his brother's side.

"I'm Webb Bryant. What can I help you with? And couldn't this have waited until later?" He looked at the federal agents with disdain.

"What did you do, Webb?" Ten asked the question quietly, but it was so silent while the surreal scene played out that it sounded like she shouted.

The blond man cut her a look and crossed his arms over his chest. "I didn't do anything, Ten. Not recently anyway. This has to be a mistake."

Wyatt looked up at the warrant and frowned at his brother. "They have a warrant for your arrest."

"For what? I haven't done anything illegal." Webb was getting angry, and everyone seemed to have forgotten we were all there to celebrate a wedding.

"For bank robbery." Wyatt tossed the warrant back to the fed and glared at his younger brother. "They have your DNA at over five different banks in Wyoming and Montana, Webb."

A collective gasp went up from the crowd as the unmistakable sound of handcuffs snapping together interrupted the festive gathering.

"Webb Bryant, you're under arrest. You have the right to remain silent—"

The end . . . For now.

I hope you loved reading about the wild Warners as much as I loved writing them. Retreat and Shelter are available now if you missed the first two books in the series. I absolutely plan on giving Webb and Ten a story someday, as long as the interest in these characters and their stories remains strong. If that's something you'd like to see, keep on reading and reviewing!

Also, if you would like to read more about the Point and see a little bit of the dark side of romance, please visit my website for the reading order of all the books in that series. Same goes for the feisty, female police officer who plays such a big part in getting Bauer home where he belongs. If you are interested in spending some more time with Officer Cross and her southern charmer, please visit my website and check out the reading order for the Marked Men series.

www.jaycrownover.com

ACKNOWLEDGMENTS

I OWE AN EXTRA HUGE shout out to my always amazing assistant Melissa Shank, Pam Lilley, Sarah Arndt, Lindsay DeRosa, Danielle Wentworth, and Meghan Burr-Martin for jumping in at the zero hour and making sure this book was spit-shined and polished up. I have the best readers and I am always amazed how quickly and how many of them stand up and volunteer their time and effort in order to help out, not just me, but each other as well. If you read Charged you know I believe that like attracts like and that is totally the case between me and my readers.

If you've made it this far, I would like to take a second and ask that you, please consider leaving a review for this book on whichever retail site you bought it off of. Those little suckers are so important to an author and to the success of a book. You can make or break this title, and all it takes is a couple of words. Love it or hate it, tell other readers what you think!

Oh, man . . . I very nearly blew the deadline for this book. I got a puppy in November right during the thick of things. She's a silver lab named Clementine, and she's cute as hell, but also a monster. The fact you have this book in your hot little hands is a goddamn miracle . . . no joke. There was also some other stuff going on this winter that hindered my usual flow. That being said I'm keeping my thanks, short and sweet!

If you have purchased, read, reviewed, promoted, pimped, blogged about, sold, talked about, preached about, or whined about any of my books . . . thank you.

If you are part of my very special reader group The Crowd . . . thank you.

If you have helped me make this dream of mine a reality . . . thank you.

If you have helped make my words better and helped me share them with the world . . . thank you.

If you have held my hand and helped me through the tough times when it feels like everyone's against me . . . thank you.

Feel free to appease your inner stalker in all of these places. I love hearing from readers.:

This is the link to join my amazing fan group on Facebook: *https://www.facebook.com/groups/crownoverscrowd* . . . I'm very active in the group, and it's often the best place to find all the happenings including; release dates, cover reveals, early teasers and you can participate in so many great giveaways!

My website is: *www.jaycrownover.com* . . . there is a link on the site to reach me through email. I would also suggest signing up for my newsletter while you're there! It's monthly, contains a free book that is in progress so you'll be the first to read it, and is full of mega giveaways and goodies.

ABOUT THE AUTHOR

JAY CROWNOVER IS THE INTERNATIONAL and multiple *New York Times* and *USA Today* bestselling author of the Marked Men Series, The Saints of Denver Series, and The Point and Breaking Point Series. Her books can be found translated in many different languages all around the world. She is a tattooed, crazy haired Colorado native who lives at the base of the Rockies with her awesome dogs. This is where she can frequently be found enjoying a cold beer and Taco Tuesdays. Jay is a self-declared music snob and outspoken book lover who is always looking for her next adventure, between the pages and on the road.

GUYS!!! I finally have a newsletter, so if you want to sign up for exclusive content and monthly giveaways you can do that right here: www.jaycrownover.com/#!subscribe

You can email me at: JayCrownover@gmail.com
My website: www.jaycrownover.com
www.facebook.com/jay.crownover
www.facebook.com/AuthorJayCrownover
Follow me @jaycrownover on Twitter
Follow me @jay.crownover on Instagram
www.goodreads.com/Crownover
www.donaghyliterary.com/jay-crownover.html
www.avonromance.com/author/jay-crownover

CPSIA information can be obtained
at www.ICGtesting.com
Printed in the USA
BVHW041835170521
607567BV00022B/281

9 781983 707704